To Ou

THIS IS NOT A PIPE

Happy reading

Tam

THIS IS NOT A PIPE

IS NOT A

PIPE

DAVID JARVIS

Troubador Publishing Lyd
Unit E2 Airfield Business Park,
Harrison Road, Market Harborough,
Leicestershire LE16 7UL
Tel: 0116 279 2299
Email: books@troubador.co.uk
Web: www.troubador.co.uk

ISBN 978 1 80514 148 8

British Library Cataloguing in Publication Data.
A catalogue record for this book is available from the British Library.

Printed and bound by CPI Group (UK) Ltd, Croydon, CR0 4YY
Typeset in 11pt Adobe Garamond Pro by Troubador Publishing Ltd, Leicester, UK

Matador is an imprint of Troubador Publishing Ltd

Beneath a painting of a pipe, Magritte wrote *"Ceci n'est pas une pipe"* (French for "This is not a pipe").

"The famous pipe. How people reproached me for it! And yet, could you stuff my pipe? No, it's just a representation, is it not? So, if I had written on my picture "This is a pipe", I'd have been lying!"

—René Magritte

CHAPTER ONE

Who could ever forget that splash?

Stepping down from the coach should have been such a relief to everyone, including Tanya, the tour guide. Morocco in summer is so hot – as in, *really* hot. The coach had been vibrating oddly since leaving the hotel, and she had been standing at the front, shaving her chin (well, that's what it looked like to everyone at the back as no one could hear a word she was saying). The photo opportunity had turned out to be the fish market in Essaouira, and almost everyone had regretted leaving the cool of the air conditioning the second that their feet had hit the dusty ground.

Tanya, who had a degree in Stating the Bleeding Obvious, was pointing out the boxes of silvery fish and the sharp knives. Over the previous three days, she had demonstrated her complete unsuitability for the job: speaking neither French nor Arabic, and having had a major charisma bypass. Norman – the tall, old man wearing the same pale-blue, seersucker shorts he had worn since his holiday had begun – was busy photographing some ticket office and ignoring the vibrant local scene. This meant he never saw Jessica, the railway station announcer from somewhere in London, trip over her kaftan and fall headfirst into the large concrete channel used to collect the fish guts and various foul-smelling liquids. Several people stepped forwards, but they stopped short of offering a helping hand. She clambered out with as much dignity as is possible when you have a fish head sticking out between your bum bag and your ample stomach.

Tanya pointed out helpfully that there was a footbridge across the sluice about ten yards away (as if any of her customers had the slightest desire to prolong the visit). Norman turned around to ask everyone if they would like a group photograph, only to be met with a range of stares. Jessica was standing with her arms outstretched and being given plenty of personal space.

One person standing nearby who wasn't interested in a record of the group or, indeed, of any photograph of herself was Michaela Kingdom. She was trying to stay under the radar, having bought a mousey wig especially that now made her sweaty, bald head itch. She was glad she didn't have to get on that coach. *I'm not cut out for fieldwork,* she had thought to herself as she cursed Leonard de Vries, her ex-boss, under her breath.

"Mike, look on it as a paid holiday," he had said.

"The last two times I went into the field for you, people died. Remember?" she had replied, noting his major concession in calling her Mike.

"Third time lucky," he had managed to say before she had killed the Zoom call.

Tanya had made the unilateral decision that Norman

2

should swap places with Jessica so the poor woman could sit on the back row of the coach, with both side windows open and the air conditioning on maximum. Norman seemed oblivious to everything happening around him and continued taking irrelevant photographs. Jessica was using her retrieved sunhat to fan away the flies as she started up the steps of the coach.

"Ealing Broadway, Slough, Reading, Swindon next stop…" she said in her best station-announcer's voice, trying to relieve the embarrassment.

Swindon? thought Mike, *That's one of the places where I nearly died,* as she tried to push Leonard de Vries's punchable face from her mind.

"Actually, the next stop is the spice souk. Let's try to keep Jessica away from the piles of saffron and turmeric…" Tanya was wondering what else could go wrong. "And remember to haggle," she added unnecessarily.

***

On Wednesday, 31st August, a little over a week earlier, Mike had been looking up a recipe on her phone when there had been a rap on her door. She had leapt up and, before opening it, had grabbed her handily placed baseball bat. She never got visitors – a benefit, after all, of living in the middle of a pine forest in Oxfordshire. It may have looked like a log cabin from the inside, but it was actually a very small bedsit above a garage, up a woodland track, which was home to a tractor and a rusty trailer.

"Who is it?" she enquired.

"Leonard," a man's voice had replied.

"What the…? What do you want, Leonard?"

"You could open the door and let me in. It's been a long journey."

"No, it hasn't. You've been chauffeur-driven from Chiswick for forty-five minutes while you slept in the back."

"True, but I had a disturbing dream."

"That wasn't a dream; that's your life, Leonard." She opened the door and stepped back.

"Nice to be back. Have you redecorated?" he said, clearly as unimpressed by the pine panelling and second-hand furniture as he had been when he had visited her once before, twelve months earlier. Three polystyrene heads stared blankly at him from a shelf: one bald, one in a blonde wig and the other with startling red hair.

"I've taken your picture down, if that's what you mean?"

"I can get you another one," he offered in his soft Alabaman drawl.

"I was using it as a dartboard."

He smiled and slumped into an armchair; this was necessitated by being both overweight and out of breath from climbing the one flight of stairs outside. He was wearing a white shirt with its sleeves rolled up and a loosened green tie.

"I'm expecting an important phone call in five minutes from a new client, so make it snappy," she said.

"Dr Rose Delavine, I expect?"

"How... how... do you know her?"

"I am her."

"What? Leonard, you are the last person on earth who cares about personal pronouns. Although it is very tempting to call you '*it*'." Mike was frowning under her jet-black wig.

"I *am* Dr Rose Delavine."

"What?"

4

"Do you think I would leave London and come out here on the off-chance you were here? My office made the appointment with you."

"Leonard, you are an utter shit!"

"Possibly… but it worked?"

"You think you're so clever."

"Yes, I do. It's an anagram of Leonard de Vries, by the way. That's pretty clever. I thought you might have worked that out, you being in intelligence?"

"You… you… I bet you didn't think of it?"

"That's true, but I employ great people… like you."

"What? You are – were – the most infuriating boss." She added, "I no longer work for you or the CIA or Five Eyes. Remember?"

It had been over three years since the accident. It had ended Mike's career, which had begun with the CIA in Oregon and then continued with Five Eyes. Leonard was both the CIA's head of station in London and the person who ran the joint venture between the intelligence agencies of the USA, UK, Canada, Australia and New Zealand (aka Five Eyes).

She was standing with her arms folded, her legs crossed at the ankles and leaning against a kitchen cabinet.

"I came to offer you a job… as a freelancer," Leonard explained.

"I don't want it."

"Don't you want to hear what it is?"

"No. You've wasted your time."

"It's desk-based."

"Your definition of 'desk-based' varies considerably to mine. With you, there's always mission creep – with the emphasis on 'creep'."

He rubbed his damp forehead with a handkerchief in the pause.

"You're head of station – or the Fat Controller, as they would probably say here in the UK – surely—"

"I just want you to find one of my guys who's gone missing," he cut in.

"The CIA has an annual budget of billions of dollars. Why can't you find him?"

"He was working on something that was under the radar."

"Radar? You should have given him better equipment. Sorry, Leonard. No can do."

He sat still for a moment – in fact, for a strangely dramatic moment – and stared up at her very-dark-brown eyes under the black Cleopatra wig. "It's Randy."

There was an inordinately long pause when nothing was said. A squirrel or something similar ran across the roof, and Leonard looked up as if expecting the ceiling to cave in. He had lived what may be called a 'sedentary and urban existence' for all his life. Half an hour spent meeting a contact on a bench in Hyde Park was as close to nature as he ever got, if you excluded the range of insects that seemed permanently attracted to his damp skin.

Mike walked over to the kitchen area and put the kettle on. She stared blankly out of the large picture window that made up most of the gable end and provided almost all the light for the room, framing the forest edge. Eventually, she carried a mug over to Leonard, who accepted the coffee even though it was likely to make him sweat even more.

"OK, you win." After a few seconds, she added, "but now I want the truth; the whole truth. Start from the beginning and don't conveniently leave things out."

Leonard sipped his coffee and tried not to look smug. "I

don't think it will take you long. It's just that I can't use my crew for various reasons that will become evident."

"Was he working for you? I haven't seen or heard from him since the funeral."

"Sort of."

"Sort of yes or sort of no?"

"Sort of unofficially. He was working for a gas company officially."

"And he's just disappeared?"

"Sort of."

"How can you 'sort of' disappear?"

"Well, OK, let's call it temporarily."

"Where do you think he might be?"

"France… or Spain or Italy or…" He paused. "Algeria or Morocco."

"Well, that's narrowed the field down. What was he doing?"

"Well, let's just say that whatever it is, it's sort of no longer US policy" – he paused to choose his words very carefully – "under the new president, and I'd like him to stop doing it and update me on the situation – fast."

"So, this is about covering your ass, not about finding one of your sources?"

"I've always been a hands-off kind of boss."

"Probably a good thing after #MeToo, don't you think? But 'lazy shit' might be more accurate."

"Will you try to find him?"

"What support do I get?"

"Just me… good old Dr Rose Delavine." He smiled and handed her a card bearing the fake doctor's name and various phone numbers and codes. "Let's keep this off the record. Don't contact me via the office."

"I'll need a lot more background." She was sipping coffee and thinking that was the understatement of the year.

"I can't tell you anything more. It's on a need-to-know basis and all that BS. It's better you don't know anything else – trust me. Just find him and tell him to phone home ASAP."

"You want me to trust you?"

He stood up at the second attempt and began to waddle towards the door. He started to say something, but stopped himself.

"If you were going to mention Dylan, don't." She was glaring at him.

"No… quit while you're ahead, eh?" And with that, he left and went down the outside stairs to his waiting car.

***

At that precise moment, 3,000 miles south of him in Algeria, an explosion disturbed the soundless desert. It would have been deafening if there had been anyone within ten miles to hear it. However, there was no philosopher in the brown, sandy expanse to discuss whether that meant the noise didn't exist. The dust plume could undoubtedly be seen from a very long way away, but there were also no photographers anywhere near; not even locals using their mobile phones.

In fact, the nearest people with serious cameras were the press pack in Algiers currently surrounding Emmanuel Macron, the French President, who was just about managing to keep a smile on his face as he stood there in his open-necked, white shirt. He was barely visible in the throng, which was a gift to his security detail, who always preferred to protect a vertically challenged target. The crowd were just beginning to turn hostile as he started to explain that his visit was to improve French-Algerian relations in a post-colonial world. However, even when he visited young entrepreneurs to discuss creating a French-Algerian incubator for digital start-ups, no one was fooled.

"*One, two, three,* viva l'Algérie," they shouted, less than two months after Algeria had marked six decades of independence following 132 years of French rule and a devastating eight-year war.

The French President seemed unperturbed, rolled up his sleeves, promoted youth culture and business development, and counted the minutes until he was on the jet back to Paris.

After the explosion, a scrap from an Arabic newspaper dated 30th August 2022 fluttered in the swirling dust storm and landed by the unrecognisable, burnt-out remains of a Toyota pickup. A feral dog was barking wildly. Just another day in the vast sandy and stony desert known as the Grand Erg Oriental.

Explosions, sabotage and all types of guerrilla warfare were regular occurrences in the region around the Western Sahara – 100,000 square miles of contested land over which Algeria and Morocco had fought for centuries. The US had been supporting Morocco in this bitter battle, but it was also claimed by the Polisario Front, which was backed by Algeria, and together they wanted an independent nation for the indigenous Sahrawi people.

The conflict had started in 1975 when Spain withdrew from what had been its colony of Spanish Sahara, and Morocco had claimed what it called 'the Western Sahara'. Their troops now occupied eighty per cent of the region, and the King of Morocco was working relentlessly to establish Moroccan infrastructure and villages in the area, as well as developing the lucrative phosphate mining, port and fishing industries.

One of Leonard's agents had been embedded in the region for over a year in an undercover role as a Spanish petrochemical consultant, with the aim of 'enabling' (a special word that mostly meant 'disabling') anything the US President regarded as needing attention. It was this agent, using a code name, whom Leonard wanted Mike Kingdom to find.

Mike was originally from Oregon, where she had joined the CIA. Early on, she had fallen for Dylan Kingdom, one of her work colleagues. He was a Harley Davidson-riding extrovert who was a field operative in the Central and South American narcotics division. It was Dylan whom she had married, and they had been posted to London together; she was the desk-based analyst, and he was the undercover operative. His younger brother Randy was also in the field, working mostly in South America, having the advantage of speaking fluent Spanish also having grown up in San Diego, California.

Despite her being desk-based, it was Dylan who had taken her on an operation in Amsterdam at the behest of Leonard de Vries, only to be ambushed in a pickup truck along some featureless, straight road on the embankment of a Dutch polder – an event that had changed her life.

Far away in the Algerian desert on that baking August afternoon, when the security patrol and special police arrived at the scene of the explosion, there was little left of the vehicle. The police officer with the unpleasant task of collecting the few remaining body parts hardly took any notice of the pale skin on one arm. Many Tunisians were blue-eyed and fair-skinned, a result of their Berber heritage.

CHAPTER TWO

On that fateful day in August, Leonard had just left Mike Kingdom's cabin.

What is it about that man? She walked to the fridge, knocked the top off a bottle of Peroni and grabbed a bag of salted cashew nuts. Her mind was completely focused on devising a way to find Randy. She also opened some windows, which was an automatic reaction whenever Leonard had been in her office – or home; this had a therapeutic effect as it allowed the sounds of the forest to enter. Today, this meant the rasping of some squabbling jays and the trill of a wren.

She removed her black wig and put it back on its polystyrene head. Rubbing her scalp, she sat down and calmly tried to work out what this was all about. Why had Leonard come to her and in an off-the-record way? He must be in trouble or he would be using his massive resources and network of contacts. Was this trouble solely because of Randy or were there other things? Leonard had asked her to stop Randy from doing something and report back to him; clearly, Randy had not completed his task yet.

This was more than finding a needle in a haystack – she didn't even know in which haystack to search. In fact, she didn't even know which country the haystack was in.

Not having access to the CIA computer network was going to make this so much more difficult. She had been given free access the last, and only, time she had freelanced for Leonard. Now, she couldn't even contact her friends at her old Five Eyes office in Chiswick. She was on her own and she had to be discreet.

At that moment, a loud plane roared slowly overhead. It was too early for the A320 on its way from RAF Brize Norton to the Falklands. *Probably a tanker plane,* she thought, and her mind drifted off, trying to decide which surveillance aircraft over the Middle East it was about to refuel. She brought herself back to the matter in hand. If in doubt, start at the beginning.

Randy; it all must start with Randy.

The obvious thing to do was to try to contact him. He was her brother-in-law after all and, of course, she had his personal cell phone number. Why not call it? She dialled and waited. There was no reply, so she sent an anodyne but teasing message: "Call me. I have some good news."

She called his landline. Number not in use. She called Eleanora, a friend from the distant past who lived in Copenhagen, and asked if she had heard from Randy. Nothing. Mike thought about contacting Randy and Dylan's parents, but she decided against it as this would only worry them. They had already lost one son.

It was all worth a try, but she wasn't hopeful.

Another Peroni seemed to be a useful displacement activity. She knocked the cap off.

He won't be using his real name, she thought. *How can I find him if he isn't using his real name and I don't know what he's doing and in which country?*

She liked a challenge. Fighting for her life after the accident had displayed her stubbornness, and she knew she was as good as anybody at searching databases – it's what had got her recognition in the CIA in the first place – but you have to get a fingerhold. You have to start with something. She went back over Leonard's words carefully. What had he said that might be useful? He wanted Randy to stop what he was doing and report back. Whatever Randy was doing was against the latest US policy. He might be in France, Spain, Italy, Morocco or Algeria. He was undercover in a gas company.

She began to address each point in turn.

What could Randy be doing that he needed to stop? He was a geologist who could speak Spanish, like Dylan, having grown up near the Mexican border in California. Was he in Spain doing something? What would the CIA want someone like Randy to do? She made a note to check if Spain produced natural gas. Even if it did, why would the CIA be interested? Curiosity got the better of her, and she immediately searched for natural gas production in Spain. It produced so little, ranking eighty-sixth in the world; this was a dead end, surely? She burst out laughing. Most people wouldn't understand that what turned her on was the pursuit. If anyone thought that being an analyst means hitting a button and the answer comes out immediately, they would be so disappointed.

She moved on to US policies. Which was the policy that had changed under this or previous presidents that would warrant Leonard leaving his office and being driven to her cabin, given that he was wedded to his big, black leather office chair in ways that were probably not entirely healthy? What had changed in relation to the five countries Leonard had mentioned? She drew a blank. As to Randy's location, she had some knowledge of the three European countries, but, again, she drew a blank. About the two North African ones, she knew absolutely nothing. She made a note to educate herself on these and quickly.

She took a swig of beer, and before she could consider the fourth matter, her train of thought was completely derailed. There, on the floor, alongside the armchair where Leonard had been sitting, was a folded newspaper. She walked over and a shooting pain shot up her left leg; this settled down after a few paces. She hadn't seen him drop it. Leonard may look like a sloppily put-together assemblage of the bits found on an abattoir floor, but he was no fool. He had dropped it on purpose. Officially, he couldn't tell her what this was all about, she guessed. This was well outside being need-to-know, and she was no longer part of the CIA. However, the paper must have been left to give her a lead.

There were no outside pages, but she could see from the date at the top that it was five months old and from London. She flicked through, looking for a highlighted section or some obvious headline. Nothing jumped out to her on her first look until she saw a small article under world news.

It was entitled "Ukraine fallout", but it was the word 'Algeria' that had caught her eye:

US Secretary of State Antony Blinken and Deputy Secretary Wendy Sherman arrived from Morocco at Houari Boumediene Airport, Algeria, yesterday (30th March 2022) for an unprecedented visit by the US equivalents of the Foreign Secretary and Deputy Foreign Secretary; they met Foreign Minister Ramtane Lamamra.

Neither Morocco nor Algeria were obvious places for such important members of the US government to visit, so the question was why? And why should it involve both of them at a time when Russia, Ukraine, China and elsewhere should be top of the list of priorities?

One reason seemed obvious: the shortage of global oil and gas supplies due to the Russian invasion of Ukraine. According to the article, "Algeria is the fifth largest gas exporter in the world."

Mike Kingdom leant back in her chair and drained the last flat, warm mouthful of her Peroni. *So, Algeria is the fifth largest gas exporter in the world,* she thought about this, rubbing her thumbs and forefingers together in excitement. Something inside her told her she had just been given the end of a thread that would lead to Randy.

Her knowledge of Africa was restricted to the fact that Egypt was at the top right and South Africa, unsurprisingly, was way down at the bottom.

She called up Google Maps and orientated herself. She started at the western end of the Mediterranean Sea, with Spain and Gibraltar to the north and, eight miles to the south, Morocco. Together, they provide the gateway from one of the largest and most important seas on earth to the Atlantic Ocean. East of Morocco, with a long Mediterranean coast, is Algeria, which is the second largest country in Africa and extends far south across the Sahara to Mali. Why had she never come across Algeria before? The second largest country in Africa and the fifth largest natural gas producer in the world. The CIA must be well represented in Algiers, surely?

She sat musing on what her brother-in-law, Randy, had to do with any of this and where he was at that precise moment.

In truth, they had never been close, mostly because he had his life in California, and she was working for Five Eyes in London. She knew deep down, however, that Dylan would have wanted her to drop everything and find Randy – or at least to keep him out of trouble.

The screaming of a muntjac deer woke her up and she realised that she had dozed off after many hours of reading long reports about the Maghreb, the area of northwest Africa that included Morocco, Algeria, the contested Western Sahara, and bits of Libya, Mali, Tunisia and Mauritania. What was Leonard trying to tell her? She decided to close the windows and go to bed.

***

Only the most malevolent of fathers would call their son Walter Cecil when their surname was Flushing. He had disappeared from family life when Walter was fourteen years old – to the relief of everyone. Unfortunately, the verbal abuse through school impacted heavily on Walter; he became introverted and studious. While emerging with very good grades, he became immune to everyone calling him W.C. In fact, for a while, he stopped speaking entirely. Inside, however, his mind was firing on all cylinders. People tended to put him down as a basket case. This was to underrate him seriously. The small mat of curly, brown hair, which sat at the top of a face with a long nose and darting eyes, disguised a sharp mind.

He amazed everyone by reading French and politics at Oxford. This in turn had led W.C. Flushing to the Foreign and Commonwealth Office (FCO) and an initial temporary position as the 'lowest of the low', supporting the staff at the

British Embassy in Algiers. He hated it more than school, but he had at least learnt Arabic on a course at the FCO language-teaching centre in the basement of its King Charles Street HQ in London. He was hoping this might all lead to a permanent post with the FCO. Sadly, his inability to fit in had been acknowledged immediately, even though he had completed all of the basic administrative tasks well and had spent six months compiling a well-received study entitled *The Current Political Tensions in the Maghreb*. At his first review, it had become apparent that North Africa was not his natural habitat (this was in his FCO evaluation report). However, his reliability, language skills and problem-solving abilities were recognised, and he was reallocated. Instead of being the 'lowest of the low' in Algiers, he was promoted to the 'lowest of the low' helping in the service section in Paris.

After a few months, he had settled in. This embassy, with its 270 staff, was much larger than the one in Algiers, and this meant he could disappear into the background as long as he performed the allocated tasks well. Outside work, he led a quiet and separate life. His living accommodation was very small and new. This suited him, as he had no interest in sharing and was unmoved by dreamy Parisian garrets on the Left Bank.

He was now called Walter, having left his nicknames behind in high school and at Oxford.

Possibly because someone saw his potential (or possibly because he was the only one available), in August 2022, he found himself in a small hotel in Colmar, the most beautiful town of the Alsace in eastern France. Trapped between the French Vosges mountains and the Black Forest in Germany, the people of the Alsace really don't care whether their government is in Paris or Berlin; the region had changed hands that many times. They took the best from both cultures. Nouvelle cuisine with German proportions. The hotel was chocolate-box pretty, with the geraniums outside each window reflected in the canal below; it was a photographer's dream.

Walter had left early to buy some pastries and a coffee before returning to meet John 'Johnny' Musselwhite in the reception at 9.00am the next day. He was tasked with making sure that Johnny, the British Minister for Energy, made it to a meeting with his French counterpart to discuss a joint Anglo-French project on Green energy using some of the old potash mine sites in the Alsace – an industry now completely closed, but that had left a similar legacy to coal mining in the UK, such as rusting winding gear and the equivalent of slag heaps.

Walter had never been to the Alsace before, so the whole experience had been like a paid holiday. The transfer from Basel airport had been easy, and as soon as he had arrived at the hotel, he met Johnny, who had promptly ordered room service and gone to bed early. It looked like it was a paid holiday for Johnny as well. He had, it seemed, driven down in his old Mercedes on his way to a break in the South of France and Spain. The planned meeting, which would take up only a couple of hours of his time, would probably make the whole trip tax-deductible. Walter was meant to be assisting someone called Brendan from the British Embassy in Paris, who had cancelled at the last moment. This did not bother Walter as the job was really a couple of hours of carrying bags for the minister and the odd bit of translation. He decided to go out to eat and found an *auberge* that served a melted cheese dish called *raclette,* which he accompanied with a large beer. He was back in the hotel by 9.35pm, slightly regretting his choices and opting to sit up with extra pillows in case any of it made a reappearance.

As arranged, he was downstairs early the next morning, wearing an unworn silk tie that he had bought in an Algiers souk. He was looking forward to a light breakfast at 8.30am. To pass the time, he was checking the headlines on his phone until he became increasingly concerned that his ward had not yet appeared. The driver was arranged for 9.30am, so Walter tried to calm his nerves and ordered another coffee. He was much happier within the confines of the embassy, dealing with minor consular or other administrative issues. 'Out in the field' was not where he felt comfortable. At 9.00am, he decided to walk up the wood-panelled stairs to Room 7 and tap the door gently. There was no response. He tapped again a little louder, thought he heard movement and beat a hasty retreat downstairs to wait. Twenty minutes later, he had released the knot on his shiny tie a little and was struggling to complete the easy crossword on his phone. With a burst of resolve he went back up to Room 7 and knocked on the door in such a way that no one inside could have ignored it. When there was no response, he ran downstairs and went straight to reception.

A few minutes later, a lanky lad with slightly protruding eyes pulled down his waistcoat and tapped the door yet again. With no response, he used his master key card and pushed it open. There was a strange smell, and the curtains were still pulled closed. He called out Monsieur Musselwhite's name and flicked on the light.

The white powder and the business card on the glass top of the bedside table rather gave the game away. Monsieur Musselwhite was still wearing last night's clothes: dark-blue chinos and a red-and-white striped shirt. He wasn't wearing shoes or a tie, and he was staring with pale eyes at a small wooden beam above him, which really did not warrant much attention. His jacket was draped over a chair next to a small table on which were his car keys.

After checking his breathing, or lack of it, and establishing that he was stone cold, the receptionist turned to Walter and said he would telephone a doctor and the police. With that, he ran out and headed downstairs. Walter had a few seconds of regretting that he hadn't become a librarian like his careers master had advised him, and then he went into professional mode. He couldn't do anything about the cocaine. However, he began to look for Johnny's mobile phone and passport, together with any briefcase or documents – he knew instinctively that these should not be examined by the French authorities. He further checked the jacket's pockets for Johnny's wallet or anything incriminating (as if taking cocaine was not a big enough problem). He found none of these items, which struck him as odd. Were they in his car? He was about to return to his room next door when the business card Johnny had been using to cut the cocaine caught his eye. He recognised the name on it and picked it up carefully before putting it in his jacket pocket. It was not, in fact, a paper business card but rather a plastic memory stick that doubled up as a business card.

Walter had already phoned his section head in Paris by the time that the receptionist turned up with two policemen, accompanied by a representative from the mayor's office – the latter's presence not being explained.

CHAPTER THREE

"Oh great. What has the idiot done now?" Victor, the British PM, was sitting in his upstairs lounge at Number Ten Downing Street, being briefed by a man from the FCO, a woman from MI6, the Chief Whip and the head of public relations (PR). It was a hastily assembled meeting.

"He's been found dead in a French hotel having apparently overdosed on cocaine and God knows what." Dennis, the FCO man, was standing there in his crumpled suit, his brown eyes slightly recessed under a large forehead.

"Has it got out yet?" the PM asked.

"No, not yet, but we have only a matter of minutes until it does." The head of PR had a concerned look.

"Have we got something ready for when it hits the fan?"

"Yes, we have a couple of hours in which we can play the 'respect for the dead and his family' card. I'll prepare the follow-ups when we know a bit more about what's happening."

"Just what we need." The PM paused. "Johnny is, was, an accident waiting to happen. But why did he have to do it in France? And why now?"

"He never got to his meeting with his French counterpart in Colmar," added the MI6 woman with the tied-back white hair and lined face.

"Terry, tell me he hasn't been up to anything else that is going to come out when the press start digging over this?" demanded Victor.

"There are enough rumours to fill the tabloids until the year after next, but nothing concrete. He was just, well, a bit… maverick." Sir Terry Kimber, the Chief Whip and keeper of the party secrets, had spent the last half hour ringing his contacts to check the situation.

"Unfortunately, his laptop, mobile and wallet haven't been found. They weren't in his room or in his car. One of our Paris embassy staff, who was looking after Mr Musselwhite, has been trying to locate them to keep them out of French hands," Dennis said, looking slightly concerned.

"God knows what was on them," pondered Lorna, the MI6 woman.

"Isn't all this covered by diplomatic immunity?" The PM was not in the happiest of moods.

"Well, on the surface of it, he appears to have driven down there alone, on his way to a holiday along the Mediterranean, using a second passport." Lorna looked across towards Dennis and Terry, who were nodding gently.

"But he's still covered by diplomatic immunity or whatever, isn't he?

"Well… that's a bit debatable." Dennis was treading on eggshells.

"Oh, for fuck's sake! Remind me, what was he down there for?" Victor asked.

"Using rehabilitated potash mine sites for renewable energy. It was a French initiative."

"Off on another free holiday, was he?" the PM asked rhetorically. "We don't have potash mining, do we?"

"Only one, but it can be applied to coal mines and the like." Dennis had a mild Yorkshire accent.

"What about his body?" The PM's mind was darting all over the place. "What about the autopsy? I suppose there'll be one. I don't want this hanging over the G20 summit in Marrakech in a week's time."

"It's all being taken care of. The relevant protocols have kicked in." Dennis sounded at his most professional.

"Terry, you had better stay behind."

With that, the others left, and the conversation moved on to who should replace Johnny, and whoever that was, he or she preferably needed to be a boring, safe pair of hands.

***

Mike Kingdom was walking down the hill, through the conifers, to her favourite pond in a marshy area near her cabin. She wouldn't be away too long, but she needed a break from staring at her screen.

She had woken early to the sound of rain on the roof above her bed. From the moment she had opened her eyes, she had been trying to work out what was relevant to Randy and what was just background noise.

A few things had caught her attention.

Firstly, there was a newspaper article that touched on

23

Algeria's gas industry and Secretary of State Blinken's visit. A few paragraphs seemed important:

In November 2021, Algeria cut off the gas flowing through its pipeline running through Morocco and across the sea near Gibraltar, to supply Spain and Portugal; Algeria has left two of the other main routes, one via Sicily and one to Almería, pumping at full capacity. Algeria used to provide twelve per cent of all the EU's gas supplies via its three pipelines under the Mediterranean Sea.

Morocco and Algeria are uncomfortable neighbours, but most worrying is that there has now been the closure of borders and airspace, plus the recalling of ambassadors.

Morocco had received its natural gas from Algeria. In addition, it was paid circa $400 million a year for allowing the pipeline across its land. This has now been lost, probably permanently.

If Secretary of State Blinken had been asking for an increase in gas exports, what had the US offered Algeria? And what might Algeria have wanted in return? Had the US administration been asked to retreat on the US recognition of Moroccan sovereignty over the Western Sahara? This would create huge regional tensions and test a relationship going back to the very first days of the USA when Morocco was the first country to formally recognise the thirteen states in 1786.

According to sources, the Western Sahara and gas supplies hadn't been discussed. It wasn't credible that Blinken and Sherman were there to buy sand or visit the archaeological remains of the Roman colonial town in Timgad. The real purpose of the visit had not been revealed.

So, of the three gas pipelines to Europe, one had been shut down by the Algerians. Was Randy working to reopen the pipeline via Morocco and Spain? And did the USA want Algerian gas – whether it came via Spain, Italy or anywhere else – so it didn't care about Morocco and Western Sahara?

Secondly, she had read about Macron's visit and concluded that he was most definitely after natural gas. This was not rocket science. President Macron was pressing for a huge increase in France's natural gas, which Algeria typically provided, to replace the seventeen per cent that used to come from Russia before the continued fighting in Ukraine. Once Putin had invaded Ukraine, oil and gas prices rocketed. He gradually turned down the supply, especially through the Nord Stream pipelines. Putin was waiting until the EU broke ranks and came begging for the energy to see them through the winter. For France, it did not take long for Macron and his ministers to realise that Algeria was the quick-and-easy way to replace the balance.

Was Randy working with the French? Was he working for a French energy company? There must have been a huge commercial opportunity while the pipeline via Morocco to Spain was shut down.

Thirdly, she read about a potential new pipeline:

Algeria, Nigeria and Niger have signed a memorandum of understanding today, 28th July 2022, to build a natural gas pipeline across the Sahara Desert, Algeria's energy minister said on Thursday.

This new trans-Saharan gas pipeline is estimated to cost $13 billion and could send up to 1.1 trillion cubic feet a year of supplies to Europe. The pipeline is expected to be about 2,500 miles long, starting in Warri, Nigeria, and finishing up in Hassi R'Mel, Algeria. Here, it will connect to existing pipelines that run to Europe.

Even more gas would flow north from Nigeria to join with the Algerian gas on its way to Europe. The pipeline routes across the Mediterranean were clearly of critical importance. Mike Kingdom wondered if Randy was involved in sub-Saharan African politics in any way (about which she also knew nothing).

Fourthly, she had read a report produced by the British FCO in Algiers entitled *The Current Political Tensions in the Maghreb.*

From it, she learnt two things that stood out to her: the Chinese were negotiating with Algeria to buy a port, and Algeria is the third largest importer of Russian military equipment – fourteen per cent of all Russian military equipment goes to Algeria. This was an absolutely mind-blowing statistic. She realised that she knew so little about this critical region of the world.

She read further and, disturbingly, saw that Russia and Algeria had agreed on 5th April 2022 to hold joint military exercises in the Algerian desert.

Mike was sincerely hoping that Randy wasn't involved in monitoring or sabotaging anything involving China or Russia.

She walked back up the gentle hill between the stands of conifers until she reached her cabin. The smell of the pines after the rain was refreshing. She went up the outside stairs, pulling on the handrail, and unlocked the door. The three heads on the shelf, looking like members of a jury, stared impassively at her – the one in the red wig looked particularly threatening.

"You wanna know something?" Mike addressed all three, "The USA supports Morocco. Russia supports Algeria. That's it in a nutshell. Which is *great* because Algeria is going to be the next Ukraine where East fights West. What do you think about that?"

Sensibly, the three stayed silent.

One hour after discovering the body, Walter was still in his hotel room in Colmar. He had exhausted the minibar's supply of chocolates. Three staff from the British Embassy in Paris were flying down in the next few hours and would take over all aspects of the case. One would deal with the police; one would handle the administrative stuff, such as the body; and one, Edward Evans, would deal with tying up any loose ends (which is FCO-speak for secret-squirrel stuff). The French police had asked Walter to stay in his room as they would need to interview him.

There was a loud knock on his door. He answered it to a group of French policemen who introduced themselves as being from a *brigade criminelle*; the shortest of the three said he was the *chef de groupe* and would be leading the investigation on behalf of the *commissaire*, who would report to the prosecutor, who would report to the judge. Walter felt punch-drunk. He had never heard of a *brigade criminelle* and felt even more disturbed when they explained they only dealt with high-profile cases. The fact that Monsieur Musselwhite was a British government minister and was about to meet a French minister meant that it wouldn't be investigated in the normal way.

They had immediately asked if Johnny Musselwhite had diplomatic immunity, as they hadn't found his passport. Walter couldn't answer that question; therefore, he stalled. *Aren't all British government ministers covered by diplomatic immunity?* he asked himself. He didn't know. *Does the involvement of drugs invalidate any immunity?* Again, he didn't know. It would be a few hours before the cavalry arrived from the embassy in Paris. He needed to keep it together until then.

This wasn't exactly what Walter had signed up for. This was too James Bond for him.

He had been drinking coffee made using the last milk capsule in his room when the *brigade criminelle* had turned up, and he had idly been musing on whether he might get a knighthood for services to the Crown – his mother in Cornwall would be so proud – or be arrested for the murder of a British government minister. Did they still have the death penalty in France? Why did things happen to him?

"What is your exact role?" the chief asked Walter.

"I'm with the British Embassy in Paris; my superiors will be down here in the next few hours. I flew into Basel yesterday. I'm here for just a few hours to organise things and look after Mr Musselwhite," Walter replied, managing to sound guilty of some unspecified crime.

"We haven't found his passport, wallet, laptop, briefcase or such things, either in his room or car. Do you have them?"

"No. He drove down separately yesterday, as I understand it. He was intending to drive south on holiday after the meeting outside Colmar with your Minister of Energy."

"Where did you both spend last evening?"

"I met him for the first time, here in the hotel, after taking a taxi from Basel. We discussed the meeting. He ordered room service and said he wanted an early night. I went out to an *auberge* and ate alone. I was in bed by 9.40pm. We arranged to meet downstairs for breakfast together."

"Do you have anything of his that might help us in this investigation?" The chief had a very un-Gallic cold demeanour.

Walter could almost feel the business card in his pocket. "No, I don't think so."

"We would like you to stay in Colmar to help. When were you intending to fly back to Paris?"

"I was intending to fly back tonight. Perhaps I should wait until my superiors arrive?" Walter was already acquiring that diplomat's knack of kicking anything unpleasant into the long grass.

"Good idea," the chief replied with a disarming look. "I was going to suggest that we wait for the prosecutor to arrive. I am sure she will have some questions."

Oh bugger! Walter thought, and then, begrudgingly, *Touché.*

"After all, it is not every day that we have the murder in Colmar of a British government minister."

Murder, did he say murder?

CHAPTER FOUR

"What are you doing, Leonard? You appear to be going up and down," Mike asked.

"Give… me… a… couple… of… seconds."

"That looks like a playground in a park. I thought there were restraining orders in place?"

"I just… need… to join… this queue." He paused. "That's better." The image steadied and the background came into proper focus.

"Are you jogging in Hyde Park?" Mike asked in disbelief.

"No, I was running to an ice-cream van that has just turned up, and the park is full of fat little shits."

Mike managed to display considerable restraint. "Why are you in the park?"

"To talk to you, of course." Mike could just about hear Leonard above the chatter of excited children. "This makes me appreciate my air-conditioned office. How are you doing?"

"Well, it's only been twenty-four hours, but I'm now the

world authority on Algerian gas pipelines. Thank you for that."

"It's an exciting, new investment opportunity."

"Leonard, why the cat and mouse? Why not just tell me what's happening? Why not tell me Randy's cover name?"

"You're… Three scoops of rum and raisin, please. You're my independent auditor. If I tell you what I think, then you'll be contaminated. I want you to come at this from… How much?"

"Is it Randy or you who's in trouble?"

"A bit of both. If we need to meet up, remind me that we should use The Goring with a decent bottle of Meursault. This park is really expensive."

"OK… well, I know enough about these pipelines."

"They're the existing ones. Why don't you look at planned pipelines? Oh, and the CFDI: the Critical Foreign Dependencies Initiative. Have you heard of it? No, thought not. Look for what's not on it."

The ice-cream van began playing a jarring, jangly jingle, which blocked out some of Leonard's next words.

"As long as you're OK, I'll head off back to HQ. That's the big, new HQ, not the shit one you used to work in. Call me if you need anything," he said, interspersed with licking his ice cream.

"I've had it up to here with pipelines and, Leonard, you're a—" But the screen faded and the sounds of a London park in summer gradually reduced to nothing.

Mike settled back down on her chair and pinched the top of her nose. One of her windows was open, and she could hear the buzz of insects. *Count to ten,* she heard a voice in her head say.

CFDI? What's a CFDI when it's at home? She knew Leonard

would be laughing to himself as he walked back to his office. While he was eating his rum-and-raisin ice cream, he was revelling in the fact that she would have to google it.

A few minutes later, she had learnt that the CFDI is a list of foreign infrastructure items, produced by the US Department of Homeland Security, which – if attacked or destroyed – would critically impact the USA. It had been part of the WikiLeaks data released in 2010.

As she read the list, three assets stood out to Mike Kingdom. Firstly, the Strait of Gibraltar, which narrowly separates Spain in Southern Europe and Morocco in Northern Africa, connecting the Atlantic Ocean and the Mediterranean Sea. Mike had never looked on the strait as an 'asset', but when she thought about it, its strategic importance seemed obvious. Secondly, she noticed the Maghreb-Europe gas pipeline and, thirdly, the Trans-Med gas pipeline; both went across the Mediterranean to Europe. Why were these of strategic importance to the USA?

Think about it. Think about it. She was trying to discipline herself. The USA was ostensibly backing Morocco over Western Sahara while prioritising Algerian pipelines to Europe. *Oh boy!*

And what isn't on the list? What a stupid question, she thought. *There are a million things not on the list.* She wandered over to the large window and stared at the wall of pine trees. The window really did need cleaning. She would get the ladder out of the garage beneath later. Window cleaning was a job that, bizarrely, she enjoyed. It was a combination of pine resin, pollen and red dust from the Sahara that had coated the glass. *Saharan dust,* she mused, *if only it could talk.*

There was an OCD side to Mike that she had recognised from her early teenage years in Oregon. It wasn't a problem and probably explained why she was so good at her job (if she had a job). After walking up and down for a couple of minutes, she went downstairs to the garage. On entering it, she ran her fingers over her beautiful Italian motorbike and walked between the tractor and trailer to a set of double ladders.

Five minutes later and thirteen feet up, she was cleaning the enormous picture window with a chamois leather. This activity was akin to therapy. Peering into her room, she felt as if she were looking into her soul. The three polystyrene heads, each with its wig, dominated her view and stared back at her, not displaying any emotion, but, perhaps, representing her mood swings. The photograph of Mount Hood on the wall brought back memories of her Portland upbringing. The various pay-outs after the accident and those from a couple of private projects meant she was very comfortable financially (if your life consisted of living in a cabin above a garage and owning an Italian motorbike). Of course, the shiny window's reflection of her bald head and pitted face also reminded her of a stark reality and, surprisingly, of the Korean war memorial in Washington, DC. She would never forget how her face was reflected in the polished granite wall with the soldiers and vegetation behind her. Suddenly, something about the ache and the deep scar on her left leg reminded her of the so-called 'accident', which she laid firmly at Leonard's door.

She was in no hurry to come down from her vantage point on what was now such a gorgeous September day, making her mistress of all she surveyed. Twenty-four hours ago, she had been relatively carefree and planning a trip back to Oregon. Now, after Leonard's visit, she was mentally in overdrive. The smells and sounds of the forest, the reflections of the coniferous trees in the window and the physical exhilaration of standing on the ladder all served to emphasise the contrast between her position and that of Randy. Was he alive or dead? Was he in some underground prison or worse? She bent her leg, stretched it out and descended.

***

The sun was shining in Colmar. This meant that the bridges over the canals were heavy with tourists taking selfies against a backdrop of half-timbered houses painted in bright pastel colours. The ancient buildings and flower boxes that were reflected in the water merely made the town doubly photogenic. All of this, however, was very low on Walter's list of priorities. After a night in the hotel, he was about to be interviewed by the special prosecutor, Madame Bettancourt.

He had spent the previous evening with three colleagues from the embassy who had, thankfully, taken control. At dinner, while he ate *magret de canard* and drank a pinot gris produced less than twenty-five miles away, they'd had a long discussion among themselves as to why Johnny Musselwhite had chosen to use his non-diplomatic passport for his trip, given that he was performing official duties in Colmar. This no longer really mattered, of course, as he was dead. The FCO had been in touch with his family and were arranging for the body to be flown back to the UK. His Mercedes was another matter, as it didn't have diplomatic plates, and the police seemed very interested in it.

It had been late morning when the chief of the *brigade criminelle* had spoken to the assembled British team and confirmed that Johnny, in all likelihood, had been murdered; all of this had quickly been communicated back to London. Presumably, the high-profile nature of the case had led to the autopsy being undertaken at breakneck speed – although that might not be an appropriate expression.

And so Walter found himself, accompanied by a senior embassy colleague called Stewart, sitting opposite Madame Bettancourt (a very striking woman of about forty-five who was wearing a black suit and pale lipstick), together with the chief of the *brigade criminelle* and a police officer in uniform. She spoke flawless English and made it clear from the outset that she was aware of the sensitivities of the case and, in particular, the diplomatic consequences.

"Now that we know Monsieur Musselwhite was poisoned, I would like to go over everything from the second you met him," she began.

Walter began to think he should have a lawyer present rather than Stewart, whom he did not know anything about – except that he supported Liverpool and drank Kir royales, but most importantly, he wasn't a lawyer.

Where's Brendan? Walter thought, *And why did he disappear, leaving an absolute junior to look after a government minister?* Brendan was meant to be in Colmar as Johnny's aide. Walter was just to be a general dogsbody. The hairs on Walter's long arms began to stand on end, and his mouth went dry. He would definitely phone Brendan when he got back to his room.

"So, from the beginning, please, Mr Flushing," Madame Bettancourt requested.

"I landed at Basel airport after flying from Paris, and I took a taxi, as agreed with the embassy. I was driven to Colmar and checked into this hotel. I rang Mr Musselwhite's room, and he came down to meet me in the foyer."

"And you had never met him before?"

"No, never."

"What happened after you met in the foyer?"

"We talked about the transport arrangements for yesterday's planned meeting with your minister and agreed to meet downstairs well before 9.00am. He ordered room service while we were in the foyer and retired to his room to eat and sleep."

"Did he mention cocaine or drugs in general?"

"No, of course not."

"He did not ask you to procure any?"

"No, of course not."

"Was there anybody else around? Did anybody show an interest in him?"

"No. Not that I remember."

The small private dining room in which they were talking seemed to get even smaller.

"Was there any contact of any sort between you after he retired and before you found him the next morning?" she queried.

"I didn't find him the next morning. The night manager, or whatever his title is, found him after using his master key to open the door." Walter sounded almost aggressive.

"Was there any contact?" she asked very calmly and patiently.

"No. None. I went out to…" He reached into his wallet and took out his receipt. "Here." He handed across his restaurant receipt, which she examined.

"Did you enjoy the raclette?" Her pale lips looked almost provocative.

"Yes, thank you."

She turned over a page in her beige file. "Let's move on to yesterday morning. What happened then?"

"I became nervous. I am quite junior," he said, looking at Stewart, who was encouraging Walter with a gentle smile. "As it got closer to 9.00am, I went and tapped on his door, but with no response, so I left. Eventually, I returned and knocked very loudly. There was no sound from inside. I came down here and asked the night manager to use his master key or card – I can't remember what he used – to get into the room."

"What happened when he opened the door?"

"Mr Musselwhite was flat out on the bed, dressed and staring up at the ceiling. He was a strange colour. There was white powder on the surface of his glass-topped bedside cabinet. We opened the curtains, and the manager checked for… signs of life…" Walter hesitated.

"And then?"

"He told me he would go downstairs and telephone for a doctor and the police."

"What did you do next?"

Walter began to think that he needed to be careful. He knew he had done nothing wrong, but these were uncharted waters. "I didn't do anything. I left his door ajar and went back to my room next door."

The prosecutor unbuttoned her jacket and leant forwards. "Did you take his laptop? His mobile? His passport?"

"No. I didn't see them."

"Do you know where they are?"

"No. Why would I?"

"They are not in his room or car."

Walter just stared at her blankly.

"Mr Flushing, do you mind if my colleague searches your room? We need to find Mr Musselwhite's laptop and mobile phone… and his passport."

"What?" He turned to Stewart who just shrugged in a vague way. "Why?" Walter asked.

"Because this is now a murder investigation, and you were the last person to see the victim alive."

"Yes, if you want. I don't have any of those things… I have nothing to hide."

The plastic business card that had been next to Johnny's bed was still in Walter's pocket. *Bugger!* he thought to himself.

"May I ask you again about the cocaine? Were you actually sharing it with Mr Musselwhite that night? Did you supply it, perhaps?"

"No. No. I've never—"

"Mr Flushing, we are not accusing you of anything, but this is a murder investigation."

"Madame." Stewart spoke for the first time. "You understand the sensitivity of all this and that Mr Flushing has diplomatic immunity. He will, of course, help you with your enquiries and stay in Colmar as long as you require."

"Mr Flushing does *not* have diplomatic immunity according to our records. He is service; that is to say, support staff at your embassy. He is not listed under diplomatic or consular – unlike you, Mr McBride." She glanced at the chief of the *brigade criminelle* and continued, "You do not have a diplomatic passport, do you Mr Flushing?"

What? Walter thought, *How could this have happened?*

***

"*Murdered?*" The PM put down his cup of tea and brushed his white hair back with his hand. He had just been told of certain events in France while beginning a meeting to prepare for a telephone call with Conrad, the US President. The British ambassador in Washington, DC, was part of the meeting via a video link and was quietly worried about exactly who had been murdered.

"The French police are saying that Johnny was murdered," a man in a dark-blue suit updated everyone.

"With cocaine? I thought he had overdosed?" The PM couldn't believe his ears.

"In addition, they have discovered poison… in the autopsy," the man in dark blue added rather superfluously.

"Get Peter in here. We need to think how to handle the PR."

An aide went out to summon Peter.

"They did the autopsy quickly, didn't they?"

No one answered the PM.

"He only died yesterday morning," Victor continued, pausing to polish off the tea and biscuit. "How big a team do we have down there?"

"We have three from Paris who arrived yesterday afternoon and someone called Walter from the embassy who was escorting Johnny and found him dead."

"Are we sending our own police down? I mean, to find out who killed him and why?" The PM was beginning to think through the implications of all this.

"Yes, they're on their way," a voice at the back chipped in.

A brief silence descended on the room before the PM switched his train of thought back to his later conversation with the President of the United States (POTUS), with whom he had a great relationship. "Stephen, what's Conrad wanting to discuss?" he asked the ambassador, who had been waiting patiently.

"The G20 in Marrakech will be top of the President's agenda," came the reply from across the Atlantic.

CHAPTER FIVE

"I have fifteen minutes." The PM was speaking to a room of half a dozen individuals, all milling around. He was sitting at his desk with a screen and keyboard in front of him. Heavy, dark-green curtains in his office at Number Ten Downing Street provided the backdrop for the scheduled call to Conrad, the US President.

Dennis walked over to the PM and bent over from the waist to speak into his ear.

"What?" Victor was nonplussed.

"An explosion," Dennis replied as quietly as possible.

"Where?"

"On one of the main gas pipelines in Algeria yesterday… Wednesday."

"And?" The PM was only open to important interruptions at this key moment.

"It's just over the Atlas Mountains from Marrakech," came the reply.

"Shit! Conrad doesn't like this sort of thing. If he hears about it, he may not come to the G20. Who did it?"

"No one is claiming responsibility at the moment, but it's early days. The President may not know about it yet. It came to us from private sources."

"You mean that I can't mention it?"

"Well… no. Not unless he mentions it."

"Don't we share this sort of thing?"

"Eventually."

"What are the implications?"

"Reduced gas to Europe."

Victor looked at Dennis resignedly. "Oh shit," he said using his word of the week.

Since President Putin's invasion of Ukraine, most international political conversations between leaders began with the supply of armaments to President Zelensky and ended with the supply of natural gas to Europe. The continental winter was approaching fast, and Germany, in particular, was about to be exposed as not having anywhere near enough gas. This whole issue would be the dominant one at the G20 in Marrakech and, even more pressingly, in the conversation in less than ten minutes. Victor grabbed a glass of water and took a sip.

Dennis came over to him again with the look of an embalmed corpse. He said quietly, "We hear that Putin isn't going to reopen the Nord Stream 1 pipeline after its so-called 'maintenance shutdown'."

"Is this general knowledge?"

"No."

"Will Conrad know?"

"Probably, through Five Eyes."

"I'm guessing the explosion in Algeria on the gas pipeline is connected. Are the Russians involved in that? Sounds likely."

"We have people checking."

"Thanks… I need to talk to Conrad."

Most people cleared out of the room, and the conversation began.

POTUS was wearing a dark-red, knitted cardigan that appeared to be his favourite when there were no cameras (or at least, no press photographers). "Victor, good morning."

"Conrad."

"What is it about you and me that we seem to begin every conversation with a geography lesson? I remember us doing a crash course on Antarctica last year. I understand that, today, we need to know all about Algeria?"

"I believe so." The British PM was trying to keep it a little vague.

"Secretary of State Blinken was there at the end of March, and within a week, Russia and Algeria had planned joint military manoeuvres."

"Why? What did he do to upset them?"

"Ha! Nothing. He was just chewing the fat. I asked him to go because I've been looking at our relationship with Morocco… you know, this whole Western Sahara thing. Why do they need to fight over a load of sand?"

"Are you interested in the Algerian gas?"

"Who isn't? That's why Macron was there. So, I just heard someone's blown up a pipeline. Who benefits from that apart from the Russians and any of a whole bunch of terrorists?"

"I take it that Five Eyes are on the case? I've only just heard."

"I'll give Leonard in London a kick. It worked last time over Antarctica."

They paused while they both thought about the implications of what might be found.

"Are you OK for Marrakech?" Victor asked, as if Conrad were coming over for dinner later.

"Yes, sure. It's a thousand miles from the gas field in Algeria. I checked. I should be safe as long as I lock my hotel door… unlike your Minister for Energy, I hear." There was no malice, and they were used to ribbing each other.

"You may not have heard that he was murdered."

"Sorry to hear that. Who killed him?"

"We, and the French, are busy checking. It's early days."

"Shall we run through our agenda, starting with Zelensky's requests?"

And with that, the general chat finished and the virtual meeting in advance of the G20 get-together became more business-like.

***

It was lunchtime, and Mike Kingdom was emerging from the shower with a large, white towel around her waist and a smaller towel wrapped around her bald head. For the last three years, she had kept strange hours – working, sleeping, eating and staring out of the window as the mood took her. Her cramped shower lined with pine boards was often where she went when she had reached an impasse in her investigations – it was either that or taking a walk through the forest. The hot water beating on her head, the noise and the steam somehow took her to a parallel world for ten minutes, away from the computer screen or cell phone. Then there were the random patterns of knot holes and wood grain, which seemed to manifest themselves as faces, objects or new ideas. Today, this hadn't happened. She rubbed herself dry, having come up with precisely zero ways to move forwards. This occurred sometimes.

Mike decided to make herself a green tea. The kettle clicked off once it had boiled, and she began pouring the water into her cup. As she carried it over to her desk, she began thinking about the kettle, electricity, switches and power supplies – like everyone, she took them for granted. She then thought about gas pipelines. Presumably, they used electricity to move the gas over vast distances. Or did they? And were the pipes underground or overground? Her mind was always running off in different directions. And what happened under the sea? There couldn't be booster stations – or whatever they're called – under the sea, could there? Presumably, these pipelines always went the shortest distance between landmasses, like the one across the Straits of Gibraltar, or they went the direct route, like the one bypassing Morocco that went to Almería in Spain. Was that why the third pipeline went via Sicily to mainland Italy?

She stopped. Did she really care one jot about any pipeline, anywhere in the world, ever? This would only be necessary if she was to find Randy. And she had to find Randy.

Leonard had mentioned planned pipelines while eating his rum-and-raisin ice cream. What route were these likely to take? She found that two were well advanced in their planning, but both had stalled for political, technical and financial reasons; the one to go via Sardinia to Italy was called GALSI, and the other was called PEGASUS and would go via Corsica to France.

Mike began to feel certain that Randy was involved, either constructively or destructively, with one of these three existing or two planned pipelines from Algeria to Europe. The reasons for his involvement could be any of a huge raft of possibilities, ranging from control of the Western Sahara to Russian interference in Algeria, and from historical tensions within the Maghreb to the EU's need for gas.

It was time for her to start hacking into a few accounts to find out what was happening. She would start with the gas companies in Algeria.

***

Stewart McBride from the British Embassy in Paris was reassuring Walter as they walked up the steps of the prosecutor's office in Colmar. He was explaining that various high-level conversations were taking place between London and Paris and that Walter was likely to be free to go after this interview today. When Stewart mentioned that a senior policeman from Scotland Yard and one from a unit of which Walter had never heard were on their way to Colmar, his mood went back down to just above panic level. As they entered the interview room, Madame Bettancourt was sitting in a high-backed, black leather chair behind a large desk. The room and its contents were nondescript, except for a big, fluffy toy rabbit slumped against a hat stand and a roll of wrapping paper leant against the wall. No one else was present.

"Mr Flushing, Mr McBride… please take a seat." The prosecutor was wearing a white blouse and no lipstick this time. She had a disarming smile. "Mr Flushing, I have some good news, I think."

Walter didn't like the final qualification to that sentence.

"The full analysis of the poison has been concluded, and it is… something unpronounceable," she said while lifting a piece of paper and looking at it over her reading glasses, "It is known as 'trick', or so they inform me. 'Tri-' followed by lots of strange letters and numbers. What matters is that it is very rare and relatively new. It is only used by certain states…" She paused to select the *mot juste*. "Certain *rogue* states. By the way, it is not radioactive or transmissible in any way."

Walter was digesting the fact that he had been in a room where someone had been poisoned when he noticed what looked like his passport, upside down on her desk. He recognised the torn-off luggage labels stuck on the cover.

"This is of special importance to our two governments. While you are still a person of interest in this case, we do not believe that you had the means or motive to use this. You are unlikely to have had access to or to have administered such a drug, although you are the last person to have seen the victim alive and the first to find him dead."

Well, that was patently obvious, wasn't it? Walter asked himself.

"We are going to allow you to leave once you have spoken to the police officers arriving later today from London and to some other officers who are coming from Paris tomorrow. Without realising it, you may have important information. We are collating CCTV footage from various sources, and we may want to ask you about anything or anybody we find of interest. This is a very serious matter with international implications. I ask you not to speak to anyone about this apart from your embassy colleagues. Knowledge that we have discovered this poison must stay secret. You understand?"

She looked at Walter and then at Stewart.

She continued, "I will keep your passport until both interviews have been completed. I understand that you are to stay in the same hotel for the next two nights. Please leave your mobile phone turned on, as we may wish to speak with you at any time. Do you understand and do you have any questions?"

Walter fidgeted slightly in his chair.

"It sounds eminently fair," Stewart chipped in as Walter glanced at him.

"Mr Flushing?" the prosecutor prompted.

"Yes. Fine. May I leave the hotel?"

"Yes, but don't leave Colmar."

Walter looked about as enthusiastic as the big rabbit.

***

Back in his hotel room, Walter was sitting on his bed taking stock. His mobile phone was on charge on the desk, and the window was open, letting in the sunshine. He wanted to phone his mother or sister in Cornwall, but he knew that was impossible. The next couple of days would drag on, he was sure.

He sensed he was getting annoyed. Up to this point, he had been scared about what had and might happen to him, but now he was just annoyed.

Shouldn't the FCO have protected him a bit more? First of all, they had sent him to Algiers on a research project that had turned into a baptism of fire, then they had sent him to Paris, but not with a full contract and the usual protections. They wanted him to assist Brendan in looking after Johnny Musselwhite for a couple of days, which would also have been no problem had Brendan not cried off and dumped Walter in it. And now, Stewart was buggering off back to Paris, leaving Walter to be interviewed by various police and investigating officers over the next twenty-four hours. *Twenty-four?* he thought. *I'm only twenty-four.*

Walter resolved that, the second he got his passport back, he would fly back to Paris and terminate his contract.

Growing up in a mobile home in the corner of a field above the River Tamar, after his father had disappeared, was not that bad. He and his sister had plenty of friends in the village, and he had the advantage of being a bright kid. The generations mixed together in a way that he hadn't seen elsewhere, whether in the pub, at the music festival or in the gig racing. He was tall with strong arms, which made him a natural choice to be part of the six-person gig team, rowing in the competitions around Cornwall and the Isles of Scilly. His artistic talents also made him a regular as the painter of the stage scenery for the local amateur dramatic productions.

While irritated at the FCO and the French authorities, he had been treated fairly by Madame Bettancourt, the prosecutor. The last couple of days had been a roller coaster, and he still couldn't bring himself to relax until the interviews were over and he had his passport in his hands.

The enormity of the situation kept welling up inside him. Who would kill a British minister, and in France? Why? The killer or killers must have been in the hotel. Had he seen them? He didn't think so, but how close had he come to being killed himself if he had stepped out of his room at the wrong moment? He shivered. The killers were probably professionals from Russia or some 'rogue' state, as the prosecutor had described them.

Why did they take Johnny's laptop, phone and passport? Or was that what they were after? They didn't need to kill him to steal those things, did they? They could simply break into his hotel room while he was out.

Whether it was because he was annoyed, affronted, patriotic, inquisitive or bored, he decided to investigate a few things himself. What else was he going to do? For the next twenty-four hours, he was trapped in Colmar, and he was intrigued. He opened up his laptop and searched 'Johnny Musselwhite'. There was enough to keep him occupied for weeks.

Having been married three times, resulting in four children, one of whom was a well-known model (warranting pages of salacious gossip herself), he was the son of Sir David Morton Musselwhite, the MP for Cheltenham. How he had ended up following his father into politics was the stuff of legend, mostly made up of privilege, luck and deep, pale-blue eyes that seemed to charm both young and old and male and female alike. Most people would agree that, for his first marriage, he had chosen well (that's 'well' in the financial, bottomless-pit sense of the word). The divorce settlement set him up for the next ten years. His second wife had a minor title from her father, who was some baronet. Then came the drinking and the drugs – and that was just her. He laughed it all off and made a success of several business ventures that various school friends seemed to front for him. Despite some financial impropriety here and there, he managed to float to the top.

Being the Minister for Energy was the pinnacle of his parliamentary career, which surprised many – not only because of his debauched and incoherent lifestyle but also because he was a vociferous Remainer and defender of the EU.

Walter took a break from the screen and wondered who would want to kill Johnny (he was thinking of those other than some madman from a rogue state). He probably had his share of enemies, but poisoning was pretty extreme and, ultimately, traceable. What was he doing that a rogue state wanted to stop – permanently? He stood up and looked obliquely down at the still water of the canal. If only the sea off Newlyn were this calm during the annual gig race.

He walked back to the desk, past his jacket draped over the chair.

On impulse, he lifted it and took out the business card that Johnny had been using to cut his cocaine. He looked at the name again: the name of someone he had seen in Algiers.

CHAPTER SIX

Mike had exhausted herself reading about the three existing pipelines, and she now knew about pounds per square inch, compression stations every sixty miles, and the comparative costs of overground and underground versus underwater. On her computer, she had spent an enjoyable five minutes on Google Maps trying to follow the underground pipelines across the desert and mountains. They sure knew how to disguise them. For most of their length, they were underground, punctuated at key points by compressor stations that pushed the gas along the next stage.

It was while searching for compression stations that she spotted an article on an explosion the previous day at what it called "compressor station no. 6". The article was in an Algerian newspaper in French and warranted only a few lines. How serious was this? Was it sabotage? Was Randy involved?

Mike's phone buzzed. The display said "Dr Rose Delavine".

"Hello, Rose. I never asked you what sort of doctor you were," Mike began.

"Well, I have to deal with assholes all day…"

"Proctologist, then?"

"…most of them above me," Leonard continued.

"That image will stay with me all week. What can I do for you?"

"I'm getting kicked by the President to find out what's happening in Algeria before he visits Morocco."

"Doesn't he have a bunch of people in Algiers? You're in London."

"Yes, but the intelligence may well come via Five Eyes. Have you found Randy yet? It's getting urgent."

"No, but I'm worried that he's blowing up compressor stations in Algeria."

"That would be unfortunate – and especially over the next couple of weeks."

"Leonard, if it's urgent, can we stop messing about? What's his cover name? What's his cell phone number? Where's he meant to be and what's he doing?"

"I wanted you to come at this from the side, but, OK, events have overtaken things." He paused. "Why not check out a name? Ramon Ramirez. And I can give you his cell phone number, but it hasn't been operational for weeks, and there's no locational data available since that time." Leonard read out the cell phone number.

"Where was he last known to be?"

"Málaga, Spain."

"Doing what?"

"Well, before Putin," he said, pronouncing it 'Poot'n', "got the hots for Ukraine, he was meant to be, shall we say, loading the dice in Morocco's – or effectively Uncle Sam's – favour."

"Doing what? Blowing up pipelines?"

"Yeah, well sort of… stuff like that… but nothing permanent."

"Why?"

"To encourage the Algerians to reopen the pipeline across Morocco to Spain. The President was hoping that it would make the Algerians play nice."

"Then, I'm guessing, the Ukraine war happened, the Nord Stream 1 pipeline got shut down, and everyone wants natural gas."

"And let's just say that the President's enthusiasm for the Moroccan claim to Western Sahara has been temporarily downgraded, and the Algerians may suddenly be our new best buddies. He doesn't want us shitting in the Algerian nest over the next few months."

"Was he behind the explosion yesterday?" Mike asked.

"I sure hope not."

"Why hasn't he made contact for so long?"

"Your guess is as good as mine."

"What a mess."

"It won't be a mess if you find him – quick. Right, I have to go. I have another appointment."

"Make sure you wear long rubber gloves." Mike saw Leonard's smiling face disappear from the line.

Mike felt like a greyhound when the gate opens on the track and the hare is in view. She now had so many avenues to investigate. Of course, Leonard had initially tied one arm behind her back (well, two, actually), but she understood why. He had hoped she could find Randy, stop him from completing his brief, and avoid any comeback on him from a change of President and policy. Not involving her by providing too many links and formal access was Leonard's clumsy way of handling everything. However, the explosion in Algeria and the US President's upcoming visit to Marrakech had changed the priorities.

She started by hacking the cell phone account using a piece of CIA software that she had helped to develop. A Ramon Ramirez appeared to have been using this phone for nine months from an address in Málaga. As Leonard had said, it had stopped completely a few weeks earlier. There were surprisingly few calls. *Perhaps, he has other phones?* she wondered, *But it's a good start.* While she wouldn't recognise any specific numbers, she scanned the country and area codes quickly. Most of the calls were within Spain and France, with some to area codes +212 and +213, which turned out to be Morocco and Algeria, respectively.

Many of the calls were to or from a number in Marrakech, which turned out to be that of a *riad*, a small urban hotel with a central courtyard. Was this his base in North Africa? Who else was staying there that he would need to call from Málaga?

She jumped up to stretch her left leg and to find a biscuit. She had to move the vacuum cleaner away from the cupboard to get access; cleaning would have to wait. Though why bother? She never had guests, and Leonard turning up twice in a year did not warrant it. In fact, she felt the need to clean *after* he had left, not before.

When she sat back down, she decided to search for Ramon Ramirez at the Málaga address. This didn't take long, and she quickly found that he worked for a gas exploration consultancy with offices in Málaga, Marseilles and some northern European locations. Málaga was the head office, and Randy appeared to live in an apartment in the suburbs. A few seconds later, she was looking at his social media accounts, all set up neatly by the CIA to give him a credible backstory. She paused over the very few photographs, which were mainly of motorbikes, some unknown men and industrial pipework on a massive scale. It was no surprise that none of his messages or photographs highlighted blowing up pipelines. In a couple of photographs, there was a girl about five years old. Was this his daughter or part of the cover? The child looked Spanish, but then so did Randy. So had her dead husband, Dylan.

It was at that moment that her phone rang again. She had never been so popular. "Hello."

"Hello, Mike, it's Charles. Charles Yelland."

"Charles, good to hear from you. How are the family?"

"They're all well. They're in Mexico at the moment. How are you?"

"Well… and surprisingly busy."

"Oh." His voice sounded disappointed. "I was hoping that you could help me with a problem. An urgent problem."

"Nobody has been kidnapped, I hope?"

Mike had worked for Charles in a private capacity a year earlier – trying to find his daughter, Angelica, who had been kidnapped. He was the CEO of Petronello Oil, an Anglo-Spanish-Norwegian oil exploration company with interests across the world from Antarctica to the North Sea and from Trinidad to Mexico. She had never completely trusted him from the first day she had ridden up the long drive to his manor house in Buckinghamshire to the day that the investigation had finished.

"No, no one has been kidnapped, but I've just had a worrying phone call. I wondered if you could discreetly check what's going on?"

"Who was it from?"

Charles had sounded a little nervous, and he had left a silence that suggested he was going through some mental turmoil. "I don't know this person, but he said that he'd seen me once."

Mike had learnt over the weeks when she was searching for Angelica that Charles's relationship with the truth was perhaps best described as 'once removed'.

"Charles, remembering last time, will you tell me everything, not just what you think I need to know?"

"He said he didn't want to talk on the phone, but asked if we could meet urgently when he got back to the UK."

Mike licked her finger to use it to pick up some crumbs of a biscuit remaining on the top of her desk. "Why's this worrying?"

"He said he thought that my life was in danger."

"What name did he give?"

"Walter Flushing. I've never heard of him. He said he would call in a couple of days, but I was to be careful."

"Was he threatening you?"

"No, I don't think so."

"Was he English?"

"Yes, but I didn't pick up any strong accent. Maybe West Country?"

"Can you give me his telephone number?"

She grabbed a pen and scribbled down on her pad what he told her. "Leaving out the BS, have you been up to anything that might lead to someone wanting to kill you? And remember it's me you're talking to."

"No more than usual. I'm in the oil business, for goodness' sake; it comes with the territory. I've already had protesters glued to the gates of the estate. This phone call is just one more thing."

"So, what are you going to do?"

"Use the helicopter more."

"I didn't mean how you were going to get home from your office. I meant what are you going to do about protecting yourself?"

"Don't worry, I'll up the protection until you tell me what this is about."

"Be careful. I'll do some quick checks."

***

It was late afternoon, and Walter was still in his hotel room, after having eaten a quiche with salad from the room service menu. The empty plate and tray were on the carpet near the bed. He was playing some music while reading the obituaries and comments about Johnny Musselwhite in the British and French press, having reached dead ends on his search for the reasons Johnny had been killed. Earlier, he had taken his mind back to his short time in North Africa when he was undertaking his research project. Walter had come across the two planned Mediterranean pipelines. He had written in his report about the political tensions in Algiers over the ways to maximise the financial return from the gas, and about the potential and sometimes conflicting routes to market.

He remembered reading about the involvement of a company called Petronello in the pipeline called PEGASUS; in fact, the 'PE' part of the name represented Petronello. There were several other interested parties, including the French government and the Corsican regional government: the

Collectivité Territoriale de Corse. Corsica was to be a key part in the long chain from Algeria to somewhere near Marseilles.

The GALSI pipeline, or Gasdotto Algeria Sardegna Italia, was the other possible pipeline; it had been mooted since 2005 and would import 283 billion cubic feet of natural gas from Algeria to Italy each year. Being roughly 930 miles long, the pipeline would follow a route that would start from the gas fields in Algeria and cross via Sardinia to Tuscany, close to Piombino.

Neither of these seemed connected to the British Minister for Energy. What was Johnny's connection to Charles Yelland at Petronello (the name on the business card), apart from the fact that they were both British. Had Johnny simply been given a business card at some trade show or industry dinner?

Walter plugged the business card into his laptop; he didn't save the contents but merely read them. There were photographs, some technical specifications and the recording of a phone conversation. What he saw and heard shocked him. He slumped back in his chair and tried to think logically what to do. He got up and paced around the room like a tiger in a compound.

An hour later, Walter was at his wits' end. He phoned Brendan, who was reassuring.

Walter was waiting eagerly for some notification from the prosecutor's office to give him the time that the policemen from London would arrive later that day. Madame Bettancourt had made it clear that she wanted to lay down certain ground rules with the British police before they spoke to Walter. He had three boxes to tick: two interviews with, firstly, the British and, secondly, the French police; afterwards, he would be free to fly back to Paris; and then, a couple of days later, he'd fly on to Exeter airport and a family reunion.

He was walking to the en suite bathroom when there was a knock on the door.

Excellent, he thought to himself. He walked across and opened it. "Oh… Hello, Brendan. I thought…"

There was the quietest of noises, which came from the raised gun. Walter never heard it. Instead, he fell backwards onto the corner of his bed, bounced off awkwardly and ended up sprawled on the carpet with his right arm appearing to reach for the napkin on the tray of finished food.

Brendan entered the room. He searched the top of the desk and Walter's open briefcase. He picked up his laptop and the memory card, putting them into his shoulder bag, then he walked past the prone figure to the door. With a quick final look, he left the room and disappeared down the corridor.

A few minutes later, Walter's mobile phone rang. It vibrated in his inside pocket, but who knows if it was enough to stimulate his un-beating heart back to life?

On the other end of the call was Mike Kingdom, who had decided to ring the number Charles Yelland had given her.

CHAPTER SEVEN

Madame Bettancourt had cut short the visit to her daughter to deliver the large, fluffy rabbit to her newborn granddaughter, Noémie. A phone call had rather taken the edge of what should have been a happy occasion.

It was early evening, and Madame Bettancourt was now standing in the corridor of the *auberge*, wearing a stylish, black coat that only went so far in protecting her against the wind. With her were a selection of French and British police, who had been expecting to interview Walter Flushing not to watch his body being carried out on a gurney to an awaiting ambulance on its way to the hospital.

Both the French and British police were trying to contact Brendan Dowell from the British Embassy, who had been at the *auberge* earlier that afternoon, making the arrangements to transport Johnny Musselwhite's belongings and car back to Paris. It might be that he had spoken to Walter and may have been the last person to see him alive. Brendan was probably travelling back to Paris and incommunicado.

Madame Bettancourt had made it quite clear to the police that, in her opinion, Walter did not have diplomatic immunity and so his phone, laptop and anything else could be examined.

Discussions were centring on why a country like Russia would use a sophisticated poison and a hit squad to kill an important British minister, then return a day later to shoot his junior assistant. What did the assistant know or have in his possession? The other unlikely theory was that Walter had killed the minister and had to be killed to cover up the tracks.

The prosecutor had quite liked Walter – he seemed like an 'innocent abroad' as Mark Twain might have said. She saw him as a hapless pawn in a much larger and darker conspiracy. Madame Bettancourt could not decide whether she thought he had seen something and needed elimination or had something from the minister that the killers had expected to find in his room. The gunman had taken Walter's laptop but not his phone; hopefully, this would reveal something.

***

In Paris, what had begun as a relatively low-priority matter (i.e., helping a British minister to meet his French counterpart in Alsace) had escalated to the top of the British ambassador's pile. This proved the golden rule in the FCO: you could forget what was top of the pile on first reading in the morning, as it would be overtaken by the day's events. He had just finished speaking to London where Dennis was about to update the PM.

***

"What? You're joking?" Victor was standing in Number Ten, looking like a slightly overfed penguin. He was about to leave for a formal dinner at the Guild Hall, celebrating the centenary of some chartered body of which he had never heard. Was it chemical engineers or estate management? Who had agreed to this? And why wasn't the Cabinet Office Minister or, his boss, the Chancellor of the Duchy of Lancaster attending this dinner? Weren't they in charge of chartered bodies? He was beginning to feel that his relaxed style was coming back to bite him.

"Unfortunately, not. This Walter Flushing has been shot – in his hotel room. He's in a critical condition in intensive care," Dennis said.

"Why?" The PM was playing with his bow tie, an action that invariably leaves it looking worse than when one first tied it.

"Nobody has a clue. Interpol and our police never got to interview him about the Minister of Energy's death. They're with the French authorities now."

"Was it to stop him speaking to them? If so, why?" Victor looked pained. "I thought Johnny was the victim of some sophisticated poisoning by the Russians?"

"MI6 are convinced it's the Russians – no one else would use that poison – but we don't have any proof yet. As to why they'd return to shoot a junior FCO man, we have absolutely no idea at the moment. He was really only a glorified lackey."

"Perhaps he saw them in the act of murdering Johnny?"

Someone indicated that Victor should be leaving for the dinner.

"Keep me updated," he requested, "I'm getting a funny feeling about this." With that, he turned and headed for the door.

Mike Kingdom was slouched in her tatty armchair with her feet on an upturned wooden wine box, which served as a coffee table. She was frustrated that Walter Flushing hadn't answered his phone, but she was glad that she had tried. When she had joined the CIA in the Seattle office, a director had told her to forget the clever and complicated theories until you have dismissed the patently obvious. She had decided to concentrate on Walter. Most things in her line of work were variants of the terminally mundane – but Walter intrigued her. Having run a quick check on him, she had established that he was on a short-term contract with the FCO and was currently based at the British Embassy in Rue du Faubourg Saint-Honoré, Paris. Why would he phone Charles to tell him that his life was under threat? It was obviously not in an official capacity.

She wanted to establish how and when Walter's life had intersected with Charles's; she didn't trust that she had been told everything by Charles. Once bitten, as they say, apply the ointment. Mike had checked Walter's social media accounts and came up with nothing earth-shattering. Mostly, she had found photographs of gig racing on the River Tamar and the sea around Cornwall. She had stared at various shots of a tall youth in surfer shorts and with a thatch of curly hair. The spy in her thought there was something missing: the mistake. Where was the mistake? Where was the out-of-focus drunken selfie or the boring photograph of a greasy breakfast? His accounts looked like a constructed backstory – or, perhaps, she was gradually becoming more cynical and more suspicious. This was a risk in her business.

She jumped up and sat at her computer; there was

something about the way her upturned fingers slid across the keyboard that was reminiscent of a virtuoso piano player. It was the sound of her nails clicking along the plastic keys. She didn't do this for effect, which was for the best, as there was nobody watching (if you discount the three polystyrene sisters). An idea jumped up out of nowhere. She remembered that she still had full access to Charles Yelland's computers and company intranet from her previous job for him, so she decided to pay a virtual visit. Unsurprisingly, he hadn't changed his password from his daughter's name – "Angelica1" (the 1 was his idea of internet security).

She tapped in "Walter Flushing", and only one match appeared.

It was a link to Walter's report *The Current Political Tensions in the Maghreb*, which he had written in Algeria. *Now, why would Charles read that?* she mused. *Petronello is an oil exploration and production company that's not involved in gas or Algeria. Perhaps his world has changed?* She was beginning to join up dots that were, in all probability, just specks of dirt on life's mucky screen.

If you've ever wondered what people in the secret-squirrel community have in common, then there's only one answer: inquisitiveness and, probably, a distrust of coincidence. Now she had access to the Petronello computer system, she couldn't stop herself from searching for, well, whatever came into her head. She started with "Algeria" and came up with a mix of items about a visit Charles had made to Algiers late in 2021 as part of some UK trade delegation. She noted this coincided with Walter's time there producing his report. She tapped in "Johnny" and "Musselwhite", but she only got very generic newspaper articles and irrelevant references. Then, on a completely random impulse, she tapped in "Randy" and regretted quickly as she ended up with several hundred hits, most of which were in his recycle bin with the remainder in his spam folder. Some of the images appeared to be upside down, but then again, perhaps not. This made her move on, and after a few seconds thinking about Randy, her focus transferred to the forest canopy outside her big window.

***

It was getting dark, and there was no light bulb in the holder hanging limply from the ceiling. The walls appeared to be rough concrete or, possibly, rock. Daylight came in from a hole where a pipe used to exit and from around the huge wooden door that fitted rather badly in its frame. It was unbearably hot and stank of a mixture of sweat and the contents of the bucket that he kept at arm's length but within reach. He was tethered by about six feet of chain to a large iron ring fixed securely to a wall spattered with unsightly, brown stains. His white linen shirt was now permanently damp, and his white trousers were torn badly and bloodstained. This was strange as he couldn't find any obvious wounds apart from superficial cuts and bruises.

The chewed bone from his meal of goat and rice was still on a plate, attracting flies. He didn't know how long he had been held in this place – almost a month? His cunning plan to save one grain of rice for each day he was incarcerated had worked for a week, until a rat had discovered his makeshift calendar. It took the rat about ten seconds to make his precious record disappear.

However long he had been here, he couldn't remember

arriving. His mind was a blank. He could be anywhere in the Maghreb, having been transported five or 500 miles. His clothes stank of camel, but whether this meant he had been carried on a camel or wrapped in a Berber camel blanket and stuffed into the back of a pickup truck, he didn't know. He could hear distant traffic and had heard goats occasionally. There had been a dog outside, but he had heard no camels or voices or much birdsong. Surprisingly, he had heard no call to prayer, so he presumed he was in the desert, away from human habitation.

His jailers wore dark-brown *djellabas*, which he thought meant that they were unmarried, and had their heads and faces wrapped in a single piece of cloth to keep out the sun and sand. Did that make them Berbers, Tuareg, or desert nomads from Mali or Mauritania? The few times that they had spoken to him, they had used broken Spanish. They had presumed he only spoke Spanish and didn't know that he had a reasonable grasp of Arabic, but this proved pretty useless as they mostly spoke to each other in a local language or dialect. Whenever he asked what was happening, their reply was *mañana*, delivered with smiling, dark-brown eyes, which was all he could see of them apart from their hands and their feet in leather sandals.

The fact that they had held him for so long and were feeding him was giving him some hope. His people would be looking for him, but in a million square miles of nondescript desert, how they would find him, he had no idea. He had spent hours and hours thinking of how he might make his rescuers task easier, but to no avail. Throwing a bucket at the wall would be the most noise that he could make, and this would not be heard by anyone beside his jailers whether he was near an oasis in Mali or a mountain village high in the Moroccan Atlas Mountains.

He looked on the positives, as they had taught him to do during his training in Texas and in Oman with the British. His captors hadn't really been violent or angry. They had made no demands except to tell him that, if he tried to escape, he would be shot. They weren't after information, or he would have been tortured immediately, and they weren't using him as a bargaining chip or for ransom, otherwise they would have cut off his ear and sent it to his family via DHL. They were also not using him as propaganda, or they would have videoed him. So why were they keeping him alive?

***

A grey US Air Force C-17 Globemaster landed at Marrakech airport and proceeded to taxi to an apron where the pilot was keen to avoid stranding his very heavy, $340-million aircraft in the surrounding sand. It was met by a small group of military jeeps and lorries. With the ramp lowered, about a dozen cargo containers and pallets were unloaded, together with various armoured vehicles and two 'Beasts', as the President's bomb-proof Cadillacs are called.

Airports always look more romantic at night given their stark geometry and their colour-coordinated illumination. Yellow signs flashed "Runway Ahead", and a network of red and green lights sparkled in the cool desert night. There was an air of unhurried efficiency.

It was one week until POTUS would arrive, and the whole preparatory protocol was being rolled out. The programme for this visit was so tight that it hadn't been possible to include an early morning round on the beautiful Royal Marrakech Golf Course, much to the frustration of the President. He would have to settle for a group dinner under the stars while being entertained by snake charmers, with their reedy pipes, and a colourful dance troupe. There would also be a group photograph taken in the Jardin Majorelle surrounding the Marrakech villa of the late Yves Saint Laurent.

CHAPTER EIGHT

"Hey, how are you doing on this fine September morning?" Leonard's beaming face filled most of the screen.

"Well, not great." Mike had just returned from filling up the motorbike with petrol, which had really been an excuse to go out for a spin. She had then decided to call Leonard.

"How may I help you?"

"It's not about Randy. Do you remember Charles Yelland, the Petronello boss whose daughter was kidnapped? Well, he phoned me yesterday to say he had been warned about a threat to his life and could I check it out. The thing is that he was phoned by a junior member of the British Embassy in Paris."

"Well, the Brits in France sure have enough to deal with at the moment."

"What do you mean?"

"The British Minister of Energy was poisoned near Strasbourg a few days back. It's not public knowledge yet, but it looks like it might have been our friends, the Russkies."

"Why?"

"We're all still checking, but yesterday a junior assistant from their embassy in Paris who was with this minister was shot; he survived – just – but is in intensive care."

Mike, like everyone in the secret-squirrel world, did not like coincidences. "What was his name?"

"Give me a second." Leonard's large face exited stage right to the sound of slow tapping on a keyboard. "Flushing, Walter Flushing. Sheesh, who calls their kid Walter C. Flushing?"

Mike took one breath while she collected her thoughts. "That's who rang Charles Yelland."

"Really?" It was Leonard's time to reflect for a moment.

"I'm wondering if the minister and Walter were targeted for the same reason that Charles's life is in danger. Were they all involved in something dodgy?"

"I doubt the kid was. He was just in the wrong place and may have seen something. The Russkies only poison people in the West to send a message to a government. They probably went back and shot the kid as a tidying-up exercise."

"Charles and the minister must have been involved in something the Russians didn't like, presumably."

"Possibly. The minister was what the Brits call a 'colourful character', which basically means that he couldn't keep it in his pants and he liked to breathe in heavily whenever he saw any white powder."

"I'll ask Charles what he was doing with the minister. Thanks for your help."

"How are you doing on finding Randy?"

"I'm getting nowhere fast. I've found his flat in Spain and a likely address in Marrakech, but there's no sign of him; he has just disappeared."

"Keep at it." With that, he rang off.

***

Two hours later, Mike was back in Charles Yelland's kitchen for the first time in twelve months, leaning against the units with her legs crossed at the ankle; it was a red-wig day. The journey over to his estate had fulfilled her need to ride the motorbike in a way that the short trip earlier to fill up with petrol had not. She stared around the enormous kitchen and produced what looked like a dark-brown cigarette – this no longer shocked Charles – and she began to chew on the liquorice stick.

"Some things don't change," he said, pouring boiling water from the tap into a mug.

"Yes, I think you were wearing that cardigan the first time I came here."

He smiled at her in a slightly patrician, rather than patronising, way. "You've probably hacked into my phone and computer, so I'm intrigued why you felt the need to ride over here."

He pressed the teabag with a spoon, removed it and handed her the mug. She sipped it, but it was too hot, which was just as well as it was undrinkable: strong Earl Grey did not pair happily with her liquorice.

"The person who called to warn you, this Walter Flushing, was connected to the FCO at a very junior level; did you know him?" She was watching his expression intently.

"Don't think so. Who is he?"

"It's probably 'Who was he?' by now."

Charles paused and his face failed to hide a nervousness. He didn't speak, so she continued.

"He was shot yesterday, after he tried to warn you." She pierced him with her dark-brown, almost black, eyes, which seemed intensified under her bright-red Cleopatra wig.

"Who shot him?" For Charles, the penny was beginning to drop.

"Probably the people who want to shoot you, wouldn't you think?"

"Where was he shot?"

A cheap reply passed fleetingly through her mind, but she just said, "In France."

Charles Yelland was one of life's cowards – one of life's lucky cowards, to be precise. It wasn't until his daughter had been kidnapped that he had ever felt threatened in any way. In his business life, everything seemed to fall into place. If there was any strategy, it came from Tony, his brother-in-law and co-director. "What was he doing in France?"

"He was supporting Johnny Musselwhite, the Minister of Energy." Mike watched his eyes for any reaction.

Charles paused and involuntarily moved a bottle of olive oil to line up with the vinegars.

"You know him?"

There was a moment's hesitation.

She waited while he weighed up how much to tell her and then she finished with, "or should I say *knew* him?"

His face had already drained of any colour during the whole exchange. "Well, of course I knew him. I run a bloody oil and gas company. I also know he's dead – I read it in *The Times*."

She waited while quietly reflecting on the addition of gas to his previous oil-based portfolio.

"We were exploring a new business venture together," he continued.

"What was it?"

"Does it matter?"

"It mattered to the people who killed Johnny and Walter, by the sound of it."

"It's in North Africa."

"Algeria?"

"Well… yes."

"That's where Walter saw you, I expect. You have his report *The Current Political Tensions in the Maghreb* on your system."

The fact she had access to his computers no longer bothered him. "I don't remember him," Charles confirmed.

"Who's pissed off at this new venture?"

He shrugged, as he wasn't used to anyone speaking to him in this way – and in his own kitchen.

"Charles, these killers are professionals. They are state-sponsored professional assassins. You can't just spend some of your millions on extra CCTV around the estate and think everything is OK. You're in real danger."

She decided to change tack. "You haven't come across my brother-in-law Randy in your travels in North Africa, by any chance?"

"I don't know anyone called Randy."

She remembered his cover name. "He's also known as Ramon Ramirez?"

"No," was all Charles said.

***

Victor was chairing something loosely referred to as 'COBRA Lite' which sounded like a beer but was actually a meeting in the Cabinet Office Briefing Rooms (COBR) at 70 Whitehall in

London. These rooms are used for committees that coordinate the actions of government bodies in response to major crises with implications for the UK. The poisoning by, presumably, Russia of a government minister and the shooting of a quasi-FCO employee had triggered enough alarm bells that a cross-agency strategy needed to be developed. More than a dozen people from various ministries, the secret services, police, military, Border Force and senior administrators were gathered in a room more suited to watching military action overseas. The whole end wall was composed of screens, only three of which were active at that moment. It looked more like the control room where a TV director selects camera views for the broadcast from a live event.

"OK, Ben," the PM began, "Where are we with Johnny's poisoning?"

Commander Ben Cox, the senior police officer present, gave out a long sigh. "The French authorities moved fast at the very beginning; for example, when they conducted the autopsy, identified the poison and started the interviews. Since then, they've managed to lose the hotel's CCTV footage covering the period relevant to the poisoning of Johnny Musselwhite; the local and national police are now blaming each other. The hotel says that a police officer collected the relevant tape, but neither the police force nor the special *brigade criminelle* investigating says it sent anyone to do this. There was, apparently, CCTV coverage showing the likely poisoners, but the French don't have the two individuals on their books. They must be new agents. The French have failed to locate them or their vehicle or establish their method of transit in and out of France, presuming that they aren't based in France and haven't gone to ground. They haven't found Mr Musselwhite's laptop or phone, and they've found nothing on Mr Flushing's phone. Actually, just before I came here, the French sent across the records for Mr Flushing's phone. I understand that, shortly before he was shot, he made a call to a UK mobile number and also failed to answer an incoming call from the UK, which must have been about the time he was shot. We're following these up."

Ben unscrewed the top from a plastic bottle of water and took a sip.

"Isn't there any other CCTV coverage – from the street or nearby businesses?" Victor asked.

"No, and you aren't allowed to film public spaces in France, anyway."

"Are the French going to release some, I don't know, photofit pictures of the suspects?"

"This is delicate," a woman with a strangely low fringe and gold earrings suggested, "The Russians haven't acknowledged anything, and we've monitored the relevant traffic between France and Moscow. We're ninety per cent sure it's them, but we're not yet certain. We don't want to give President Putin any advantage, should it prove not to be him. He would probably say they were tourists, like in Salisbury, looking at Strasbourg Cathedral."

"What about the hotel's CCTV footage of when this Flushing chap was shot? They haven't lost that as well, have they?"

"No, we haven't seen that yet."

Victor turned to a nondescript man in a grey suit whose only distinguishing feature was that he had absolutely no distinguishing features. "Robert, what have you found on Johnny or this Flushing chap?"

In a surprisingly high voice, Robert explained, "Well, we

started with the cocaine and have established from sources that Johnny had been back using again. It's likely that he took it down with him in his car as there's no mention of it on his phone or email traffic. We're going through his communications, but we've found nothing strange so far. He may, of course, have had a separate phone – in which case, this will all take a bit longer and come via our French counterparts, using the hotel as a location for unidentified devices. As to what Mr Musselwhite was about to do next, his family say he was going on down to Spain, and we have an address just outside Málaga. We're checking it out. Mr Flushing appears to be whiter than white. He doesn't even have three points on his driving licence, if you know what I mean? He was just in the wrong place at the wrong time."

"May we go back to the poison?" Victor asked, "Is Porton Down checking it out?" He wanted to know if the UK's Defence Science and Technology Laboratory near Salisbury was engaged.

"No, it's being tested by the DGA [Direction Générale de l'Armement], the French agency, in their laboratory at Vert-le-Petit in Essonne. We are in contact."

"Then, I only have one question: why? Why Johnny?"

There was a wide selection of blank faces, but one person offered the only plausible theories without any additional facts – namely, that Johnny was seriously up to no good outside his official duties or that the UK or something in his portfolio was upsetting the Russians.

***

Mike was at home transferring money to her landlord for her share of the electricity when her mobile trilled. "Mike Kingdom."

"Hello, Miss Kingdom, I'm Inspector Maslen from the police. I was hoping that you could help us with one of our investigations?"

Mike was looking at her screen, which was displaying "Caller ID withheld". She didn't trust random callers, especially ones not revealing their number.

"Hello, Inspector. Which police division are you from?"

There was a pause before the inspector replied, "Special Branch… in London."

Mike was about to ask him for a number on which she could call him back when he said, "This may not take long. All I'm interested in is the reason you called Walter Flushing on his mobile at 4.02pm on Thursday, 1st September. I just want to eliminate you from our enquiries."

The word 'eliminate' did not sit easily with Mike. Having heard of Walter's attempted murder via Leonard, she needed to play along – if, indeed, this was a real policeman on the line.

"I've never met a Walter Flushing, Inspector." This gained her a few seconds while she thought this through.

"So why did you phone him?"

"To ask him about a report he had written."

"Which report?"

"*The Current Political Tensions in the Maghreb.*"

"Why are you interested in Algeria?" This was beginning to sound a little more like an interrogation.

"I have an academic interest."

"And this was the first time you had tried to contact him?"

"Yes," she answered truthfully.

"How did you get hold of his number?"

"A mutual friend gave it to me."

"And who's that?"

77

"Sorry, Inspector, I'm not discussing this further until I know a lot more about you and your investigation."

"Did you know Johnny Musselwhite?" He seemed to have changed tack.

"No."

"We may need to interview you formally. Will you give me your address?"

"Inspector, if you *are* from Special Branch, my address is up on your screen right now as we speak – or it can be in two minutes."

"Thank you, Miss Kingdom, we'll be in touch."

With that, Brendan Dowell made some brief notes, looked at a printout of calls from Walter's phone and prepared to call Charles Yelland.

CHAPTER NINE

Charles Yelland was standing drinking a mug of tea in the arched gateway to his Victorian walled garden. One of his staff was far behind him, cutting the lawn using a ride-on mower, while another gardener was weeding the rose beds with their low box hedges that formed a geometric pattern in front of him. It was a beautiful day, and his family were still away in Mexico. He was enjoying the noises of the countryside and the freedom from his usual weekend routine. Unexpectedly, his personal mobile phone rang. He knew this must be important as very few people had this number. The caller display came up as Jo, his so-called 'PA' who was, in fact, probably better described as his confidante and the actual managing director of Petronello.

"Hi, Jo."

"Charles, I've got the police on the line. Should I transfer them?"

It was unusual for him to be called on this phone, so

they must have dialled a dedicated work number that Jo monitored.

"Sure. Did they say anything?" He was beginning to worry that there was some sort of trouble in Mexico.

"He's an Inspector Maslen from Special Branch, London. He wouldn't say anything else to me."

"Thanks, Jo. Please put him on."

He allowed a couple of seconds to pass while the sound of mowing grass and rooks arguing in the avenue of limes took centre stage.

"Inspector. Charles Yelland. How may I help?"

"Hello, Mr Yelland, and sorry for disturbing you on a Saturday. I was hoping you could help me with an ongoing investigation?"

"No problem. Fire away."

"Do you know a Walter Flushing?"

"Sorry, but I've never met a Walter Flushing. It's quite a distinctive name. I think I'd remember."

"Sadly, he's been murdered… in France."

"Again, sorry, but I don't know anyone with that name in France or anywhere else."

"I'm calling you because you were the last person he rang before he was murdered." The inspector paused to let this information permeate.

In such situations, the brain looks for a distraction from the main event. In Charles Yelland's case, this meant he suddenly noticed that the tractor had stopped and the background sounds of Buckinghamshire in autumn were at their most vibrant.

"Who was he?" Charles asked eventually.

"We're currently checking, but can you think of any reason why he might have phoned you just before he was murdered?"

"Inspector, as I've said, I've never heard of this man. That means I have no idea at all why he might phone me."

"The phone records show that you answered the call. What did he say?"

Charles stood there, frozen. A billionaire with the world at his feet who was at a complete loss for words. He wasn't one to think ideas through – he just reacted. In truth, he couldn't exist without Jo to organise his life; Tony, his brother-in-law, to push the business forwards; Maria, his wife, to schedule his private life; and Mike Kingdom to sort out any problems that came in from left field.

"I remember a strange call now you come to mention it," he admitted. "I have no idea what it was about."

"Yet he got straight through to you? Someone who is notoriously private. How did he get this number?"

"No idea." Charles was walking back to the kitchen, which might have been to satisfy a natural craving to be in a safe place.

"What did he say?"

Charles was right out at the end of the plank, looking back at the sharp end of a pirate's sword. The sharks were circling beneath.

"He said something odd about my life being threatened." Charles regained his composure. "I just assumed he was a crank. Inspector, you have to understand that I'm in the public eye and thus the target of so many crackpots."

"Do you have any idea who might want to kill you?"

"Inspector, I run an oil and gas exploration company that operates all over the world; you can imagine the list of my enemies is quite long." He had reached his back door and was about to turn the handle.

"Out of all these people, who might be near the top of the list?"

"No idea."

The inspector didn't bother to say that he himself was probably at the top of that list.

***

Charles had barely reached his study when his phone rang again. He was staring up at a kid's sketch of Antarctica on the wall, which had been drawn – or rather, coloured in – by his daughter. He saw that the caller was Mike. "Good morning, Mike."

"Have you had a call from an Inspector Maslen?"

"Yes, I've just been speaking to him."

"He's not for real. What did you tell him?"

"The truth. That my life has been threatened."

"Did he ask to see you?"

"No. Who is he?"

"I'm checking, but I don't think he's going to become your best buddy."

Charles sat down at his desk and stared out of the windows of what had been a loggia before he had got it glazed and turned into his office, his snug, his safe place.

"Have you organised any protection yet?" she continued.

"What?"

"Bodyguards. Have you arranged any yet?" She sounded like his mum asking if he had ordered his grandmother flowers for her birthday.

"No, not yet."

"You are taking this seriously, Charles, aren't you?"

"I think I'll go to Spain," he suddenly blurted out, not having given it any serious consideration.

"Are you safer there?"

"Probably. I won't tell anybody except Tony and Jo… and you."

"May I come too?" Mike equally made an on-the-spot decision. She hoped she could kill two birds with one stone: specifically, to watch Charles at close range and visit Randy's flat in Málaga.

"If you want. Can you be at Northolt airfield at 10.00am tomorrow? I'll ring the crew."

"Yes, I'll be there."

She finished the call and it dawned on her that, despite all her protestations to Leonard, she was back doing fieldwork.

***

Patrick Redwood was the senior British police officer in Colmar looking into Johnny's murder and Walter's attempted murder. He had spent a few hours with Prosecutor Bettancourt and the *brigade criminelle* in a sequestered office in the main police building. His head was full of the investigation, and this had been stretched further by the language issues. Needing fresh air, he was now sitting on a bench in a tree-lined avenue, eating a baguette. The weather was warm, and the sun was filtering through the leaves. Something, however, had been bothering him all morning.

He was about to call Commander Ben Cox, his ultimate boss, who had attended the COBRA meeting with the PM. Patrick waited to make the call until after he'd chewed and swallowed. Unfortunately, the sliced cured ham in the sandwich was a bit stringy, and he regretted his choice. He breathed in. For a few seconds, he savoured his life and the fact that he was being paid to sit on a bench in the Alsace while his colleagues were trying to nail some Albanian drug dealers in the arse end of East London.

Commander Ben Cox, who had worked with Patrick for a long time, was waiting for a progress update. Ben's office was about ten stories up in an office block in Central London, with views across the urban fabric that never quite reached the countryside. He, too, was a little frustrated. This wasn't any annoyance with Patrick and his colleagues but rather as a result of not being in control or, at least, having to devolve the investigation to another jurisdiction. He knew how a murder (in fact, a murder and an attempted murder) would be dealt with in London, but this was different. He liked the idea that the French had very quickly appointed a special team to take this over once they had realised that it was a high-profile international character. Next, a special prosecutor had been appointed to drive things forwards; this matched or bettered the British system. Then it seemed to fall apart.

"Patrick, where are you?"

"I'm sitting on a bench in a quiet street – called Rue Camille Schlumberger – having a sandwich," he replied, subtly communicating the level of conversation they might safely have.

"The boss is asking questions." The commander was equally subtly communicating that the PM was personally very interested.

"Well, I would suggest that things are going swimmingly on the surface."

"And below the water?"

"Well, I'm not sure. I would sure like to swim back to the shore. I'm beginning to think things aren't quite what they seem."

"I'm intrigued."

"It's all going too well." He paused. "You and I know how these things usually progress… and we aren't adding a British minister dying on foreign soil into the mix."

"So, what's bothering you, Patrick?"

"Let's start with the prosecutor, Madame Bettancourt. She's superficially charming and efficient, but her priority seems to be on PR. She says all the right things in TV interviews, but then applies no pressure on what I'll loosely call her 'team'… and they're all muppets. They've 'lost' the hotel's CCTV footage covering the period when the poisoners were in the hotel, which is the only real way that we're going to identify the killers. If you wanted to screw up the investigation, I cannot think of a better way to do it." As if to give some sort of physical demonstration, he screwed up the paper bag in which his lunch had been and put it in his jacket pocket.

"Had anyone looked at the footage before it got conveniently lost?"

"Yes, apparently, and whichever officer watched it can give a description of two men whom he describes as 'typically Slavic'. But it gets worse. They're now saying that the special lab in Lyons may have misidentified the poison. It may not be some special Russian concoction but something more run-of-the-mill."

"It sounds as though, right at the beginning, they jumped to the conclusion that the Russians were to blame and have tried to shoehorn any evidence into their theory… or they've been nobbled."

"I agree. Blaming a foreign power is terribly convenient. They clearly don't want it to turn out to be a French plot. I've spoken to the hotel night manager, and he can't remember two Russian-looking men and, by the way, is certain that they weren't staying at the hotel."

"What about the shooting of Walter Flushing?"

"This is what's making me really suspicious. The night manager told me that he saw a plastic business card next to the cocaine on the bedside cabinet when he went into Johnny Musselwhite's room with Walter Flushing. He told the local police about it because he says it wasn't there when he went back into the room with the doctor a bit later. I asked the prosecutor and the *brigade criminelle* chief, and they deny any knowledge and say they've never found a business card in Johnny's or Walter's rooms or on their bodies."

"That's bizarre. I presume the night manager didn't see the name on the card?"

"No, no such luck, but you see that it must have been Walter who took it or hid it, as he was the only person in the room until the manager and doctor turned up."

"Why take it? Of all things, why take that?"

"And where is it now? The French say they didn't find it in Walter's room or on his body... and they found nothing on his phone to frighten the horses."

"Are you thinking that this is why Walter was shot? To get this card?"

"Well, if not, why come back at great risk to shoot a very junior assistant? It can't be because he saw and could identify Johnny's killers, since Walter would have already told the manager, doctor or police when they interviewed him several times. Whoever is behind this failed to get what they wanted when they killed Johnny. They presumably thought it was on his laptop, on his phone or in his wallet. I don't think the poisoners were looking for a business card. I think they were told to bring back his laptop, phone and wallet."

"So how did whoever is behind this know that the card existed and Walter might have it?"

"I don't know, but this is why I'm suspicious and not entirely buying this Russian-hit-squad scenario. I specifically asked the manager if he had told anyone about the card apart from the police and me. He said no one."

"So, it looks like it had to come from the French police and prosecutor or someone with access to their files?"

"I can't see who else. I'm going back to the police HQ now, and I'll try to find out more about the card and missing CCTV footage. I also want to look at the hotel footage from when Walter Flushing was shot."

"Let me know what you find out," Ben said.

"Oh, and another thing to add to the list is that Brendan Dowell, the senior bod at the British Embassy who was down here sorting out the transport of Johnny Musselwhite's belongings back to the UK, has gone AWOL or at least isn't answering his phone. He was travelling to Paris late last night, but he's not answering his phone this morning. He may have spoken to Walter or seen something."

With that, the call ended, and Patrick walked slowly back towards the town centre.

CHAPTER TEN

The first thing Mike had noticed on boarding the plane was that there weren't any overhead lockers; this wasn't a problem as all of her luggage had been whisked away from her at Northolt. *Why would they have overhead lockers?* she wondered. *Stupid girl!* The second thing was the enormous sofa that faced across the aisle halfway down the cabin, with a large TV screen opposite. She was shown past this by a flight attendant, who looked like a model in a casual white blouse and skirt, to a large seat ready for take-off. Everything was either ivory-coloured leather, polished wood, or carpet in a bold pattern of greys and black.

Mike was also colour-coordinated: black Cleopatra wig, black leather biker's jacket, black trousers and black trainers. She was even wearing dark eye make-up and dark lipstick. She had covered up her orange-peel complexion with foundation. The latter was a time-wasting exercise she had undertaken in her cabin. Private jet travel was a whole different world to her.

As she had pulled into Northolt on her motorbike, she had wondered exactly what she was doing. Hadn't she told Leonard that she would never go back into the field?

Before they were over Brittany, the flight attendant had served gin and tonics. Charles was sitting opposite her in a light summer jacket, chinos and loafers. He looked across and lifted his glass in a silent toast. He seemed to be enjoying her nervousness – normally, it was *her* making *him* nervous. She had said yes to a gin and tonic, but this wasn't her normal drink, and the bitter taste made her grimace.

"Would you prefer something else?" Charles asked, and without anything being said, the flight attendant reappeared and asked her what she would like.

"Do you have a beer?" Mike requested.

"Of course. Peroni?"

"Thank you."

Two minutes later, she was presented with one in a tall glass on a small, white tray with a bowl of crisps. Charles was still smiling. What was it about this man that irritated her so much?

Halfway through the flight, Charles left his seat to talk to the captain and first officer in the cockpit. The flight attendant, who was called Sylvia, came over to ask if Mike wanted anything, although this might have been more to relieve her own boredom. Mike, for her part, had started to relax and had decided to enjoy the experience. How often do you get to fly in a private jet? She asked if she could sit on the leather sofa and watch the TV, to which Sylvia smiled.

Sitting sideways on a plane – a seemingly empty plane as Charles and Sylvia were now out of view – felt strange. On the screen, she flicked through the channels before settling on the UK news. The PM was being interviewed by someone called Karen, against a backdrop of a newsroom seen through a glass wall.

"Prime Minister, may I ask you about the G20 summit next week in Marrakech? Why Marrakech?"

"Well, I recognise that it's a break with tradition, but we've had summits for forty years, mostly in the cities of the member countries. It was a joint decision to pick destinations that widen all of our horizons going forwards. Apart from Saudi Arabia and South Africa, there are no African or Arab members of the G20, so it's a great opportunity to include Morocco. I'm very excited about that."

"Will Western Sahara be discussed?"

"I'm sure many things will be discussed, both in the formal sessions and outside." Victor was giving his boyish smile.

"But Western Sahara is the bone of contention in the region. Is the UK changing its stance?"

"No, the UK and the USA – and Spain, I might add – are very supportive of the UN resolution and eventual autonomy for Western Sahara."

"But Morocco occupies eighty per cent of Western Sahara and has done for decades. The UN peacekeeping force has been there longer than anywhere else on earth. There is stalemate, isn't there?"

"It's complex, I won't deny that, but we're all working towards a solution. Hopefully, this summit will help."

"Nothing will happen without Algerian agreement. Are they invited?"

"No… but this isn't a one-issue summit. Western Sahara is just one of fifty subjects that will be discussed. There are other important ones, such as the war in Ukraine." He was trying to deflect the questioning.

"And in the Ukraine war, Algeria supports Russia?"

"No, no, that's not true. Algeria hasn't supported Russia. In fact, despite their close relationship, they've stayed resolutely neutral."

"May we move on to energy? And speaking of Russia, how are the investigations progressing into the murder of Johnny Musselwhite in France?"

"I know there are rumours, but we need to let the French police and authorities investigate. We're in close touch with our counterparts over there."

"If it is the Russians who have murdered a British minister, what reprisals against them are left? We've used every economic one already as a consequence of the war, haven't we?"

"Well, let's not jump to conclusions. Let's wait and see."

At that moment, Charles came down the aisle of his private jet, carrying a cup of coffee, and sat next to Mike on the sofa.

She nodded at the screen. "Are you involved in any of that?"

"What do you mean?"

"Morocco, Algeria...?"

Charles looked a bit sheepish, but then he always looked sheepish. He took a sip of coffee. "I'm interested in lots of areas. That's my job."

"What were you doing in Algeria when this Walter guy saw you?"

"I presume he saw me at the British Embassy. I don't make a habit of travelling around Algeria."

"And?"

"Sorry, I don't remember him."

"What were you doing there?" Mike persisted.

"Is it relevant? I was exploring business opportunities – that's my job."

"Charles, I know what you think your job is. I'm trying to do my job, which means asking if it's relevant because this Walter Flushing rang you up a couple of hours or so before he was shot to warn you that your life is in danger."

"OK, I was talking to people there about a new pipeline in which I'm investing."

"Where will it go?"

"The project is called PEGASUS. It's planned to go to mainland France via Corsica from Algeria."

"Bypassing the pipeline that crosses from Morocco to Spain?"

"That one's been shut down by the Algerians for a year, and anyway, there are already other pipelines direct to Almería and across to Italy via Sicily."

Mike smiled to herself on hearing Charles use the word 'anyway', which was his daughter Angelica's favourite word – or possibly her second favourite word after 'like'.

"The Moroccans and, probably, the Spanish aren't thrilled about your new pipeline, I'm guessing?" She muted the TV, turned and stared at him. "Could this be a reason for someone to shoot you?"

"I, well… I…" He hesitated. "It could be… but no more than other things I'm involved in around the world."

She then made a connection in her mind. "You said that you knew this Johnny Musselwhite. Was he involved in this pipeline?"

"Well, we had discussed it." He was leaving things a bit vague.

"Charles?" Her voice had the tone of an exasperated parent.

"He wasn't directly involved. Anyway, it's none of the UK's business if Algeria exports its natural resources to Europe by one, two, three or four pipelines. He was, however, interested in the security of gas supplies to continental Europe. The UK wants Europe to have secure gas supplies."

"For selfish reasons?"

"Yes; if Europe has Algerian gas, it isn't competing against the UK on the world market."

"Charles, from what I've heard, Johnny Musselwhite would make Nixon look like a reliable witness… and from what I've read, he spent more money on cocaine than Oliver North sent to the Contras."

"That may be true, but he was a good minister."

"Is there anything else I need to know about pipelines that might be relevant?"

"There's another one called GALSI that aims to go to Italy via Sardinia."

"Are all these pipelines needed? Are you all in competition?"

"Well…" He began to look sheepish again. "A bit, but PEGASUS is different in that it also has two power cables linked to it, delivering electricity to France from a massive solar farm in the desert. And I mean massive: 12 million solar panels covering an area of 600 square miles."

"*What?*" Mike needed to pinch herself. What was a girl from Portland, Oregon, doing on a private jet discussing solar farms in Algeria with a billionaire oil-and-gas magnate? She didn't even know what 'magnate' meant.

"It's no different from the XLINKS proposal from Morocco to Devon – that would use cables 2,400 miles long."

"Huh?" This time she didn't even manage a "What?"

"These are big projects."

"I noticed. How much would they cost?"

"PEGASUS will cost £12 billion or thereabouts."

Mike thought these figures were probably enough to

explain why someone might want Charles dead. She had entered another world. One as far removed from her own as it was possible to imagine.

There was a pause while she weighed his answers. She changed tack. "Have you sorted out any personal protection?"

"As a matter of fact, I have. You'll meet him at the villa. He was recommended by a friend."

"A bit like me?"

"No, he's much bigger." Charles smiled.

"I meant that he was recommended by a friend like I was."

"How true."

Charles returned to his seat to take a phone call. As if prompted by this, Sylvia wandered over to ask Mike if she wanted access to the Wi-Fi. A few minutes later, she was on the phone to Leonard.

He picked up immediately. "Hi…" There was a pause. "Either you've got a grant to do up your cabin or you're on board a Gulfstream… I recognise the windows."

"I forgot how you CIA directors travel."

"Hey, it wasn't always like that! Sometimes, we had to go first class. Where are you?"

"On Charles Yelland's plane on my way to his villa in Spain."

"What?" He paused to take it all in. "Are you on speaker?"

"Wait, I'll turn off speaker and video."

"Good; I can live without pictures of your inner ear. I'm about to eat in the Subway."

"It's called the Underground. How many years have you lived in London?"

"No, I'm in the branch of Subway near the office, having just ordered a festive turkey snack."

"Most people just have a mince pie. Wait a minute, isn't it a bit early?"

"It's midday."

"I meant for Christmas."

"Shop early to avoid disappointment. I might pick up an Easter egg on my way back."

"Why don't you eat in the office?"

"Nah, it doesn't feel right; there are too many people watching your every move."

"They're spies; that's their job."

"Nah, I like to keep work and leisure separate."

"How do you know the difference?

"Work is when I speak to you… What did you call me for?"

"Well, it wasn't to discuss food – although all I've had today is Peroni and some cheese-and-onion crisps."

"They have Peroni and cheese-and-onion crisps? What is it, a 777?"

"Well, this cabin is much bigger than mine in the woods. Can we leave the food for a second – anathema to you, I know – but I'm picking up funny vibes."

"That's the Peroni. Very soon you'll have a following wind." He sounded as if he had taken a huge bite out of something both wet and crunchy.

"Charles has started to tell me about the gas pipeline he's promoting across the Mediterranean."

"And why not?"

"Leonard, I'm beginning to smell a rat. To save you embarrassing Subway and calling the local authority health inspector, the rat is you."

"Are you one of these conspiracy theorists?"

"Only when you're involved." She could hear more munching, which bothered her as she couldn't imagine what crunched in a festive turkey roll. "What am I going to find when I get to Randy's flat in Málaga? Am I in for any surprises?"

"Never been there. Are you going to his place in Marrakech while you're only an hour and a half away?"

"What place in Marrakech?" she asked in mock innocence.

"No idea. So you haven't found an address yet? I don't believe it."

As with everyone else faced with Leonard's barbs, her hackles rose. His persona was so carefully crafted that even he didn't know where reality and fiction started or finished. After only a second's thought, however, anyone would conclude that he didn't occupy his elevated position because he was a bumbling idiot. Most people forgot this.

CHAPTER ELEVEN

The walls went on for miles, or so it seemed. They were terracotta coloured with yellow accents on the pillars; they didn't look Spanish, maybe more Mexican. So many of the other walls they had passed during the half-hour journey were the more traditional white, in various states of repair. Mike could feel Maria's influence even before the solid, dark-grey gates slid back to let them enter. The large, black Mercedes purred across the paved drive, all the way up to the villa. On either side, the lawns and palm trees were being irrigated by mists of water.

The chauffeur pulled up under the porte cochère; he didn't get out. Charles opened his own door and waited while Mike found the handle and let herself out. She had to stop herself from waiting to collect her bags from the boot. Instead, she joined Charles, and they walked up the tiled steps to a medieval-looking, large, studded oak door. The villa was bigger than the manor house where he lived in Buckinghamshire.

The hall was two stories high with life-size Roman statues in alcoves and a full-length tapestry that hung down from the vaulted ceiling to the floor. As a piece of Spanish art, it was very modern and surprisingly three-dimensional, having been made from (among other things) thick ropes and what looked like flotsam and jetsam. It was in stark contrast to the cool, pale marble floors and the sweeping wooden staircase – she was in another world.

"Inez will show you to your room and give you the password to the Wi-Fi – although I expect you've already got it," Charles said with a warm smile.

Mike snapped out of her reverie, not even noticing the maid who had appeared, as if by magic. "Yes, thank you," she replied, unconsciously acknowledging that, yes, she did have the password: he was using "Angelica1", which was the same as in the UK. Charles was conservative with both a small and a large 'C'.

"We'll have lunch in twenty minutes, is that all right?"

"What? Yes, perfect. I'll be down then."

"Ask Inez if you want anything; she has been with me for years."

With that, he disappeared through another oak door, this one with an armorial crest above it. Mike was fascinated by the motifs included in the crest and assumed it was from Maria's family, descended from the conquistadores.

***

A few minutes later, Inez was opening the door to a suite consisting of a bedroom, dressing room, lounge and bathroom. Heavy curtains, which were pulled closed, were hiding a large balcony that most people would call a terrace. The air conditioning was silent and discreet.

Mike had never stayed in such unadulterated luxury. Any time she had seen pictures of places like this, they were owned by Mexican or Colombian drug lords whom she was pursuing from her CIA base in Seattle, Washington or Los Angeles. Typically, there were hippos roaming the grounds. It wouldn't surprise her if Charles had a menagerie outside. Everywhere she looked was a mixture of old and new, seen through a gifted designer's eye and applied without financial restrictions. She could see Maria's influences – an odd mixture of old Spanish, Mexican and her years in private education in Switzerland – and all of this with the limitless money through her marriage to Charles.

Mike's eye was immediately attracted to her embarrassingly awful bags that were already on a bench near the door, along with her crash helmet and leather jacket. She clasped her face as it registered that – having ridden her motorbike to Northolt, where she had handed over everything – they had put it all on the plane. For a millisecond, she wondered if her motorbike was already in the garage here in Spain. Actually, it might have proved useful.

She pulled the cords that opened the two pairs of double curtains; this almost involved leaning back as they were so heavy. The view across the gardens to the sea was breath-taking. It was cosmopolitan. There were palm trees that, unbeknown to her, had been flown in from Hawaii aboard a cargo Boeing 747, and pencil cedars more reminiscent of Lombardy in Italy. The collection of very tall cacti was, probably, the most dramatic. There were opuntias and saguaros straight out of the Mojave Desert – literally.

It was then that she noticed the smell. A deep fragrance that she associated with Arab men. Was it in the air conditioning? Oh, and the music. The Spanish guitar gently but passionately coming from where? Small speakers in the ceiling.

She felt like a fish out of water – one in the baking heat of southern Spain.

Having temporarily lost herself, she came back to reality. She had a job to do – actually, two: protect Charles and find Randy.

She opened her small backpack and took out her laptop, together with a couple of small pieces of hardware that helped her access places that were normally out of reach. She pulled out her washbag and the liquids in a see-through, small plastic bag. Her feet finally reached terra firma when she pulled out her red and what was best described as 'mousey-brown' wigs; the latter being a new purchase. She didn't have her polystyrene heads, so she moved two blue-and-white vases and a bust of Caesar to be together on a table and used them instead. She temporarily took off her black wig and rubbed her itchy scalp.

She went into the bathroom to freshen up before going down for lunch. It wasn't the size of the bathroom or the selection of all of the most expensive perfumes that caught her eye, rather it was the black remote control. She picked it up and pressed the red button; the music stopped. She looked into the mirrored wall and wondered whether she should go downstairs without her black wig. Hmm, probably not. Her dark eye make-up was still fine, but her pock-marked skin was showing through her greasy, thin foundation. *Whatever,* she thought. The scar on her nose from where it had been broken on her previous job for Charles seemed to be more prominent under the downlights. She was ambivalent about her appearance.

Some minutes it mattered, but at others, she wanted to show herself off in the raw.

Mike was hungry before she set off from her bedroom, with Inez having reappeared to escort her down, but by the time she had followed Inez down the corridors and flights of stairs, she realised she was ravenous.

Charles was waiting for her in a cool and airy dining room with a side wall made of glass. The table was at the back, away from the light, under two contrasting paintings. Mike walked up to them before she sat down. One was a loud, crazy mix of graffiti with primitive heads and the other a rather enigmatic woman in Edwardian clothes who was smoking a cigarette while sitting on a rattan chair.

"Basquiat and Ramon Casas, respectively," Charles said, without her having asked who they were by, "not entirely to my taste. Especially the Basquiat."

"Too off-the-wall for you, I expect," she concluded.

"Not far enough off-the-wall, in my opinion."

There was a love of the literal and obvious that probably explained why he didn't like Basquiat.

"And who wants to stare at a woman smoking?" he continued his musings.

I wish you could, Mike thought to herself. Her craving for a cigarette, especially before she ate, was getting strong.

A man she hadn't seen before, Paco, who was wearing a white shirt and black trousers, brought in two trays of warm tapas. The table was already covered to bursting with salad and breads. Inez was not far behind, carrying two bottles of wine that she handed to Paco before retreating.

"White or *rosado*?" Charles asked.

"White, please."

Paco poured them both a glass. After a glance at his employer, he left the room.

"Here's to a long life." Charles was not only proposing a toast but also being provocative.

"Charles, I came out here to make sure you're taking this threat seriously."

"Paco and Inez have been with me for over five years. So have most of the others. The villa and gardens have every security device that money can buy. I'm careful without limiting what I do."

"This is all great, but you either don't know – or aren't telling me – who's behind this threat. If I knew this, we could deal with it at source, not after the threat has been attempted."

"I genuinely do not know. I don't know this Walter chap. He didn't say what was on the card. It was a very short phone call."

"What do you mean? What card?"

Charles adopted an enigmatic look that Ramon Casas would have enjoyed painting and realised that he had perhaps relaxed while having the upper hand on Mike. An easy trap to fall into when you receive someone into your thirty-room villa. "He said that he had my number from a business card."

"You said he didn't say what was on the card."

"No, well, it's both a memory card and business card. It's just a sales gimmick. It's, like, the thickness of two credit cards stuck together. Plastic... with your name and number on it."

"Where did he get one?"

There was a pause. "From Johnny Musselwhite."

"What was on this card you gave Johnny Musselwhite?"

"Details of potential projects." Charles conveniently left out quite a lot, including the recording of phone conversations.

"PEGASUS?"

"Yes."

Mike leant forwards and put her head in her hands. Her black wig formed two black curtains on either side of her head. What was it about shits like Charles and Leonard that they couldn't tell you the fucking truth up front? You were expected to help them with one hand tied behind your back. "How did this Walter get hold of the card?"

Charles took a sip of his Penedès. "He said he had found it next to Johnny's bed. Johnny had been using it to cut coke."

Neither the gifted Jean-Michel Basquiat or Ramon Casas i Carbó could have done justice to Mike's face, which was frozen in some strange other-worldly look. Actually, it was probably better to go with Basquiat.

"For fuck's sake. What are you involved in? And you think the lovely Inez and state-of-the-art motion sensors are going to save your life? And, yes, I did see them. I came out here to protect you, but I'm now worried about all of us in this villa."

She had eaten two tapas and swigged one glass of white wine, but her appetite was gone.

"Charles," she continued, "you remember what happened last time? You do trust me, right? Tell me the f—" – she restrained herself – "truth, the whole truth and the commercially sensitive, personally embarrassing truth." She stood up and took the wine bottle out of the ice bucket and poured herself another glass. She looked up at Charles and poured him one too. Initially, he made no comment and didn't press the button on the underside of the table that he used to summon Paco.

"I'm guessing that the memory card had commercially sensitive information on it. Everyone knows Johnny was a cokehead. That wasn't any problem. The fact that he was using it to cut coke before he was murdered is… unfortunate," he said.

"Unfortunate? Do you ever think ahead? I don't give a shit that he was cutting coke with it. What bothers me is that Walter helpfully took it, and this meant that the killers had to come back" –she paused – "because they weren't after Johnny or the unfortunate Walter. You understand that the killers were after this memory stick and, in case I need to spell it out, the contents?"

She took another gulp of wine and spelt it out very firmly: "What was on that memory stick?"

Charles matched her and more, taking two big mouthfuls of wine. "I don't know. Really, I don't know, but it probably had details about the pipeline. Sensitive details. Does it matter? Johnny and this Walter are dead."

Mike stopped any movement. "Who told you that Walter Flushing is dead?"

"Inspector Maslen."

"Inspector Maslen is probably one of the killers. He obviously doesn't know that Walter is in intensive care. It might be better if we keep it that way."

She changed tack: "How much were you paying Johnny Musselwhite?"

Charles stopped. "I thought I was paying him enough to be a bit more careful."

She finished the glass.

***

At Northolt, near London, it was early afternoon and starting to rain. The rented white Gulfstream 700 with orange and green stripes was taxiing to the private terminal while a black Range Rover pulled up on the tarmac at the front of the building. The steps were lowered, and an American flight attendant peered out at an England in gentle autumn sunlight.

A few minutes later, Maria Yelland and her daughter, Angelica, were on their way through the necessary but perfunctory formalities at passport control before they were whisked off to their estate twenty-seven minutes away in Buckinghamshire. England looked green but somehow more mellow than the lush, tropical greens of Cuernavaca in Mexico where they had been staying at one of Maria's family *haciendas*.

After a journey along fast roads, the Range Rover slowed down in preparation for turning into the estate between the stone gatehouse and some large pillars. The gates opened, and the Range Rover vibrated across the first of several cattlegrids before heading up the long drive shaded by an avenue of lime trees. Beyond the deer fencing on one side, they could see the familiar sight of Charles's Highland cattle herd, which barely paid any attention to their arrival. These same cows hadn't even raised their huge horns earlier that day when a white van had stopped opposite the entrance gate and discharged two highway engineers in hi-vis jackets, one of whom proceeded to push a measuring wheel along the edge of the road. The other man appeared to look for, and find, a small manhole, which he sprayed with blue aerosol paint. His task of identifying it for future maintenance was over in a matter of minutes.

The first man, now fifty yards away from the gatehouse, tied a mini-surveillance camera surreptitiously to the black metal deer fencing and walked nonchalantly back to his van. They need not have worried as there was nobody in the gatehouse and no one was watching the entrance on the estate's own

CCTV camera at that moment. However, there was someone watching now. Brendan Dowell was sitting fifteen miles away, checking the newly installed camera and confirming to his installation team in their van that all was OK. He wouldn't have to wait long until the camera was automatically triggered by Maria and Angelica returning early from their Mexican trip.

CHAPTER TWELVE

Lunch in Spain had come to an abrupt halt when Charles had to take an urgent call from Tony (his brother-in-law and finance director of Petronello) about test results from a drilling rig off Mozambique. Mike was in desperate need of a cigarette and was pleased to have an excuse to clear her head and digest what she had just heard. She didn't know where she could smoke, and so she made her way out into the sunshine and around the side of the west wing of the villa. She found herself outside the kitchen, from which she could hear the sounds of staff chopping and preparing food against a background buzz from the extractor fans. She leant against the end wall and lit up. The first deep drag into her lungs and the stunning view across the back lawns lifted her spirits.

"That'll kill you," came a voice from behind her.

She spun around.

"You should try vaping," the voice continued.

A chunky man with his arms covered in tattoos was

leaning on a yellow metal bin as if it were the bar in his local pub. He was puffing on an e-cigarette whose smell was not that distinct from the rotting vegetables and salad waste in the bin. He stood up to his full height, revealing a neck and forearms that were seriously testing the fabric of his white tee shirt.

"I'm Wazz," he said, using the trainer on his right foot to tap out a rhythm on the brake release at the bottom of the mobile bin.

"Does that mean piss or wank? I can never remember."

"It means snake in Polish, and you must be Mike?" he said, not missing a beat. He spoke with the merest trace of a central European accent, as filtered through a broken nose.

"Only to my friends."

Wazz, or Waldemar Wasielewski, stared back at her, and his face gradually relaxed into a smile. He stepped to the side but did not approach Mike or offer a handshake. "Paco said you would be here soon."

"Charles told me that he had organised protection. I didn't realise he meant protecting the bins."

Wazz continued to evaluate her. "Do you have a problem?" he said, but the smile never left his eyes.

"Lots, but I was hoping they'd cancel each other out."

"How did you break your nose?" he asked as he walked towards her.

They ended up next to each other, both facing the terraced back lawns.

"Someone didn't like me looking through a back gate. You?"

"Boxing as a teenager."

The ice was beginning to thaw between them.

"You sound British," she said.

"I am British. My parents are Polish. You sound American."

"I am American, but I've lived in the UK for a while. My parents are Czech."

Three small parrots flew across and landed in a tall, thin Washingtonia palm to continue their squabbling. A brown leaf frond spiralled to the ground. Wazz watched it fall onto the manicured lawn, contemplating it in silence.

"Were you special forces?" she asked him.

"More like special delivery. I was a postman."

She smiled. "Why Spain?"

"My son and his mother live out here. I was fed up with only seeing him twice a year, so I decided to move out permanently. Personal protection was the easiest job for me. It was either that or working in a bar. And you?"

"Computers and research," was all she said.

He turned to face her with a quizzical look.

"For the CIA," she clarified, having made the decision that she liked and trusted him.

"Good. That means you know what's going on. I was hoping you'd fill me in. I've been here about four hours, and I'm not sure what I'm meant to do in the villa. Am I just to protect Mr Yelland when he goes out?"

She was standing with her arms crossed, one hand holding an elbow and the other the cigarette. She looked at him sideways from under her black wig. "I'm partly here to find out, but let me say that he's not being threatened by amateurs. Are you armed?"

"Yes. I have a special licence."

"Good." She looked at him, wondering where his gun was concealed. "Have you looked over the villa?"

"Yes, it has thirty rooms but no panic room, which is a bit odd. There's a small room with a metal door and a large safe in it, but it isn't what I'd call secure."

"That sounds like Charles. He's more likely to protect his money and business than his family. And for your information, he has a problem with the truth – he seems to be allergic to it."

"What's the threat? Kidnap? Or is his life under threat?"

"A business partner was poisoned, and the person who rang Charles to warn him about the threat to his life has been shot at."

"I think I prefer escorting rich widows shopping in El Corte Inglés."

"What did Charles say to you?"

"I only met him for five minutes while you were upstairs. He just said I was to wander around the villa and gardens… and go in the car with him if he leaves the place."

"Unbelievable. I must get back to him. Hopefully, he has finished the call to his brother-in-law."

***

It was Sunday morning, and Brendan Dowell was sitting looking out of a cottage window a few miles outside London at the last act of the harvest: the loading onto trailers of the bales of straw for the short trip to the two barns. Although his work colleagues thought he was in Paris, having returned late from Colmar, he would in fact never go back to the embassy again. The cottage was a safe house, but not one belonging to the British secret services.

***

Six weeks before, he had stayed over a weekend at the Auberge du Pont Neuf in Colmar, where he had befriended the staff and reconnoitred the place. In particular, he had noted the locations of the cameras inside and near the *auberge* and where the CCTV recording device was hidden in the cupboard at the back of reception. He had chosen the hotel carefully because it was old-fashioned and had three points of access, if you included the kitchen. He had subsequently recommended it to Johnny Musselwhite, with Brendan being Johnny's liaison while in France for his meeting with Yves Dubuisson, the French Minister of Energy. On Wednesday, 31st August, under instructions from Brendan in Paris, two of his colleagues had unplugged the recorder before getting the final instruction to kill Johnny Musselwhite.

Everything had been planned, right down to the selection of the innocent Walter to accompany Johnny during his overnight stay. It was well known in FCO circles that Johnny would spend the evening in his room on coke, as he always did when he was away from home and his family. While shooting him would have been easier, it was important to send the right message, and only poisoning would do this. It was also critical that Johnny's laptop and phone were taken as there would be information on them that Brendan's real employers needed desperately. This was where the plan had started to go wrong.

The key information hadn't been on either of them.

However, his phone had revealed a WhatsApp message from Charles Yelland earlier in the evening on which Johnny had been killed asking him if he'd had time to check and agree to the structure outlined on the memory card. His killers hadn't been tasked with finding a memory card, nor had they noticed one. Brendan, as had previously been planned, was in

Paris so he would be perceived to be unconnected with events in the Alsace.

On hearing about the card, he knew he had to return to the Alsace. He had immediately set off in his car from his flat in the southern suburbs of Paris. He hadn't wanted to go through airport security. His trip was easily disguised as a final tidying up of the logistics surrounding Johnny Musselwhite's belongings. His first port of call on arrival had been a catch-up with the prosecutor. He had sat listening to a litany of barely disguised excuses and downright lies. More than anyone, he had known that the CCTV tapes hadn't mysteriously been lost after having been handed over to the police – they never existed in the first place. Brendan had relied on all of his acting skills and considerable restraint. He needed to know whether the police had found the business card and asked in a roundabout way, trying not to emphasise his interest. Finally, he had settled on requesting a list of Johnny's belongings that had been taken from his room. This was, he had been told, not a problem.

A few hours later that afternoon, he had been sitting alone outside a café with a cup of coffee as he read the short inventory. He had really been interested in only one thing on it, and that wasn't mentioned. Did he trust the French police? He had ordered a piece of patisserie and another coffee. A noisy refuse lorry had reversed up towards him, and the large waste container nearby had been emptied into it. The lorry had driven off in a puff of black smoke that had added nothing to the subtle taste of the pear in his slice of *tarte tatin*. He had regained his train of thought. The card was either still in his room or had been collected up in Johnny's belongings and was in storage at the hotel, being of no further interest to the police. As a representative of the British Embassy, it would not be difficult for him to gain access to these. In fact, the French authorities had wanted to know the plans for the transportation of the body, together with the removal of his Mercedes and remaining belongings. If it wasn't in one of these places, the remaining possibility was that Walter Flushing had taken it.

He had rung Stewart to tell him what he was planning to do. Afterwards, he had informed the *brigade criminelle* that he was going to the *auberge* to deal with these administrative and logistical matters. He had begun to feel the pressure from his real masters: people who did not take failure as an option. His task was to find this business card. He had swallowed the last mouthful of tart, put some change on the table and set off.

He had crossed the bridge and had walked alongside the black metal railings separating him from the canal. At the *auberge*, he had pushed open the old oak door and accustomed himself to the dim light and the smell of polish. He was a consummate actor, and in situations like this, he adopted his 'person in authority' aura and had spoken to the young lady behind the reception desk. Before she had responded, the manager had come out from a door behind her. The expression behind his eyes had said, "Please take everything away and let the hotel return to normal."

Brendan's first port of call had been Johnny's Mercedes. The manager had given him the keys that had been returned by the police. There are so many places where something the size of a plastic credit card could have been hidden or dropped in innocence. It had taken him twenty minutes to check everywhere that wasn't covered by a glued- or bolted-on surface. He hadn't been optimistic at the start. Johnny had not been alert to the possibility that he might be killed and may not have realised the full potential contained on the card, and therefore may not have thought that it was necessary to hide it.

Next, he had checked the things in the locked store cupboard. Almost everything had been packed into Johnny's suitcase or briefcase. It didn't take long to sift through the pieces, being ever wary of hidden places in the linings.

Finally, he had gone into Johnny's room, which was still officially out of bounds and under the control of the authorities; it had been emptied but not cleaned. Brendan had closed the door behind him and had quietly begun to look everywhere. He had looked on the top of every wardrobe, at the back and bottom of every drawer, in the toilet cistern, and at so many other places. In passing, he had noticed the wastepaper bin was empty. Its contents couldn't have been thrown out, collected and on the way to the incinerator? No, Johnny had only been there one evening and overnight. He had probably generated no waste.

Brendan had sat on the bed for a couple of minutes to calm himself in preparation for going next door to Walter's room and the likely result. The gun had been in his coat pocket. It wasn't the probability that he would have to shoot Walter that had been prominent in his thoughts. Rather, it was that this represented a pivotal moment with no going back. For seven years, he had been a sleeper for the DEGD, the Moroccan Directorate General of Foreign International Studies and Documentation; this was the very active and respected Moroccan intelligence agency that was best known for its infiltration of the EU at the highest level – particularly, it was alleged, on behalf of Qatar. Brendan had spent this time within the British FCO, firstly in Belgium and more recently in Paris.

His phone rang. It was an agitated Walter, asking him about the card.

There was now no debate. Brendan waited a few minutes and then, with a cold heart, he had gone and tapped on Walter's door. He would have preferred to have found the card earlier in his searches, but this had always been a very long shot. It had always looked likely that Walter had found it and may even have been a willing partner. On opening the door, Walter was shocked to see Brendan, whom he presumed to be in Paris. Brendan had fired at Walter, who had slumped onto the bed and fallen onto the floor. The room had smelt of recently eaten food. He had reached outside to put the do-not-disturb sign on the door handle.

Having put Walter's laptop and the all-important memory card into his bag, he had taken a minute to check the bedroom and en suite bathroom for anything relevant, but he'd found nothing.

Once back at reception, he had thanked the girl at the desk, said that he would be back in the morning and walked straight out to his car. Forty-five minutes later, he had been driving into Basel airport. Two hours later than that, he had flown to London on a false passport. He had arrived at the safe house by midnight that Saturday night.

***

The next morning, Brendan had been staring at the harvest when he was snapped out of his reverie by an alarm. He walked over to his laptop to see live images of the entrance to the Yelland estate. His colleagues, who were based in the safe house, had been monitoring Charles's phone traffic and were aware that Maria and Angelica would probably be arriving home about now.

This meant that a version of his plan could be put into action.

CHAPTER THIRTEEN

Mike had been researching the easiest way to get to Málaga. She had settled on the forty-five-minute train from Fuengirola, which ran every twenty minutes. It gave her a slight problem at the Málaga end because Randy's flat was out in the suburbs. She changed her mind. She would hire a motorbike – after all, she had her own helmet – as a bike would give her more flexibility. The Yellands' chauffeur ran her to one of his friends on the outskirts of Fuengirola, and an hour later, she was riding along the fast road cut into the low hills with views down to the built-up coast. She passed under the ski lift near Benalmádena that was ferrying tourists up to Mount Calamorro and, a few minutes later, swept down towards the airport on the western edge of the city.

She didn't go straight to Randy's apartment. Dylan had taught her a few techniques, and she could hear him telling her to take care. She pulled over and took off her helmet. A cigarette later, she was happy that she wasn't being followed.

A pine tree provided her with some shade under which to park the bike, and she took a few minutes before setting off again, with her bag over her shoulder, towards the entrance to the apartment block. It was about five stories high with a large glass door giving access to a communal entrance hall, lifts and stairs. Mike looked up at the small balconies outside and saw caged birds, mountain bikes up on end and lines of drying washing. There was nobody around, and in the foyer, no camera was pointing at the mailboxes that made up one wall. She had a screwdriver ready to force her way into the box marked "Ramon Ramirez". Having done so, and after quickly putting the contents into the bag slung across her shoulders, she made her way up the stairs to Apartment 8 on the first floor. *Typical CIA,* she thought to herself. The ground floor is generally too vulnerable and accessible, and too high up limits the possibilities and speed of escape. *Yes,* she told herself, *this is Randy's apartment.*

The corridor on the first floor smelt of burnt cheese, but she couldn't work out if this was the remains of breakfast or the start of lunch. She assumed that the neighbours might look out of their spyholes, so she acted as normally as possible. Her back-up plans involved on-the-spot variations of "I'm his sister-in-law; can you help me?" But plan A involved a beautiful, small jemmy that would open most doors that weren't reinforced, barred or double bolted.

A couple of seconds later, she was inside with the door closed behind her. Immediately, she took off the shoulder bag and put it to the side. If anyone in authority came in or challenged her, she was Randy's sister-in-law visiting from the US. She put on latex gloves.

Mike knew that speed and efficiency were the bywords.

The first thing she noticed was that the apartment was clean and tidy – nobody had left in a hurry or, worse, had been killed messily. Secondly, the fridge was empty of anything that wouldn't last for weeks. There was no milk, salad or fresh meat. This meant that Randy had planned to leave the apartment and for a reasonable length of time. She checked the waste bin in the kitchen, and it was empty. So, it was a planned trip – but where to?

This place is sterile, she mused. *How much does he sleep, let alone live, here?* The first door she opened revealed a small second bedroom that could have come straight out of a show house. Nobody had used it, and there were no personal effects. Next door was the master bedroom, but even this – while evidently in use – was uncluttered.

The contents of his desk, bedside drawers and shelves turned out to be of little interest. She did note that there were a couple of five-centime coins from Morocco in a small dish on a side table. The dozen-or-so books were mostly thrillers by Michael Connelly or Jeffrey Deaver. There was one very thick paperback that looked anomalous. It had *1421* emblazoned on the spine and was by Gavin Menzies. "The year China discovered America," she read. What was Randy doing reading this? It didn't sound like his sort of book. What interest did he have in the Chinese exploration of Africa and America in the fifteenth century? She began to suspect that this apartment was used by more than one person. There was a half-drunk glass of water by the bed, the contents of which she emptied into the toilet and then she quickly stowed the glass itself in her bag, along with the toothbrush from the small bathroom. These might provide fingerprints or DNA if that were ever necessary.

Mike had made her name devising software that

searched for what was *missing* from any scenario or what was incongruous; this was a way to eliminate people from a long list of possibilities and/or identify a residence. If you knew the suspect was male, eighteen years old and lived in a particular town, he probably doesn't subscribe to *Woman's Weekly* magazine, have his nails done every week or buy Spandex pants. He might do any of these things, but the percentages were heavily against it. When added to a hundred other possible activities that an eighteen-year-old man is very unlikely to do, the potential houses where he might live are reduced considerably. If that sounds boring, it's because it *is* boring, but if you can reduce 10,000 possible houses in a town to 100 or fewer, this is invaluable.

It wasn't surprising, therefore, that she was trying to spot what was out of place or what was missing from this apartment. Firstly, she noticed that the only handwriting in all the rooms was in the kitchen on a magnetic reminder pad on the fridge door. There were three words in English, one of which was 'hake'; the writer had not used the Spanish word '*merluza*' for the fish. She wouldn't know Randy's handwriting, so she tore the page off and put it in her pocket.

She was now clutching at straws. She went back into the bedroom and pulled back the sheets, looking for some evidence of sexual activity – nothing. Cursing herself for being inefficient, she ran back into the kitchen and opened drawers and cupboards. Nothing. She looked down at a wine rack with five bottles in it. They were all red. *Randy drinks white, doesn't he?* She tried to remember. She pulled one out and found it had a tag around its neck. Mike couldn't read the printed message in Spanish, but she could see that it was clearly a corporate gift from Petronello. *If Charles Yelland has lied to me again...*

After ten minutes, she could still hear no sounds in the adjoining apartments, but she didn't want to tempt fate. She wasn't a trained field operative – just an inquisitive amateur who had no idea if she should stay ten or twenty minutes. She lost her nerve and decided to get out. Before leaving, she placed a small listening device somewhere out of sight. This would be triggered by any sound of activity in the apartment and relay this to her phone. Looking around, she couldn't resist lifting a couple of rugs on her way out, but she found nothing. She had brought some kid's plasticine with her from England, which was in her bag together with the jemmy and some other tools. Having formed a small lump of it, she used it to prevent the front door from swinging open – it was enough to fool anyone passing by.

As she walked down the stairs, she found herself imagining Randy doing the same on his way out, but to where? *Where are you?* she asked herself.

Stepping into the sunlight, Mike put on her sunglasses, and her mind wandered on to transport. Did he have a bike, scooter or car, or just use the train? There was nothing to help her in the apartment: no keys, documents, used tickets or helmets. She walked around the side of the block to a small car park. There were a dozen cars, mostly small Seats, Fiats and Fords. She took some photographs on her phone to record the registration plates.

Fifteen minutes later, with warm air blowing on to her face, she was roaring westwards up the *autopista* towards Fuengirola. An easyJet plane above her was coming into land at Málaga airport as she passed by.

***

Mike pulled up at the gate to the villa and stood the bike on its stand while she rang the bell. A voice she didn't recognise asked for her name. Wazz, who was watching the various security cameras, told the man at the gate to allow her access. The man pressed the button inside the gatehouse and then stepped outside to watch the visitor first-hand. Mike rode in through the gates and slowed to acknowledge the new level of security. She noticed he was missing his left eye, which didn't seem to qualify him for this line of work. He then focused on her with his right eye, which told her that he did indeed qualify – the intensity of his stare bored into her soul.

She rode up to the villa and parked to the side of the garage complex. On removing her helmet, she was reflecting on the fact that her trip had revealed little – and that Randy was still out there somewhere and in trouble. She knew this instinctively.

"Haven't found what you're looking for?" came a voice from the outside stairs.

"Who are you? Bono?" she replied, feeling tetchy.

"Sorry, your face is, well, demonstrative." Wazz was almost at the bottom step.

"That's what faces are for." She had said that she was going into Málaga to have a look around.

He held up both arms and smiled in a conciliatory way. "Want a cigarette by the waste bins?"

"I can see why you're single if that's your best chat up line."

"Or we can talk in my office?"

"Where's that?"

"By the waste bins."

While her stance in the black wig, the black leather jacket and the black helmet gave off an air of confidence, her eyes did not.

He didn't speak but just shrugged and used his head to indicate rather unnecessarily where the bins were.

"You are a…" But she didn't, or couldn't, finish the sentence. A strange vulnerability persisted in her eyes.

He held his arms open wide. His tight, white tee shirt rode up as he breathed in gently and he offered his chest to her. "You need to punch something?"

"I'm just a bit too tall, but possibly, if I knelt down?" There was no venom in her response.

She acquiesced and followed him around the outside of the kitchen to the first area where they had met.

"Don't tell me that you went to visit the Francis Bacon exhibition at the Picasso gallery and it was closed?"

"No." She lit the cigarette that was twitching in her fingers.

"Want to tell me why you needed to hire a bike on a Sunday morning to go to Málaga when you're meant to be here watching Charles?"

Her right hand was rubbing her left ear, and her left hand was holding the cigarette. "It's not as it seems."

"When I said I was boxing when I broke my nose, I failed to say that I wasn't in a ring or wearing gloves. Life is never quite what it seems." He was checking the batteries before vaping, but whether this was to give her a moment to reflect was not evident. There was a significant pause.

Mike realised that she was alone – not at that moment, but in life generally, she was alone. Weren't moments like this meant to occur when aged parents died in your arms, not outside of the double-glazed kitchen door of a Spanish villa? Her parents were in Oregon and, apart from them, she had, well, nothing. No husband, no siblings, no *anything*. It made her realise that Randy, her brother-in-law, was part of a very small group.

On top of all this, her body was still recovering. Her left leg was only half-functioning and her hair had now completely fallen out, all a consequence of the incident in Holland – or the 'accident' as Leonard liked to call it. *Damn!* Why had she brought Leonard into her thoughts?

"I was looking for my brother-in-law," she said after exhaling smoke towards the rear gardens.

"And you didn't find him?" he asked gently.

"No."

"This sounds like a two-cigarette conversation. Or more?"

"I'd probably get lung cancer before I finished telling you."

"Then you'd better start telling me."

"My husband, Dylan, was killed in a road accident in Holland. I was in the passenger seat, hence my leg and the wigs. His brother, Randy, is meant to be living between places in Málaga and Marrakech. I don't know him well. A mutual friend" – here, Mike paused, imagining that describing Leonard as a friend would have made him smile – "thinks he has gone missing and asked me to check out his apartment."

"Does he do this regularly? Disappear, I mean?"

She looked across at Wazz. "He works for the CIA."

"Ah. So, you don't really know what he's doing in Málaga?"

"I have an idea, but whatever he's doing, I don't think he had been in the flat for weeks."

"And you didn't find anything to help you?"

"No."

"What are you going to do next?"

"Try to avoid going to Marrakech." She stubbed out her cigarette.

"Do you have an address?"

"Yes, a *riad*."

"Marrakech is an hour-and-twenty-minute flight from Málaga. You can see the Moroccan coast from here on a clear day."

"Have you been there?"

"Yes, twice. Escorting nervous wives on shopping trips."

She smiled knowingly. "We had better check up on Charles," she said, changing the subject.

"He's talking to his wife and daughter on Zoom."

"They're hardly awake, I wouldn't have thought. He's probably forgotten the time difference with Mexico."

"They are at home in England. They flew in yesterday."

"*Oh for...!*" Mike's eyes were wide open. "And they're alone at the Manor, I expect, while we're all cosy in Spain." With that, she rushed off to find Charles.

CHAPTER FOURTEEN

"You need to fly out here," was all he had said.

"Charles, we've only just got back from Mexico and we're jet-lagged. You know that I can't sleep on planes. Why can't this wait?" Maria had asked.

He was trying to strike a delicate balance between frightening the life out of them and communicating the urgency of the situation. However, this was taken out of his hands, literally, as Mike had grabbed his phone.

"Maria, you trust me, don't you?" This was rhetorical, and she didn't wait for an answer. "You're both in serious danger. This is no joke. You need to get out of the house now and fly out here. Fast!"

There had been some mumbling from Maria and a shriek from Angelica.

"Maria, everything will be fine. Just do as I say. I'll get Charles to sort out the transport."

"OK." Maria had tried to take all of this in.

Patrick Redwood had needed a day off from his police work and so had spent a very pleasant Sunday in the city of Mulhouse, twenty-eight miles to the south of Colmar, forgetting about murdered ministers and their hospitalised aides. Having been car-obsessed since he was a child, he couldn't miss the opportunity that a random visit like this to the Alsace offered to someone like him. He drove to the Musée National de l'Automobile, which was housed in an old spinning mill in the French textile city of Mulhouse. It exceeded his wildest dreams. He couldn't believe his eyes as he gazed on the largest collection of old cars in the world. There were over 400 Bugattis, Hispano-Suizas and every other make he could think of.

His disbelief was not dissimilar to that experienced by the textile-union activists who, after a stand-off in March 1977, had staged a sit-in strike at their employer's offices and broke into one of the Mulhouse spinning mills to find not textile machinery but an astounding number of rare and valuable cars. Their employers, the secretive Swiss Schlumpf brothers, had built up a huge private collection of cars under the noses of the entire workforce. When the brothers got into financial difficulties in the late 1970s, the French government and unions concocted a plan to keep the collection together under group ownership. Hence the Musée National de l'Automobile.

After the short drive back to his hotel, Patrick Redwood received an update from London. This was to be no relaxed Sunday away from work and family. He was so pleased that he had managed to snatch a few hours of joy because he now knew he was involved in a major ongoing international incident and there would be no let up.

It was his boss, Commander Ben Cox, who had phoned. "Patrick, sorry to ruin your Sunday in sunny France, but I think everything has just hit the fan, including the brown stuff. We haven't told the French yet, but this Brendan Dowell from our embassy in Paris has gone missing. He was Walter Flushing's boss… well, sort of."

"Where and when was he last in contact?"

"He went back to Colmar on Thursday from Paris to begin sorting out the shipping of belongings, cars… and stuff. Apparently, his colleagues say he felt guilty that he had opted not to escort Johnny Musselwhite on Wednesday and had left it to such a junior member of staff – well, he was on contract, actually – to look after him."

"Have they tracked his phone?" Patrick wondered.

"Yes, he was connected and in Colmar until 5.30pm on Thursday. Then, his phone went dead with no location service – nothing."

"I presume he wasn't staying at my hotel. Where do FCO staff stay?"

"I'll check, and someone will get back to you. He might have enjoyed a fun evening away from home and is sleeping it off, but that doesn't explain the phone. Everyone here is a bit twitchy."

"So, he went to the Auberge du Pont Neuf on Thursday?"

"Yes, but, Patrick, be careful if you go back there – or anywhere, actually – until we have half an idea what's going on. Someone seems to have it in for Brits in Colmar."

"I have an appointment at 10.00am tomorrow with the prosecutor for an update on progress over the weekend. I'll see what they've discovered about the two events at the *auberge*. Brendan might have surfaced in Paris by then."

***

In Buckinghamshire, it was late afternoon. There was a weak sun, and the sky was washed out with the only cloud consisting of a few patches of indistinct grey. The shadows from the tall cedars on the Yelland estate were long, faint smudges that barely reached the clipped box parterre. A heron was standing incongruously in the middle of the park, waiting for a frog or, failing that, for a vole to venture out from among the cow pats left by the Highland cattle.

Out on the road, two white vans with false number plates were approaching the farthest corner of the estate. One van stopped, and a man dressed in black leapt over the deer fence and began to jog across two fields to the back of the gatehouse. He peered into the windows, but could see no one. Walking out onto the drive, he triggered the sensors that automatically opened the gates for departing vehicles. The two vans swept in. The second one picked up the man in black and took off behind the first.

They drove fast along the tarmac drive under the avenue of mature limes, but they stopped before entering through a set of pillars topped with stone eagles. There was no gate to open, but this was the transition point onto the gravel immediately in front of the house. It also had a second set of sensors, which would sound a bell inside the house. Three men exited the vans, rolled under the beam and ran around the house to reach the glass door to a loggia; the two drivers remained in the vehicles.

The red metal battering ram that was slung over one man's shoulder wasn't needed – a jemmy opened the door with ease. They pushed into the glazed-in loggia that served as Charles's snug and office. The men were well prepared. They had studied the plans of the house and had looked at dozens of internal photographs from the glossy sales brochure that had tempted the Yellands into buying the estate in the first place.

Outside, the two vans pulled onto the gravel, making a tight loop so as to park alongside the steps to the front door; the engines were left running. They slid open the side doors, ready to receive Maria and Angelica. Looking around for any signs of unwanted activity, they stood waiting.

Inside, the three men entered the hall and crept along, with their guns drawn.

Having heard the bell, two animated female voices were coming from the kitchen.

***

Mike had gone back to her bedroom. She was sitting in a small armchair, reflecting on the fact that she was spending her life working for older men who seemed to think that withholding information – or as she liked to call it, lying to her – was acceptable behaviour.

She had carried two bottles of Estrella Galicia beer, with their caps removed, up from the kitchen as she was in a thinking (and, perhaps, drinking) mood.

It had taken four days for her life to be turned upside down. Four days since Leonard had turned up at her cabin. Four days since she had learnt of Randy's disappearance. And what had she learnt, even with a visit to Randy's apartment? Nothing, in all reality. Well, she now knew a lot about gas pipelines and had an address of a *riad* in Marrakech where he might have stayed, but how useful was any of it? In all her years of searching for people, this was one of her worst in terms of meaningful progress. Often, she had failed to find or identify someone, but this had been because there was too much information or too many possibilities. With Randy, it seemed as though he had simply disappeared, leaving no trace.

As if this weren't frustrating enough, Charles Yelland had resurfaced, deflecting her from the task of finding Randy. She had tried to kill two birds with one stone by coming to Spain. In one case, the bird had flown, and in the other case, what? What was Charles up to? Whoever was after him would now focus completely on the villa once Maria and Angelica arrived – a villa that was neither heavily fortified nor easily defensible. The villa in which she was sitting right now, drinking her cold beer.

Mike knew deep down that there was only one potential ally available to her. Starting to drink from the second bottle before it warmed up, she decided to spend a few minutes checking up on him. Wazz wasn't on any of the very restricted databases that were still available to her illegally, she was relieved to see. He did, however, have a criminal record and had spent eighteen months in prison with parole refused after he had got into a bare-knuckle boxing match that he had claimed was an act of self-defence. His submission to the Parole Board had cited his otherwise good behaviour and his progress in his Open University degree in International Studies; however, his early release had been refused.

Mike had made her decision. She would go and find Wazz and confide in him.

Inez was at the bottom of the stairs and told her that Wazz was up in the tower room at the other end of the villa, a rather pointless box room created in an architecturally dubious mock bell tower. It did, however, provide good all-round observation and wasn't used by the household. She tapped on the trapdoor and clambered up. He was looking at a screen displaying four camera views around the grounds.

"So, this is where you hang out?" she enquired.

"Yes, but I suffer from claustrophobia, so it's not great for me."

Prison can't have been much fun either, she wondered.

The small staircase came up through a trapdoor and into a whitewashed room that was perhaps thirteen feet by thirteen feet with matching windows in each wall. It was furnished with a desk and a typist's chair. There was a small crucifix on one wall; perhaps it had been used for quiet prayer by a previous owner?

"Nothing happening?" she asked.

"No. Just a few deliveries. I feel happier now Diego is on the gate. I've worked with him a few times. And in case you're wondering, he can spot more with his one eye than you can with two."

"He looks hard."

"He was in La Legión – the Spanish Foreign Legion, that is. He was in the *tercio*, or regiment, based in Ceuta on the African coast across from Gibraltar."

"We may need him, Wazz," she began her confession. "I need to come clean about a few things."

She was resting on a small windowsill with her legs crossed at the ankle, her default pose. He rotated the chair to face her directly.

"I'm going to trust you with some stuff that no one knows, certainly not Charles and his family. I told you that I'm ex-CIA, and I still freelance for them occasionally. My brother-in-law, Randy, still works for them and has gone missing. They want me to find him. There's a slim chance that what he was working on overlaps with Charles and his future projects. I don't know at the moment, but it can't be ruled out." She paused for this to sink in. "Separately, Charles has received a warning that his life is being threatened. He called me to investigate. He was tied up in some way with Johnny Musselwhite, the British minister who was poisoned in France. You may have read about it? It was Johnny's assistant who rang Charles to warn him, just before the assistant, too, was shot."

Wazz sat there quietly, but he was slowly forming the word 'wow' with his mouth.

"I was happy that Charles came out here. I thought it would be safer, as only two of his work colleagues know... and Maria, obviously. I was hoping that I and the police could find whoever is behind this before they came looking for him. I'm no longer sure this was a great idea."

This time, Wazz did say, "Wow."

"I didn't factor in Maria and Angelica cutting short their trip to Mexico and flying back to Buckinghamshire. When they get out here, at least they'll all be together, but I just wonder how many people now know where they all are?"

Wazz was digesting all of this while watching as Diego – in one of the views on Wazz's screen – was standing under a palm tree, talking to a delivery van driver just outside the gates.

He eventually replied, "Where do I start? Let's leave you working for the CIA until we have an hour together with nothing better to talk about. Top of my list at the moment is where the threat to Charles and his family is coming from. From what I've read online, Johnny Musselwhite was poisoned by Russian agents. If these are the people after Charles, then this is above my pay grade."

"Mine too, probably. Wazz, do you have a couple of mates who can come here and help? And I don't mean any deadbeat you eat with in a tapas bar down by the sea."

There was a level of genuine hurt in Wazz's eyes, but he reflected for a moment before speaking. "Actually, I know a half-dozen people around here whom I would trust with my life, including Diego. What you've said is really insulting. None of us would eat in a tapas bar by the beach. We eat in Italian restaurants up on the main drag." His smile broadened.

"Can you get four of them to come over… discreetly?" she requested. "No screaming from the rooftops."

"Will Charles pay?"

"Yes, he earns enough to cover it in the time it takes me to stand up. I'm going to see him next before Maria and Angelica arrive. In the unlikely event that Charles puts up any resistance, I'll get the money from Maria, and that will cost Charles a hundred times more."

CHAPTER FIFTEEN

He no longer could smell the contents of the bucket or his dried sweat as he had grown so accustomed to them. The limited exercise routine that he had devised was both to keep him physically fit and to stop himself from going mad. His programme had to be based on whatever he could manage using the floor, wall, chain and iron ring – all such activities were limited by the length of the chain. Every couple of hours, or what he guessed to be a couple of hours, he would do a series of pull-ups, chin-ups, handstands and yoga positions. By sunset each day, he knew how wrong he had been with his estimation of two hourly intervals. Some days he did his routine six times and other days eight.

The frequent visits by the rat had become a welcome distraction and a form of entertainment. He now purposely held back some bones to see how close the rat would venture. He had also tried over several days to fashion a small piece of goat bone into a very crude key by rubbing it on the stone floor, but this was never going to work. It might be more useful as a stiletto blade, but that, too, was fanciful thinking. What was the point of trying to stab one of his captors while still chained to a wall? This would just bring on retribution from the other one or from both.

He had speculated long and hard about why he was being held and for so long – there was precious little else to do. They were keeping him alive for a reason. He must have some value to them, but for what? He killed another fly and threw it into the bucket six feet away. This was his favourite sport after tempting and teasing the rat. Why was one day more important than the next? What were they waiting for?

He had come to the conclusion that the only thing it was likely to be was the G20 meeting in Marrakech. Having lost track of the days, he wasn't sure when this was.

One other thing was bothering him. Why had they not tried to find out what he had been up to and why? Did they already know and so didn't need to ask? Or did they think he was genuinely an American gas exploration geologist based in Spain, who was interested in meeting people from the Western Sahara. Was he simply a convenient American to kidnap, and then what?

These thoughts led him to think about his bosses. Surely the CIA was looking for him? It had been weeks now. The thought made him despondent; therefore, he killed another fly and took aim at the bucket.

***

Brendan had watched, with quiet satisfaction, the white vans leave the gates of the Yelland estate and drive off up the road.

At last, his project was back on track. Killing someone in

their hotel room and stealing their laptop was not the most difficult task to be given, especially as he had a large team at his disposal and had been hiding in plain sight at the British Embassy in Paris. Johnny's laptop, however, hadn't contained the expected data, and the French police had been less than efficient (or, perhaps, too efficient?). The need for Brendan to blow his cover by getting overtly involved was a high cost, but Walter Flushing had needed to be removed and his laptop or devices recovered. The memory card had revealed nothing; it was empty. Brendan knew, however, that Charles Yelland was at the heart of the whole dilemma. He needed to be encouraged into falling in line and as quickly as possible.

Sometimes, things don't go according to plan, and sometimes, everything falls into your lap. The fact that Charles's wife and daughter had flown back from Mexico was an unexpected blessing; they had been outside any plan. Things have a habit of providing opportunities to the winners. Brendan now had the means to apply pressure on Charles Yelland in a controlled way.

He was in the safe house, a cottage a few miles north-west of the M25 in Hertfordshire. When Maria and her daughter Angelica were delivered to him, he would be able to force Charles to do what he wanted. He walked up to a window in the lounge and peered out, all he could hear was the honking of geese flying overhead on their way to or from one of the local reservoirs. The cottage was hidden by hedgerows and large trees on two sides and surrounded on the other two by old brick-built sheds and outhouses; it wasn't overlooked.

He settled down to enjoy the rest of the film on TV – they would only be another twenty minutes.

The film's plot became ever more obvious, and Brendan

didn't mind whether he saw the ending or not. In fact, the credits were speeding across the screen as he heard the engine of a van outside. He turned the TV off and walked to the kitchen door.

His colleagues, dressed in black, drew back the sliding door and pulled out the two handcuffed captives, each wearing a hood over her head with tape beneath it across her mouth. The two women were manhandled into the cottage and carried upstairs to one of the bedrooms.

***

Charles took the call beneath the white dome of the echoing atrium. This meant that several people could hear his side of the conversation.

"Charles Yelland," he said, and then he sat himself down on a carved wooden bench that had come from some castle near Santiago de Compostela.

"Mr Yelland, we have your wife and daughter. Listen to me carefully and nothing will happen to them. Do you understand?" Brendan was speaking very clearly from a secure phone.

Charles, for his part, was experiencing a form of déjà vu. "What? Who are you?" Charles had not twigged that this was Inspector Maslen, whom he had spoken to a few days earlier.

"It doesn't matter who I am. In fifteen minutes, I'm going to phone back, and when I do, I'll give you an email address. You'll be waiting and ready to send me the file covering the details of the PEGASUS contract that you have set up with Johnny Musselwhite. Do you understand?"

"What's so special about PEGASUS?"

"Don't you worry about that. May I suggest that you worry about your wife and daughter?" Brendan's voice was at its coldest. "We know what you've been proposing under cover of the gas pipeline. You'll send me everything, and I mean *everything*, related to PEGASUS and all parties concerned. Again, do you understand?"

"Yes."

"You'll then announce to the world that the PEGASUS project is dead and buried. You and everyone party to the project will forget all about it. If you try to resurrect it, your family will die like Johnny Musselwhite. I repeat, do you understand?"

"You aren't giving me any option."

"Well done, Charles, so you do understand. Now find the contract on your system, and remember that, if you conveniently leave anything out, your family will die. In fifteen minutes, I'll give you an email address, and you'll send me the contract that you have with Johnny and the other parties. Simple?"

The line went dead.

Upstairs, Mike was trying to digest what she had heard. She came down the stairs to find Charles staring at his phone as if he had discovered that he was holding a fly whisk.

"Charles," she said on stepping from the bottom step.

"Did that just happen?" He was still staring at the phone.

"Did what just happen? I only heard your half of the conversation."

"I've just been blackmailed again," he said.

"About what?" Mike asked, unaware of the bargaining stakes.

"Someone has kidnapped Maria and Angelica."

"*Charles!*" Mike raised her voice, and her black hair was flicked back as she raised her head skywards, or at least towards the dome. "I told you to get them on a plane out here as fast as possible."

He raised his hands, palms upwards, and shrugged.

"What do they want? A percentage of the production from your Antarctica field?" she asked cynically.

"Sight of a contract and the parties involved."

"What's this contract?"

"An agreement with Johnny Musselwhite and some other people, plus the full details about PEGASUS."

"Charles," Mike said very slowly through gritted teeth.

"It's a commercial agreement. What do you want me to say?"

She didn't move. She didn't say anything. Instead, she stared at him intensely from under her black fringe.

"It's commercially sensitive."

"Of course it's sensitive. I can work that out. I think it was the murdering, shooting, kidnap and blackmail that gave me the clue. We need to talk... somewhere private." She pivoted on the spot with her arms crossed, waiting for Charles to lead the way.

He led her down a corridor into a study with two walls lined with books (although Mike couldn't imagine that he would ever have touched anything on these meticulously arranged shelves). He closed the door, and they sat at a desk inlaid with red leather with a decorative gold border. It looked like an interview for a job; perhaps it was?

He pulled out a laptop, turned it on and tapped in some password while she sat in silence, wondering how a room like this could look so photogenic, but at the same time, be totally devoid of any character. Did Charles have any opinions, views or preferences of his own? Did he really simply react to what was before him?

"I need to get this file ready to send to… them." He couldn't bring himself to say 'blackmailers'.

"Can you talk while you are doing that?"

He didn't answer.

"Obviously not." She didn't sound sympathetic. She kept going. "Is this really about PEGASUS? Is this all about a pipe? Or is PEGASUS not a pipe but a cover for something else? Are there people, governments… I don't know… who would prefer you not to build a pipeline that goes from Algeria to mainland France via Corsica?" She was trying to provoke him, but he seemed obsessed with the screen and the keyboard.

"Wait a second. I'm not very good at this. I have Jo and ten other people who use these damn things for me." It appeared that he wasn't avoiding the question but concentrating on applying his limited computer skills.

"May I help?"

"Yes," he said begrudgingly. "You know the passwords anyway."

She moved around the desk and leant over to the keyboard. "What are you trying to do?"

"I want to move that file called PEGASUS so that it's ready to email when they give me the address."

Less than thirty seconds later, she said, "There. Done. Now relax. I'll attach it for you when they call back, if that's what you want."

She was tapping away at the keyboard while he began pacing up and down.

"So, who doesn't like the idea of PEGASUS?" She stared at

141

him, trying to encourage him to tell her the truth and not beat about the bush.

"The Moroccans... and the Americans and the Spanish."

"Are we talking governments or private interests?"

"Both," he replied. "Their governments don't like it, and neither do certain industrial groups and their backers. It would mean that Algerian gas goes directly to France and across Europe. The pipeline to Spain via Morocco would be redundant. It's almost redundant already, but the Moroccans cling to the hope that it will reopen one day – if the politics change."

"So, they want the details of the project and to kill it?"

There was a long pause.

"PEGASUS is a complicated project," he said.

"Do you want to send the MEDUSA project file as well?"

"No! Good God, no. How do you know about MEDUSA?"

"Relax. It's in the same folder as PEGASUS. I've just seen it."

"No, no... please separate the PEGASUS stuff from the MEDUSA file; that's a different project."

There was a period of quiet while Mike rattled the keyboard and undertook Charles's instructions. This moment of peace was broken when Charles's phone rang.

"Charles Yelland." His voice was steady, but his eyes betrayed a fear.

"Mr Yelland, do you have a pen? I'll give you the email address."

"Wait. I have no proof that you have my wife and daughter. Put them on the phone."

"Mr Yelland, they have tape over their mouths at the moment, and it will hurt if I tear it off... and you don't want them to get hurt, do you?"

"I'm not sending you a confidential contract without some proof."

"I don't have time to cut off your daughter's ear and post it to you. You're stalling. You'll have checked your security at the Manor and will have seen the broken French windows. You'll have seen your wife and daughter bundled into the two white vans." He paused. "May I say that the red and yellow tiles don't look right in your kitchen?"

Charles would tend to agree with him on that, but now was not the time.

"I want to see my wife and daughter." Charles was adamant.

"It will only distress you… but if you insist, I'll show you. They're in the next room. I'll open the door." He started to walk. "Then, there will be no more discussion."

Making sure of what was in the view, Brendan turned on the camera phone. The door was opened.

"Maria! Angelica!" Charles jumped up.

On his phone, he could see two people with grey tape across their mouths and terror in their eyes.

CHAPTER SIXTEEN

On hearing Charles shout, "*Maria! Angelica!*" Mike read the situation very quickly.

She, too, leapt up and made a gesture to Maria and Angelica, who had just appeared in the study doorway. Mike walked quickly towards them, ushering them into the corridor. She kept a finger to her lips until they were well clear of the door.

"We'll explain later," she said as she hugged them both.

"What's happening?" Maria asked.

"Later." And with that, Mike walked back into the study, closing the door behind her.

"Nice try, whoever you are, but those two are not my wife and daughter. Goodbye," Mike heard Charles say, before he ended the call.

He jumped up, ran to the door and walked into the hall, where Angelica ran up to him. She had her jet-black hair in a ponytail and was wearing a loose, pink shirt and baggy, white trousers.

"What's happening, Charles? Why the mad rush to get out here? We're both jet-lagged from the flight back from Mexico. You know I hate flying. Why can't this wait?" Maria walked over to him, and they kissed, albeit briefly and coldly.

"I'm not sure what's happening, but my life has been threatened," he said.

"And we couldn't leave you unprotected at the Manor. I think someone has already broken in there," Mike added. She then turned to Charles. "Didn't you get any notification of a break-in?"

"It will have come into my other phone... it's in the bedroom," he explained.

"Well, can I see it? Now!" Mike had stood there in disbelief. *How does this man run an international company?*

He went up three steps and began to walk along a corridor with Mike following.

When they were well out of earshot, she said, "I want to see this break-in, if there is one."

"Oh, there is one," he said while walking into his bedroom, "They've kidnapped Gabriela and her daughter, Camila."

"Who are they?"

"Our Mexican cook and her daughter, who live in the gatehouse. I don't know how to tell Maria and Angelica; they're all close."

Mike registered the almost complete indifference Charles had displayed once he knew his family were safe. Nobody else mattered, it seemed.

He turned on the mobile, tapped in a code and handed it to Mike.

"Charles, you do realise that the kidnappers will phone back? You aren't in the clear yet."

"I know, I know; I just needed time, and seeing Maria and Angelica threw me."

"Go and reassure them, but don't mention the kidnap. Then, speak to Wazz and get him to get a couple of his friends over here pronto. Whoever the kidnappers are, they now realise you're all here in Spain. I'm going to look at the security footage and will ring the police."

Charles seemed frozen to the spot.

Indicating the door with a nod, Mike said, "Before the grape harvest would be good." Although as she had said it, she didn't really have any idea when this might actually be.

Five minutes later, she was sitting in her room, scrolling through Charles's phone. She had taken off her wig, only to put it straight back on again as she had felt the cool breeze from the air conditioning. She spent a few minutes downloading much of the recent activity on to her own phone and her laptop. She needed a drink, but she had no idea of time – perhaps thinking of the grape harvest had increased her thirst?

Neither Mike nor Charles could have known that their decision to use a helicopter may just have saved Maria and Angelica from being kidnapped. If they had used a car, it would have triggered the camera near the gatehouse, and this would have alerted Brendan and his colleagues. The team from one of the white vans had already been sitting in a layby a mile away. As it was, it had been only a matter of minutes later that the two vans had turned up, unaware that their targets had lifted off from the helipad in a piece of parkland half a mile away from the back of the house.

***

"Leonard, are you on the Underground? Turn on the camera; this I have to see."

"No, I'm not. I'm shaking a box of popcorn."

"What? Where? It sure sounds like you're on the Tube," Mike declared.

"I've just parked at the office, and I'm walking to the elevator."

"Leonard, your car parking space is so close to the elevator that the 'S' of 'de Vries' wraps around the call button."

"Someone parked in my space."

"Who?"

"Let's call him Lance Armstrong because he'll be cycling to work from now on. Call me back in five."

He rang off, and Mike leant back in her chair. It was Monday morning, and she was still digesting what had happened yesterday. Most important for her was that Maria and Angelica were safely in the villa after their flight from Northolt. Unfortunately, Maria was now heavily sedated and lying in her room. The realisation of what was happening and the flashbacks to a year previously had set off a panic attack. Angelica had gone to her room and locked herself in, but not until after Mike had read the Riot Act to her, having explained that she must turn off the location services on her phone and she couldn't tell anyone that she was in Spain.

"Yes, Angelica," Mike had said, "that does mean no selfies."

"How long are we here for? I'm going to the Ariana Grande concert next week with Pippa."

"Just leave it a couple of days while we sort out what's happening. Sorry."

Angelica had locked the bedroom door.

Now in full operative mode, Mike had asked Charles

to describe what he had seen on his phone while talking to the kidnappers. It was no surprise that he wasn't the most observant of people and could only describe Gabriela and Camila with tape across their mouths. He thought he had seen a chest of drawers to one side, but he wasn't sure. This fact contributed absolutely nothing to the search, but this seemed to pass Charles by altogether. Mike and Charles hadn't told Maria or Angelica about the break-in nor that the blackmailers had rung back a little later once they had established who they had kidnapped. Their demands were the same, and Charles had written down the email address that Brendan had given him. It ended in '.ma' which was Moroccan.

"Just as I thought, the bastards are in Morocco," Charles had said.

"Not necessarily," Mike had replied.

"Why are you always so cynical?"

"Charles, when the magician keeps waving his left hand in the air, look at his right. Just a piece of advice."

Charles had shrugged.

For several hours previously, Mike had tried to piece together why a well-spoken British man was holding two females who he thought were the Yellands, while demanding that commercial information was emailed to a Moroccan email address. This didn't ring true, but then again, what did she know?

Not long after Maria's arrival, and as promised, Mike had made the call to one of her contacts in the London police and reported the events in Buckinghamshire. She had forwarded the security video from Charles's phone. A police team had gone out to the Manor to investigate, and a scene-of-crime unit was currently gathering evidence. However, it was obvious that the gang was professional and had only made one mistake: assuming that the two people in the kitchen were Maria and Angelica. An easy mistake to make given that both mothers were Mexican, and they all had jet-black hair.

Mike was surprised that the kidnappers hadn't been monitoring the Manor. Hadn't they seen them leave for Northolt? Here, she was wrong because she didn't know that they were indeed watching, but they hadn't seen the mother and daughter being ferried to the airport in a helicopter from the rear of the estate, which had therefore not triggered the surveillance camera at the front gates.

She grabbed her phone. She had forgotten to call Leonard back.

"Where've you been?" he said when the call she made connected.

"How's Lance Armstrong?"

"He's been selected at random by me for an invasive drugs test."

"Aren't you confusing him with the real Lance Armstrong?"

"Well, whatever. All I know is that he won't be able to sit on a bike for a while."

Mike winced and, as an involuntary reaction, squirmed on her chair.

She told Leonard all about the events in Buckinghamshire and that she felt she was under a lot of pressure. He, for his part, told her that she didn't know what the word 'pressure' meant and that she ought to feel the heat that he was getting from above. Leonard wanted her to forget about the Yellands and find Randy.

***

On a bright Monday morning, Patrick Redwood walked up the steps of the prosecutor's office in anticipation of his 10.00am meeting. While stopping at a kiosk to buy some chewing gum, Ben Cox had rung to confirm that Brendan Dowell still hadn't been in contact or been found. The FCO was presuming he had decided to spend his weekend completely away from work and would be back in his office on Monday – so far, he hadn't reported for duty at the Paris embassy.

Madame Bettancourt was sitting at her desk, wearing a collarless black suit with a dragonfly brooch. She invited Patrick to take a seat. "Mr Redwood, how was your weekend in the Alsace?"

"Very enjoyable. I visited the Schlumpf car museum in Mulhouse yesterday. It's very impressive."

"I am ashamed to admit that I have never been," she confessed.

"Are you from the Alsace originally?" He couldn't bring himself to use the word 'Alsatian' for some reason.

"No, I am from Lorraine, which is the region to the north... not far away."

Patrick reflected on this and, after a short pause, asked, "How's Walter Flushing?"

"Alive but still on the critical list. He is under police protection, which you might also be interested to learn." She moved a notepad on her desk and looked directly at Patrick. "You did not spend the weekend with Mr Dowell from your Foreign Office?"

"No, no; I think he has gone back to Paris. I don't know him. I've been liaising with Stewart McBride on this case – or should that be cases?"

She smiled in a knowing way. "Over the weekend, we tried to contact Mr Dowell, but his phone has been turned off."

Patrick wondered why the French investigative team should be trying to contact Brendan. "Have there been developments?"

"Several… beginning with our examination on Saturday of the hotel's CCTV footage over the period that Mr Flushing was shot."

"What have you seen?"

She paused while she rotated her gold bracelet. "It is rather what we have not seen. As you know, it is an old *auberge* and does not have the most comprehensive camera coverage. We cannot be certain, but it looks as if Mr Dowell was the only person, beside the staff and other guests, in the *auberge* at the time Mr Flushing was shot." She paused again to let this sink in. "He was visiting Monsieur Musselwhite's room to collect his remaining possessions. It is the room next door to Mr Flushing's."

Patrick began to get an uneasy feeling as several thoughts began to develop in his head.

Madame Bettancourt raised her eyes to look directly at him. "Mr Redwood, while you were looking at the Bugatti collection yesterday, I was in here." She indicated her temporary office. There was no one-upmanship in her voice, just a recognition of the reality of the circumstances.

Patrick stayed quiet, but his face betrayed a sympathy borne out of nights, weekends and even Christmas Days when he had been hauled away to deal with emerging crises.

"I can see that you have realised the implications. Mr Dowell is now the prime suspect."

Patrick shook his head gently as the enormity dawned.

"For the record, we know that he has diplomatic immunity, unlike Mr Flushing and Mr Musselwhite. We have spent the last twenty-four hours trying to find him," she said.

So, they haven't found him yet, Patrick thought.

"As we are speaking," Madame Bettancourt continued, "my colleagues in Paris are contacting their London counterparts."

"I'll also be on the phone after this meeting. I think this will have to go right to the top."

"Just before you arrived, I was given an update from the Immigration Office. The good news is that no one called Brendan Dowell has left by plane, sea or road." She paused. "The bad news is that someone called Habib Bennani flew from Basel to London Heathrow on Thursday, 1st September. He was identified by facial recognition."

"Has this name or passport been used in France before?"

"That is being checked, but you grasp the situation. It looks as if your Mr Dowell from your Foreign Office is either a British spy or a Moroccan spy."

"Moroccan? Do you really think that?" There was genuine surprise in Patrick's voice.

"He was travelling on a Moroccan passport." She took a deep breath. "If we assume that your Foreign Office has not decided to kill a British minister and his assistant on French soil, we are left with a very worrying situation, are we not?" She placed her hands together on top of her notepad.

Patrick's mind was full of possible scenarios, but he was trying to keep focused on the murder and attempted murder that he was investigating; others would pursue the political and other consequences. "Brendan, either using his own name or his alias, wasn't here when Mr Musselwhite was poisoned, was he?" he asked.

"I have asked for this to be checked, but my guess is that it was the two large men in the lost or imagined CCTV footage who poisoned Mr Musselwhite. Mr Dowell came back because something was not… resolved." She hesitated over finding the right word in English.

"I think I agree."

"I wonder what poor Mr Flushing either saw or, perhaps, had found out?"

Patrick's mind went back to the missing memory card. "That's what I'm asking myself."

Twenty minutes later, standing on the corner of a quiet street, Patrick was on the phone to Ben Cox.

CHAPTER SEVENTEEN

Victor was chairing a Monday morning meeting that was meant to sign off the final details for the G20 meeting in Marrakech later in the week. To use one of his favourite expressions, he was feeling quite bright-eyed and bushy tailed. This was about to change.

Dennis walked in and waited for the PM to signal to him. When beckoned, he bent over and whispered in the PM's ear.

"Really?" Victor looked at him in disbelief as Dennis, with his large forehead covered in sweat, continued his update and suggestions.

"Now?" Victor asked, to which Dennis nodded. "So who needs to leave this meeting?"

There followed a temporary exit by some people not cleared to a sufficiently high security level, who were then replaced by two other people, including Ben Cox.

"What's happening?" Victor stared at the head of MI6, who had joined the meeting with Ben Cox.

"We have a major problem. We've just been updated by our French colleagues and our own people out there that one of our Paris embassy's FCO men, whom we know as Brendan Dowell, may have shot Mr Flushing and be involved in the poisoning of the minister."

"Shit!" The PM had reverted to another of his favourite expressions.

"I'm afraid it may be much worse," the MI6 head continued.

"What can be worse than that?" The PM's face had begun to sag at the cheeks.

"He may be a foreign agent" – there was silence – "working for the Moroccans."

"You are…" But Victor never finished articulating his disbelief and exasperation.

"He didn't return from Colmar to the Paris embassy, as expected; instead, he flew back from Basel to Heathrow on a Moroccan passport. This is all very new. We're checking his whereabouts, obviously."

"But why kill Johnny? Is this Brendan really working for the Moroccans? How long has he been at the FCO?" the PM asked.

"All questions I'll have answers to as soon as possible."

"I need to know if this will have any impact on the G20… We need to keep the Moroccan passport bit quiet until we know more. Give me another update when this meeting is over in an hour. May we call the others back in?"

**

Ben Cox had then joined Simon, the head of MI6, in a separate meeting of half a dozen people who were solely investigating who Brendan really was, whom he was working for, and why he had murdered – or been party to the murder of – Johnny Musselwhite and made the attempt on Walter Flushing. They were in a modern office with black leather chairs, dark-grey desks and nothing to relieve the starkness of the white walls.

Violet Anderson, who had been looking at Brendan's personnel file, was giving the meeting an update: "Brendan Dowell grew up in Lancashire. His mother is English and his father's Irish. He got a first in French at Durham. He was fast-tracked through Basingstoke into the FCO, where he has been for twelve years. During this time, besides London, he has done a year in Brussels, three years in Rabat and the last two years in Paris. His annual reviews are all excellent, and there are no major criticisms or suspicions mentioned. I've been in touch with someone who was at our embassy in Rabat while Brendan was there to ask whether he had worked with anyone specific on the Moroccan side or whether any approaches had been made to our staff in general. It was about the time that we were using the Makhzen heavily to combat Islamic terrorism after the 2015 Paris bombing."

"Who are the Makhzen?" someone called Alice asked.

"They're a part of the security services from Rabat, tied closely to the King of Morocco and his court. They've been very useful to us, being non-Christian and – how shall I put it? – sufficiently removed. They've infiltrated several organisations and provided us with good intelligence," Violet confirmed.

"The Moroccan intelligence agency and secret service have been getting a little out of hand," Simon, the head, said. "Look at what they did this year in Brussels: apparently bribing EU Commissioners on behalf of the Qataris. They're growing like Topsy."

"I'm not sure why they would want to turn a British FCO member of staff, though? And what with? Money? Blackmail?" Violet was not convinced.

"Was Brendan involved in anything off-piste?" Alice asked Violet.

"No, not that I've found so far."

"May we concentrate on the events in the Alsace? What was he meant to be doing – for us, that is?" Simon asked.

"Johnny Musselwhite, through his department, had been very keen on those Green initiatives that the French have been trialling using the old potash mines as test sites. He has been in frequent contact with his French counterpart, Yves Dubuisson. Brendan was tasked with setting up this latest meeting near Colmar. He went down some weeks ago to make the arrangements from the British side: hotels, transport, timings – that sort of thing. Really nothing too complex and, certainly, not secret," Alice explained. "Oddly, he seems to have made excuses not to actually escort the minister on the day, and instead, he sent Walter Flushing. It was assumed in the embassy that Brendan couldn't be bothered to go down to Colmar for what would only be a couple of hours."

"Then, two heavies – nationality unknown – kill Johnny using a rare poison and steal his laptop, etc.," Violet suggested.

"Are these heavies Russian, as we might expect, or Moroccan? If the latter, why?" Simon questioned.

"Surely, it rather depends on what Johnny was up to? And he must have been up to something; countries don't kill each other's ministers for the fun of it," a new voice offered.

"We haven't found anything in Johnny's calls, office or home to link him with anything serious, if you exclude his penchant for cocaine, which doesn't look like it would be reason enough. If it were the Russians, there are many things to do with energy and minerals that they might not like… but the Moroccans? What could Johnny have been involved in that would have bothered them?" Alice put her hands together as if praying for an answer.

"He was enthusiastic about a new gas pipeline from Algeria to France, called PEGASUS, which might not be to the Moroccan's liking. They want as much as possible of Algeria's gas to go via a pipeline through their territory to Spain," Violet commented.

"Is that enough to want him dead?" Simon asked her.

"I wouldn't think so, but possibly."

"Whether it was the Russians, Moroccans or anybody else, what went wrong? Clearly something did." Simon wanted to get to the crux of the matter.

"This Walter had something in his possession or saw something that meant Brendan had to nip down there sharpish, look for it and silence him. Could it be this mysterious memory card?" Alice was following her own logic.

"And to blow his cover flying back to London on a Moroccan passport," someone added, "Whatever it was, therefore, it was of the highest importance."

"Have we located Brendan?" Commander Ben Cox entered the conversation. He was, after all, responsible for the criminal aspects of the case.

Violet updated everyone: "No. We're going through CCTV footage from when he landed at Heathrow, but so far, we don't have anything useful. Unsurprisingly, he hasn't gone home, contacted friends or family, updated any social media, used his phone, or used his bank account and credit cards."

"Neither has his alias, Habib Bennani, by the way," Alice said.

"This is something big. Well, of course it's big, given that people are being poisoned and shot, but just think if it were the other way around. If we had spent years getting someone of medium rank into a foreign embassy, we wouldn't blow the whole asset on some minor commercial disagreement, would we?" Simon wasn't looking for any reply, just stating the obvious. "We're missing something big, and I mean *big*," he emphasised. "Whatever it was, I'm sorry to say that it went wrong to such an extent or so quickly that he didn't even try to hide his covert identity."

Ben Cox was applying his policeman's logic to all this. "I don't think it was something Walter saw. He had already been interviewed several times by the prosecutor and the *brigade criminelle*; he would have already described everything that he had seen. I also don't think that it was something Walter knew. Brendan didn't have time to get it out of him. He appears to have shot him very quickly on entering his room. My money is on Walter having something – an object such as this card – that should have been in Johnny's room, but for some reason, was in Walter's instead."

"The only thing that appears to be missing is Walter's laptop… and the CCTV footage shows Brendon with only a small bag that's just big enough to carry one. He didn't even take Walter's phone," Violet confirmed.

"So, what wasn't on Johnny's laptop but was on Walter's?" Simon asked.

"Or what did Johnny give to Walter for safekeeping? From this, we can infer that Johnny knew his life was in danger," someone else added.

"Nobody has ever found the memory card that the night manager saw, have they?" Ben looked around the room, seeking an answer.

There was a pause in the proceedings as a connecting door opened and closed, although no one came in.

"May I go back to this PEGASUS pipeline proposal? Is it worth us checking out the British company involved and asking quietly what the international reaction has been?" Simon enquired.

"We should be careful; this PEGASUS proposal is also for power cables transporting – or is it transmitting? – electricity from a solar farm in Algeria. Actually, it's the size of twenty farms," Violet declared.

Simon changed tack: "The Moroccans must know that we know about Brendan. What are they saying, Alice? We have friends out there, don't we?"

"They're saying nothing. Absolutely nothing."

"That does bother me."

"Nobody's mentioned the G20 meeting in Marrakech. The PM and POTUS will be there in three days' time," chimed in someone else.

"The timing just doesn't stack up," Simon said, patently not convinced. "Are we seriously thinking that the Moroccans, for whatever reason, would poison a British minister a week or so before they host in their country their first G20 meeting ever? I don't buy it. Is this Moroccan passport just a smokescreen or an irrelevancy?"

"It could be either of those, but if it's the Russians, they could have given him any passport. They may have seized the opportunity to muddy the waters. Giving Brendan a Moroccan identity would be credible given his past time in Rabat, and it might mess up the G20 meeting – that would be attractive to the Russians and, possibly, some others," Alice replied.

"I wonder if this is about gas. The Russians don't want more gas coming into Europe, so scuppering a new pipeline might be on their agenda. I wonder if Johnny was a bit more involved in this pipeline than we realise – in which case, they might want him taken out? Violet, will you speak to those involved in this PEGASUS pipeline and find out what's happening?" And with that, Simon closed the meeting.

***

Mike Kingdom was with Charles Yelland in his study when the call came in from Violet, who was using another name.

He answered immediately in case it was the kidnappers. "Charles Yelland."

"Mr Yelland, I'm ringing from the Foreign and Commonwealth Office in London. We're investigating the murder of a British national in Colmar last week and wondered if you could help us by answering a few questions?"

"I have no idea who you are. I'm rather preoccupied at the moment. How did you get this number?"

"From Jo at your office. She phoned me back at the FCO and can therefore vouch for me, if you would like to check with her? If it's easier, I can email the questions to Jo? However, it is rather urgent."

"I was rather hoping that you were the police ringing to say that you had found the kidnappers of my cook and her daughter."

"I'm sorry, Mr Yelland, but I don't know anything about the kidnap." Violet was thrown off by this, and she was having to think on the hoof. "Which police force is investigating?"

Charles asked Mike Kingdom and then gave the name of the investigating officer to Violet.

"Our principal interest is the PEGASUS project. We know that Mr Musselwhite had supported it widely in the media, but may we ask whether he was involved in the project in a personal capacity?"

"Johnny did stand to gain financially if the project went ahead. Please remember that this project isn't on British soil, doesn't conflict with British interests and would lead to lower gas prices, for example."

"Mr Musselwhite hasn't detailed any of this in the minister's register of business interests."

"I'm sorry, but I don't know what he did or didn't list."

"Have you or he been threatened?"

"As you will find out when you contact the police, the kidnappers of my cook and her daughter have demanded a copy of the PEGASUS agreement and for me to effectively and publicly quash the project."

"Was Mr Musselwhite party to this agreement?"

Charles hesitated. "Yes."

"Was Mr Flushing party to it?"

"No, definitely not. I don't know him, although I believe our paths may have crossed once at the British Embassy in Algiers."

Mike Kingdom was listening to this conversation intently.

"Do I understand from" – Violet paused, presumably to check the name – "Jo, that you're at your residence in Spain?"

"Yes, with my wife and daughter… and a lot of protection. It was they who were the kidnapper's real target. I'm staying here until this thing blows over."

"Good. I'll phone you back if Her Majesty's Government has anything else you may be able to help with, if you don't mind?"

"Happy to help."

After the conversation, Violet was straight on to Simon, Ben, Dennis, Alice and the others who had attended the meeting at MI6. A series of working groups was set up given that the likely motive for the murders was now known.

CHAPTER EIGHTEEN

It was 9.00am on Tuesday, 6th September, and in Spain, the sky was free of any cloud. The sun was still at a low level, blinding Mike Kingdom as she sat on a terrace eating a croissant with apricot jam. She had come to a decision while drinking her cup of tea: she was happy with the security arrangements at the villa under Wazz and, with the three Yellands safely in one place, she could fly to Marrakech and check out Randy's room. His apartment in Málaga had yielded little other than tempting her to think that he didn't spend much time there.

She was frustrated. She felt she had made so little progress finding Randy and this was mostly due to the distraction of having to organise Charles Yelland's life for him. The man was a nightmare.

Angelica walked out onto the terrace, wearing a pink dressing gown and carrying a *Love Island* water bottle; she was barely awake. She sat down at the other end of the marble table without saying good morning. The sun was shining straight into her eyes, which forced her to stand up, walk around the table and sit opposite Mike.

"Happy birthday." Mike was holding her mug of tea in both hands.

"It doesn't feel like it," came the flat response, with Angelica's bleary eyes barely opened. She took her phone from her pocket and started flicking with her thumb.

"You aren't posting any pictures or telling your friends where you are, are you?" The sun was glinting off of Mike's cropped, bright-red wig.

"I'm seventeen not seven, and I don't want to be kidnapped… again. Keep your hair on."

"Bit late for that."

"Sorry."

"I'm as frustrated as you, believe me. I'm meant to be finding my brother-in-law, not baby-sitting your father." Mike was trying to engage the surly teenager.

"Where is he?" Angelica asked without looking up from her phone.

"I hoped that he might be in Málaga, but now I'm guessing Marrakech."

"Where's that?"

"Over there." Mike nodded at the mountains on the horizon, which were just visible across the Mediterranean Sea.

Angelica looked up and turned towards the sea below them. "Is that Marrakech?"

"No, that's Morocco. Marrakech is in Morocco but an hour away by plane."

"Why don't you go?" She looked back down at her phone.

"I'm seriously thinking of flying out there this afternoon

now the three of you are safe. If I go, you will listen to Wazz, won't you?"

Angelica raised her head, took a drink of water and stared at Mike. "Why does everyone treat me like a child?"

Mike was about to reply when her phone vibrated on the table. She picked it up. "Leonard."

"Wait while I turn the brightness down," he said.

"Wait while I turn the screen off."

"Hey, I bought this new tie especially."

"Did you keep the receipt?"

"I'm gonna retie it. I got dressed real early this morning."

"Are you in the office already?"

Angelica stood up, grabbed her water bottle and walked back inside, mumbling something about being in prison.

"Yes, I was called in. When POTUS is about to fly across the pond, everyone gets twitchy. Have you been to Marrakech yet?" Leonard asked.

"I'm going today. I'm just about to book a flight."

"Great. The last thing I need is our friend Ramon Ramirez muddying the waters while POTUS is in town."

"I'm more interested in finding him safe and well."

"That too. By the way, I have some intel for you, but don't let it stop you being 'Morocco-bound'; you know, like Webster's dictionary?"

"I know the song, Leonard. What's the intel?" She put the last piece of croissant in her mouth and brushed a flake off of the table.

"Five Eyes has just been briefed on the poisoning and stuff in France. The Brits are chasing their collective ass all over the place. It seems that one of their spooks in the Paris embassy, Brendan Dowell, is in the frame for the poisoning of their minister and the shooting of a lackey who was helping out down there. Apparently, this Dowell has disappeared somewhere in the UK. You'll be interested because he was travelling on a Moroccan passport in the name of Habib Bennani. He flew back from Basel to London after shooting Walter Flushing." Leonard waited for his bombshell to drop. He began to undo the knot in his tie.

"Surely he's not Moroccan?"

"Nah, this smells like the Russkies to me. The passport is just smoke and mirrors. The Russkies are best buddies with the Algerians so they really want to wind up the Moroccans, you know, while the G20 is on."

"The Russians really don't want this PEGASUS pipeline, do they?"

"Probably not; they want Europe freezing and dependent on their gas or paying big bucks for it."

Mike was still catching up on some of the implications. "So this Brendan Dowell killed Walter Flushing?"

"He tried to. The Brits are keeping it quiet, but this Walter guy is in intensive care under armed guard."

"Thanks for the intel, Leonard; I appreciate it."

"Now book that flight to Marrakech and find out what you can. Ring me quick. I need to redo this tie again. The back bit is twice the length of the front." With that, he rang off.

Mike jumped up and made her way back to her room. *Coincidences; we don't do coincidences.* Unlike Leonard, Mike wasn't fixated on Russia. It was Morocco that was uppermost in her mind. A 'Brit' using a Moroccan passport shoots Walter and a 'Brit' who telephones Charles is using a Moroccan email address. Both these 'Brits' appeared not to want PEGASUS to go ahead. Were they the same man? The more she thought about it, the more she became convinced that was the case.

Mike would find it hard to describe how elated and how pumped-up she felt once she had something tangible to which she could apply her skills. She fired up her laptop and attached all of her peripheral equipment that would aid her in her searches. Firstly, she booked a Vueling flight from Málaga to Marrakech, leaving in four hours, which gave her a couple of hours to find Brendan or Habib Bennani, depending on whom he was exactly. Secondly, she booked a room at the Riad des Tailleurs, the *riad* where Randy might be. She did this in her own name. Randy would have used the surname Ramirez, which meant that they wouldn't make the connection.

With a big intake of breath, she began her search for Brendan Dowell.

It took her fifteen minutes to find his flight to Heathrow from Basel in the name of Habib Bennani. She saved the details in case she needed to track him from the arrivals lounge at Heathrow to his safe house. This was something she didn't want to do and something she expected that the police and secret services were already doing with their extensive manpower. She hacked into an account that provided her with the address he gave when booking the ticket. Unsurprisingly, it was false, but it's essential to eliminate the obvious first.

She accessed Charles's second phone, the one with the notifications from the security system at his estate, Beswick Manor. She watched the various sequences as the two white vans arrived, the building was entered, and the two hostages were bundled into the vehicles. She made a note of the registration numbers, but she didn't expect these to lead anywhere. Most importantly, she made a note of the exact time that they drove out.

On Charles's other phone, Mike looked at the exact time that Brendan, if it was him, had telephoned. Next, she started to play the percentage game. Of course, Brendan could have used any means of transport – in which case, the hostages might be anywhere in most of West London or South East England – but he was unlikely to do that. What were the average times, rates, speeds, etc. for the two vans, assuming that he would want five minutes with the kidnapped mother and daughter in the house in case he needed to prove they were in his control and, perhaps, to be photographed?

It was twenty-six minutes from the kidnap before he called Charles. Allowing one minute for them to clear the estate and five minutes at his end to get them into their room, that meant the vans had travelled for approximately twenty minutes. They wouldn't have broken any speed limits or drawn attention to themselves – this was a golden rule. Being aware of the general area, she knew they were unlikely to exceed an average of thirty miles per hour, probably less. That meant they were within a circle with a ten-mile radius. However, as was quite evident, they had turned left out of the gates of the Manor, and this theoretically reduced the circle by half. Again, this might mean nothing in reality, but they were unlikely to turn back in some act of deception with the attendant risk of being in the vicinity of the Manor for even longer.

Using a piece of town-planning software that she had modified, her computer calculated the area accessible by the local road network at that speed and in that time frame. Her screen revealed a kidney-shaped area, mostly composed of parts of east Buckinghamshire and a small part of south Hertfordshire. She unconsciously held her breath when she hit the button that would reveal the number of households.

Her screened showed 42,133. Her heart sank, but she tried to encourage herself, as she had searched much, much bigger areas over the years. *Come on,* she told herself, *there are 19 million households in the UK; it could have been much worse. You can do this.*

She began by removing all properties with only one bedroom, all properties with outstanding council tax bills, all properties with children of school age and so on, until she had applied over forty factors that weren't likely to be applicable to a safe house that might be used by Brendan. Three-quarters of an hour later, she was down to 127 properties.

Mike had an hour before she needed to leave for the airport. It was at this point that Inez tapped her door and brought in pizza with two bottles of ice-cold beer. Inez left with a broad smile on her face.

With a slice of margherita pizza in one hand, Mike began to click through the list of properties, selecting the view via satellite from above. Now she was flying by the seat of her pants. It was more about feeling rather than fact. Was the property overlooked? Did it have a long, shared drive? Was it next to a garage or business that would have CCTV outside? She quickly put each property into one of two virtual piles: likely and unlikely. Nearing her hundredth property, she had a breakthrough. A large brick cottage with outbuildings that wasn't overlooked and was away from the road caught her eye – or rather, a white van caught her eye. It was impossible to see any registration plate from this view vertically above, but it was of the same type as those used in the kidnap and there was room for another in the garage alongside. She forced herself to continue checking and finished up with twelve possibilities – of which, the one with the white van was leaping out at her.

She looked at her watch. She had to leave for the airport. With a final swig of beer, she telephoned her friendly police contact and told him she was sending a list of properties, of which Holly Cottage with the white van might be worth a look.

Mike also told Nigel, her Special Branch friend, that she was sure Brendan Dowell wasn't just the ringleader with regard to Johnny Musselwhite's murder but that he was also coordinating the kidnap and issuing the threats to Charles Yelland. Nigel knew her reputation well enough to take her thoughts seriously.

She didn't have time to ring Leonard. Instead, she sent him a simple text explaining her thoughts on Brendan.

That done, she divided her computer gizmos between her check-in and cabin luggage, changed her wig to the black one, and clattered down the marble stairs.

Wazz was near the door. "Need a lift?"

"That would be great. I'll be back as soon as I've checked out his room."

"Want to tell me where you're staying in case I have to come and find you? Or is that top secret?"

"Riad des Tailleurs in Marrakech."

"If I asked you to be careful, would it make the slightest bit of difference?"

"No."

"Let me know when you've checked out his room."

"Yes, Mum." She smiled at him in an impish way that didn't look quite so cute under her black wig. "And you let me know what happens here."

A couple of minutes later, they were leaving the villa gates under the monoscopic gaze of Diego, whose right hand never left the gun tucked into the back of his waistband.

In Colmar, Patrick Redwood had also been updated by Commander Ben Cox. He now understood the situation and was one of only a handful of people who knew that Walter was still alive. They agreed it was crucial to let Brendan, or whatever his name was, continue to believe he had killed Walter.

"Patrick, as soon as Walter gains consciousness, we need to find out what he knows about Brendan. I have a feeling that he suspected something," Ben explained.

"I'm almost at the hospital now. In a minute or two, I'll ask for an update and I'll probably hang around. There's not much else for me to do out here."

"I hear that Stewart McBride is arranging for his secure transport back home – assuming he comes out of his coma."

"I'll send you a message once I've spoken to the doctors. Oh" – he suddenly remembered something that had been on his mind – "one other thing, have Porton Down tested the poison?"

"Yes, while the French have been backtracking, Porton Down think this is serious stuff from the big boys, probably from the Russians or Americans, but not exclusively so. Of course, they may have given it to a third party."

With that, the call ended, and Patrick, in his pale linen suit and white shirt, walked towards the hospital entrance. At the door, he met Madame Bettancourt, who was on her way out.

"Mr Redwood. I have just been speaking to the doctor. He tells me that Mr Flushing has not gained consciousness yet, but he is stable, which is good news."

"Oh, that is good news, I think… Thanks," he replied. There was something deeply attractive about her beyond her constantly smiling eyes, but the policeman inside him was always suspicious. Why had she driven to the hospital rather than ringing the doctor?

"Have you had lunch?"

"What? No, I haven't," he said.

"I am on my way to a favourite place just around the corner. Would you like to join me?"

"*Pourquoi pas*," he answered, not able to think of a reason not to. Whether this was because he might learn something about the case or because he found the idea of lunch with an attractive French lawyer too tempting, it didn't delay him unduly.

***

While Patrick was listening to Madame Bettancourt's lunch recommendations, an easyJet flight had taken off from Basel-Mulhouse-Freiburg airport forty miles to the south. In seats 1A and 1B, two large men had taken advantage of Speedy Boarding and were staring, without actually engaging eye contact, at the flight attendants sitting wearing their harness seatbelts opposite the men.

In the overhead locker was their minimal hand luggage. One had a transparent plastic bag with a selection of liquid toiletries. The roll-on deodorant was unlikely to interest any customs officer, but if it did, it would be last thing that they ever examined.

CHAPTER NINETEEN

The cabin crew were also still in their seats on the Vueling flight to Marrakech. It was three minutes after take-off, and Mike Kingdom was staring out of the window at Gibraltar and the incredibly small eight-mile gap between Europe and Africa. The plane banked to the left and flew down the western coast of Morocco. She looked out at the enormous expanse of the Atlantic Ocean. After an hour, the plane turned sharp left and flew east across the centre of Morocco towards the Atlas Mountains. As it approached the brown foothills, the captain turned on the 'fasten seatbelt' sign. She looked down at the suburbs of Marrakech and wondered where Randy was holed up. Probably not in what looked like a collection of royal palaces with their manicured grounds. She prepared herself for the landing.

The airport was modern and made from a lattice of white concrete. Once she'd disembarked and reached the echoing hall, she joined a large queue, which snaked to a series of booths. She handed over her American passport to the officer.

"G20?" he asked. Mike failed to understand him, and he repeated, "Are you in Marrakech for the G20?"

"No, no. I'm on holiday for a few days." She was trying to look non-descript in her black wig, brown gilet and dark-brown trousers.

"Where are you staying?"

"Riad des Tailleurs."

"Enjoy your stay." He stamped her passport and returned it.

Fifteen minutes later, she was pulling her battered suitcase from the carousel and, soon after that, getting into a people carrier. This seemed excessive for one person, but it was the same price as a small saloon. Of prime importance to her was that the air conditioning worked. Looking at Marrakech seen through the various van windows was like watching a bank of TVs in the window of a Currys shop. There were goats being carried on mopeds, a stack of mattresses being pushed on a handcart and so many men in leather jackets on old motorbikes weaving through the lines of traffic. Marrakech was a blend of pink and brown. Whether this was the original colour or a covering of dust was not evident.

After driving alongside some very high, windowless city walls for what seemed like hours, the scene changed to a maze of small streets in which the traffic and pedestrians mixed in a lawless chaos that should have brought the city to a standstill but instead proved to be an efficient system – if you accepted that there were no rules.

Outside an open-fronted, small clothes shop, where rolls of fabric were being turned into assorted shirts and trousers, the van pulled up. The side door slid back, and she found herself on the pavement with her luggage next to a pile of rubbish in the gutter and an open manhole into which her suitcase could have fitted. She stepped through a small arch into a high-sided alleyway no more than three persons wide; the surface was of uneven, compacted earth. A donkey pulling a small cart was coming towards her. She pressed herself against the side, edging into an arched recess with a large wooden door held together by wide metal hinges. A small brass plate, unreadable from less than a foot away, confirmed that this was Riad des Tailleurs.

A door within the larger door opened inwards to reveal, well, absolutely nothing. It was pitch-black inside. She jumped back as a boy in a gold waistcoat stepped over the wooden lip and stood there smiling at her. Keen to get out of both the surprisingly busy alley and the heat, she started to lift up her suitcase, but without saying anything, he took it from her, and together they almost fell into the black void. Her eyes tried to adjust to the darkness gradually, but she had to squeeze them tight as protection from the acrid smoke from an incense burner lurking in some corner.

"Would you turn on a light?" she asked the boy in as unaggressive a tone as she could muster.

"It's all part of the *riad* experience. Leave your bag and come through here."

She couldn't work out where the voice was coming from.

Eventually, she stepped past a row of neatly arranged Moroccan slippers, with one incongruous pair of Nike trainers, into a dimly lit, small sitting room. It was, in fact, the hotel reception, and it consisted of a wooden desk behind which sat a blonde-haired woman tapping at a keyboard. A grey cat was curled up on an armchair, which was the only place for a guest to sit.

"Welcome."

Mike spun around to see a man emerging from a side room or cupboard – or perhaps a cave. She was beginning to get irritated by the 'authentic' *riad* experience.

"You must be Miss Kingdom?"

"And you must be… Oh, sorry, I can't read your name badge in the dark."

"Hassan. I am the manager. Welcome to the Riad des Tailleurs, a once-in-a-lifetime experience."

"Almost certainly. How often are the power cuts?"

Hassan tried a conciliatory tack. "You must be tired. The Royal Air Maroc flight from JFK to Casablanca is very good, isn't it?"

"I have no idea; I didn't fly from New York." She turned around to the woman at the desk. "If you'll just give me my key, that would be perfect."

"We don't have keys here. Nobody can come in except through that small door past Gharib and us here in reception," Hassan replied.

Is he taking the piss? she thought, but her real concern was that she couldn't imagine Randy would choose this *riad* as a base in Marrakech. *This place must surely break every rule in the CIA manual,* she considered, but then again, she hadn't read them. *Has he really been here?*

She decided that now was not the time to discuss Randy or anything else with Hassan. She just needed to get to her room and regroup.

"May I have your passport?" The woman spoke with an Eastern European accent.

"Which room is Miss Kingdom in, Karolina?"

"It's 127."

Mike handed over her passport and was assessing whether Karolina was Polish or Czech. Actually, it didn't matter because she was another potential route to finding Randy, although Czech would be a bonus.

"Would you like to follow me? You can collect your passport later. I will carry your suitcase," offered Hassan.

With that, Mike began her journey through the labyrinth that this group of five old town houses provided. Each house was centred on one of three small courtyards, which were open to the sky; two of them were filled with a mature fruit tree that touched the walls on almost every side. With Hassan, she went up to the first floor in a glass lift that was the centrepiece of one atrium, and then she walked along the open-sided and carpeted corridor. Hassan slid back a bolt and opened a tall, glazed wooden door into a room that was mostly red – everything was red or leather or red leather.

When he had left, she tried to take stock. After a minute, she gave up and sat at a leather-inlaid table below a mirror surrounded by a black beaten-leather frame. The walls and floor were made of stitched leather rectangles – the floor black and the walls red. There was something disorientating and oppressive about the décor. She put her head in her hands and told herself quietly that she was out of her depth. *You are not a field agent!* she screamed silently to herself yet again.

Standing up, she pulled back the long curtains that were across the windows on to the open-sided corridor and stretched her left leg while taking off her black wig. A brass pot seemed to be tailor-made as a wig stand. She began to relax. The built-in wardrobe revealed a standard hotel bedroom safe, into which she put most of her personal items. All of her special computer bits went behind a leather sofa.

Seeing a kettle, she opened a bottle of water, filled it up and made herself a mint tea.

She was halfway back to normal. The Wi-Fi was accessed via her phone, and she had attached a small piece of kit that gave her one level of encryption. Mike checked her messages, put her wig back on and decided to go for a walk around the hotel. There was no room key, so she jammed a small piece of paper between the door and frame. Later, this might give her an idea if anyone had been in the room.

Each courtyard was tall and narrow with the sole original purpose of cooling the residents during the hot months. There were no external windows or openings on to the streets or alleyways, except the one thick door. All of the threats were outside the houses, or now, the *riad*. Inside was calm and safe – except it wasn't. Every sound in the hotel echoed off every surface and reverberated through the courtyards. As to safety, she felt like she was locked up in a prison – a prison during a fire.

Look on the bright side, she said to herself, *Randy's room won't be locked.*

She walked up to the roof terrace with its views across the rooftops to the Koutoubia Mosque, the central tower of Marrakech, and peered down into each courtyard. Disorientated and suffering from vertigo, she made her way back towards reception, having taken several wrong turnings.

Why had Randy chosen this place?

***

A couple of hours earlier, an attractive couple had been sitting in the corner of the Restaurant des Trois Lapins.

"You could try the *salade automnale au sanglier légèrement fumé*," the woman had said.

"What's that?" the man had asked, "*Sanglier*, I mean, not salade. My French extends to *automnale* and *salade*."

"It's wild boar, shot here in the Vosges mountains."

"A sort of roast pork?"

"Well, yes, smoked pork." Madame Bettancourt had broken some bread on her side plate. "My late husband used to shoot them."

"In the Vosges mountains?"

"Yes, but only to put them out of their misery."

Patrick Redwood raised an eyebrow.

"It was very dangerous. No, really." She had looked at Patrick in mock offence. "If hunters wounded a large boar, it could not be left in the forest. They would telephone my husband, and he would try to kill it." She had spread some butter on a piece of bread. "He had two huge Bordeaux mastiffs on leads, which would follow the trail of blood from the boar. No, really." She was reacting to Patrick's smile. "He had to wear overalls, eye protectors and carry his gun over his shoulder. These dogs would drag him through the forest and branches following the scent. Then, he would put the poor pig out of its misery." She had popped the bread in her mouth.

"You must have got fed up eating the stuff?"

"It's on every menu here in the Alsace."

"OK, I'll have it. Although you may have an inflated idea of what British chief inspectors are paid."

"I will charge this lunch to my account. It does mean that we must talk about this case for at least one minute."

He had smiled back at her. "Thank you. I'm sure we can manage that."

She paused. "Tell me what's bothering you while I try this wine."

"I will," he had said, while lowering his eyes and then raising them to stare directly at her, "if you tell me what's bothering you, afterwards? And this is off the record."

Whether there was more sexual, rather than professional, tension was hard to judge.

"I am Jacqueline, by the way."

He had grinned and leant back in his chair. "I'm Patrick. OK, let me fire a few things at you. Let's start with losing the CCTV footage of the two poisoners."

She had sipped her wine. "Incompetence, nothing more."

"Secondly, why no progress on finding the two poisoners?"

"That is not surprising. We have no photograph. No names. No fingerprints. No vehicle. No leads. Plus, they were professionals." She paused. "They knew what they were doing."

It had been his turn to sip some wine. "Thirdly, what about the conflicting results from the lab on the poison?"

Some of the light had appeared to leave her eyes. "I am nervous about that," she had said, "I am nervous of political interference." But she went no further.

"I have two more things. Are autopsies normally undertaken that quickly in France?"

"They can be… especially when the victim is a high-profile individual."

"Finally, how active are the Moroccans in France – I mean the secret services?"

"I have never come across them. It is the Algerians who cause us the most problems."

They had both paused.

"Now it's your turn," he had said.

She had looked around to catch the waiter's eye, but he had been out the back.

"Why do you think your minister drove down here and didn't take a one-hour plane trip?"

"Johnny Musselwhite is, or was, a maverick." He looked at her to check that she understood the word. "I don't even want to speculate what dodgy business he was involved in, and I don't just mean his cocaine addiction. Apparently, he was driving down to the Mediterranean and on to Spain to stay at the villa of the CEO of Petronello. He was an avid supporter of the PEGASUS pipeline project from Algeria that Petronello are promoting. He was probably getting backhanders; I mean bribes."

Her face had slowly changed. "What do you know about Yves Dubuisson, our Minister of Energy?"

"Nothing."

"What if I said that I, and many others, have grave suspicions about him, especially about this potash mine project?"

"Do you think Johnny Musselwhite and he were involved in this together?"

She had shrugged.

"And PEGASUS?" he asked.

With that, she had turned to catch the waiter's eye.

CHAPTER TWENTY

Mike Kingdom had stopped on her way down to reception. Her first idea had been to talk to Karolina and find out which room was Randy's and when she had seen him last. She was now having second thoughts. Where did Karolina's loyalties lie, and would Hassan overhear any chat she might have with her? Mike began to think that she needed to be extra careful and use other methods to find his room.

Standing outside her room in the open-sided first-floor corridor around the courtyard, she dialled the *riad*'s phone number. Karolina answered. Mike squeezed the top of her nose to change her voice and asked to speak to Randy Ramirez.

"I don't think that he's here at the moment," Karolina said.

"Will you try his room, just in case?" Mike asked.

"Sure."

Mike lowered her phone and listened carefully. She couldn't hear a phone ringing in any of the rooms above or below her, even as she walked around the corridors on the four sides.

"There's no reply, sorry," Karolina said. "Would you like to leave a message?"

"No, thanks." Mike rang off.

The first part of her plan hadn't worked; although she had eliminated twenty-four of the rooms, that left forty-eight or so to check. However, the buzz inside her was almost uncontrollable as it registered that Randy really was staying in this hotel. She walked through an enclosed corridor to the next courtyard and sat on a daybed covered with cushions of every shade of pink and green imaginable. She was considering phoning Wazz and getting him to fax an innocent message to the *riad*, asking them to put it under Randy's door for his return when a maid in a black dress came out of a room nearby.

"Hello," Mike asked in her most friendly tone of voice, "maybe you can help me? I'm looking for my friend's room. He's Randy Ramirez. I have an urgent message for him."

The maid indicated for Mike to follow her.

They walked only a short distance, through a couple of corridors and up some narrow stairs to the furthest courtyard. She pointed to a temporary wooden door made from an eight feet by four feet piece of chipboard. It had "KEEP OUT" scrawled on it in yellow paint, along with something in Arabic. The maid smiled and retraced her steps. Mike looked around to check there was no one watching and no CCTV. She pulled gently at the piece of board that was acting as a crude door. It barely moved as it was secured by several plastic tags and a small padlock. There was no way she could see anything beyond it, even when pulling at the edge of the board.

She walked back to her room, where she had a selection of specialist miniature tools inherited from Dylan. They were often disguised as something harmless, and she had distributed them throughout her luggage so as not to draw the attention of anyone. She sat on the bed playing with them and remembering how Dylan had told her of his exploits. *And now they're going to help find your brother,* she thought to herself as she tried to hold back some unexpected tears.

She wiped her eyes and, on the way out, checked herself in a mirror whose surround was made in a rather rustic style using pewter or gunmetal. How many mirrors does a room need?

Distant voices echoed around each courtyard as she made her way back towards Randy's room. The expectation of what was inside built as she cut through the plastic ties and picked the small padlock. She breathed in as she lifted the board with both hands. She was mentally preparing herself for finding, well, anything. With adrenaline pumping she said to herself, *Here goes.*

Moving the board to allow access and closing it behind her had made more noise than she expected – the scraping sounds echoed around the atrium. Fortunately, most of the guests were tourists and away during the daytime. It was Hassan, his friends and, possibly, Karolina who were bothering her.

Disappointingly, she found herself not in Randy's room but in another corridor with no light except at the far end. It gave out onto yet another open-air courtyard, but this had not been viewed by a tourist's eyes for a very long time. It was filled below by a dying lemon tree, stacked dusty furniture and an air of decay. It was, as any estate agent might say, ripe for redevelopment. She moved purposefully around the four sides, checking the doors to each room. They were mostly full of old furniture or unopened carboard boxes of crockery or electrical equipment, according to the labelling.

Having moved around each side of the atrium and almost

back to where she had begun, she pushed open a glazed door into a bedroom that was clearly in use. She pulled back the long, dusty curtains in preference to turning on the light. There didn't seem to be any movement detectors or cameras, but she couldn't be sure. She tried to work methodically, beginning to the right of the door and moving anticlockwise. She noticed that the TV, lights and kettle were all plugged into the wall. Opening a wardrobe revealed shirts, trousers and one summer jacket. They looked like Randy's size. At the bottom of the wardrobe was a bag, which she unzipped; it was full of rock samples, some fossils and a geological hammer. This all began to look promising.

The bed had been made, but not by hotel staff. There was nothing under the bed or under the pillows. She opened the matching wardrobe on the other side of the bed to find a suitcase, but this appeared to be newish and barely used. Certainly, it had no luggage labels or tags, and it was empty. A small flight of steps led to a bathroom. These *riads* were, after all, just a collection of rambling Moroccan town houses of random design, sharing only the one common feature: a narrow central courtyard into which everything faced. There was a bath, toilet, basin and, sitting incongruously in the corner, a free-standing, large, black safe that was at least three feet high. She checked the spinning arms in the centre of the door, but it was locked firmly. After walking over to the corner, she looked in the small waste bin, but it contained only one item: a screwed-up luggage label in the name of Ramon Ramirez. A warm feeling washed over her.

Back in the bedroom cum living room, she looked at the desk and at the bookshelf above it. There were more paperbacks by authors such as Jeffrey Deaver and Michael Connelly. This seemed to confirm that the Málaga apartment was his, at least in part. She was lifting some newspapers in French from the bin when she spotted another copy of Gavin Menzies's lengthy book on the shelf. Was Randy really that interested in the Chinese maritime exploration of Africa in the fifteenth century? She took it down, but no handy scraps of paper giving her a pointer fell out.

The phone on the desk trilled, frightening her.

She was torn between answering it and making a hasty exit. She chose the latter, but not before standing in the two rooms and quickly taking a few pictures on her phone.

On the way back to her room, however much she lifted the piece of chipboard, it made a scraping noise on the tiled floor. She clicked the padlock shut and checked that it all looked passably the same as before. She began to move back through the labyrinthine hotel corridors and alleyways to her room. *Why is Randy's room behind a barricaded and padlocked entrance?* she wondered. *I must be careful.*

She leapt as Hassan stepped out of a recess. Her burglar's tools suddenly weighed heavy in the small bag hanging from her shoulder. "Oh… Hi, you scared me."

"So sorry. Are you lost?" His slightly hooded eyes managed to look menacing while his voice sounded friendly.

"No, I was taking some photographs of your *riad*. The courtyards are beautiful."

"We are about to start a major redevelopment. We will have another twenty-four rooms next year around another courtyard. You must come back and visit us."

"That sounds exciting."

"Let me know if you would like us to arrange a guide or a driver? Marrakech is also very beautiful."

"I will."

He gave her an extra wide smile and disappeared down a stairwell.

She entered her unlocked room, leaving the long drapes closed to prying eyes. She turned on the lights and walked over to the small fridge to grab a bottle of water. Her heart rate slowed as she drank half of it. Sitting in an armchair, she took stock. Randy's room, beyond the barricade, was still connected to the hotel telephone system. Why? Had the barricade gone up after Randy had 'disappeared'? *Or,* she thought to herself suddenly, *is there another entrance?* Actually, there must be another entrance to the original townhouse, but there wasn't another door onto the dusty alley outside, she remembered. This meant that any access was via the tiny shops at the front; the clothes shop, perhaps?

She wavered between thinking that she should have answered the phone in case it gave her a new lead to thinking that she did the right thing by not alerting anyone, including Hassan, to the fact she was in there. The wig was making her itch, so she lifted it, rubbed her scalp and replaced it; stress didn't seem to help her skin condition.

Presumably, Randy hadn't found this room and *riad* himself? Yet it didn't fit the usual criteria for a safe house in a foreign country. There must have been alternative accommodation that the CIA would have organised. Or was it chosen precisely because it was relevant to whatever he was up to?

Thinking of the CIA and safe houses made her wonder why Leonard hadn't asked the local CIA desk in Rabat to find Randy. They would have been involved in sorting out the accommodation, surely? She would ask Leonard the next time they spoke. Knowing Leonard, Randy was probably working in Morocco without the local CIA desk knowing he was in-country. That would possibly explain why Leonard needed this tidied up.

Had Randy chosen the *riad* because it was the centre of something? Or because he wanted to monitor someone like Hassan? Or because it was a well-located base that was well hidden in plain sight, to use one of Dylan's phrases.

Mike had finished her bottle of water. She was still thirsty, but the only thing now available to her was a single tea bag that had the words "Moroccan Mint" on the little label, but it smelt of absolutely nothing. She decided against it.

Fortunately, her phone rang, and she was temporarily distracted from her thirst. "Hello, Wazz."

"I hope that you're going to bring me back a fez?" he asked.

"I thought that they came from Egypt or Turkey or… somewhere. Anyway, I haven't been out of the damned *riad* yet."

"Have you made progress?"

"I've found his room here. It's in an unused bit of the hotel."

"How is the hotel?"

"It gives me the creeps."

"Is the shower curtain torn?"

"No… that would be an improvement. If Mrs Bates is in the room next to Randy's, I wouldn't be surprised."

"Have you got any new leads?" Wazz had a calm and reassuring voice.

"Not really, but I am in the right place, I know. I'm guessing that any leads are in the refrigerator-sized safe in his room. That's my next big problem. I just wish it was the size of the safe in my own room, which is about as big as a shoebox and, I discovered, not even attached to the shelf in the wardrobe."

"Be careful… I need you back here."

"Are you missing our chats by the bins?"

"No, I've run out of cigarettes," he said.

She changed hands and put the phone against her left ear. "And I thought you were ringing to ask after my health." There was a slightly awkward silence before she continued, "What's happening at the villa?"

"Charles is walking around as if his football team is on for the treble, Maria is ordering a new cover for the swimming pool, and Angelica comes out of her room, argues with the first person she meets and goes back in with a tray of food."

"An everyday tale of billionaire folk?"

"Except that Diego is getting suspicious. He has seen the same two men in a Mercedes pass up and down outside a few times. He's keeping an eye on them." Wazz waited for her obvious reaction. There was none, and he could feel that she was completely distracted and scared stiff.

"I can't handle both the situation with Charles and the mess out here with Randy," she confessed.

"Then put all of your effort into finding Randy and leave me to look after the Yellands."

***

"Patrick, I have some news for you. Brendan Dowell isn't just in the frame for the events in Colmar; he's also the orchestrator of the kidnap of Charles Yelland's family. This is all linked, obviously."

"Really? This is bizarre."

"Patrick, any developments at your end? I have to update the PM first thing tomorrow before he flies to Marrakech on Thursday." Commander Ben Cox really wanted some resolution to events in Colmar.

"No, and yes. No, because Walter Flushing is still in a coma. Yes, because I've just eaten lunch with the prosecutor, Madame Bettancourt."

"Was she forthcoming on anything?"

"I'm tempted to say, 'No, and yes,' again. I'm pretty good at reading people, but I find her inscrutable. She's charming, attractive and professional, but there's just something that doesn't click with me."

"Do you trust her?"

"I think so. Our lunch was off the record, and it was just the two of us, but I don't know what political pressure she's getting from those higher up the food chain. She was open about police incompetence and the difficulties of the investigation, but she said she was nervous about the lab results. What have Porton Down said is their final analysis, by the way?"

"I don't have their final report, but they've told me that they've never seen the poison before or at least not in this form. They think the French analysis was a bit faulty. However, they tell me that this was made in a state laboratory; this couldn't have been developed and manufactured by amateurs."

"Did they think Russian or Moroccan or someone else's?"

"They thought that it was unlikely to be Morocco, but that is possible, of course, and it also could have been supplied by another country… or anyone else."

"One other thing she asked me about was Johnny Musselwhite and the PEGASUS gas pipeline. You remember that he was meeting Yves Dubuisson, their Minister of Energy and Minerals, about the potash mine rehabilitation project? Well, she made it clear that Yves Dubuisson was about as dodgy as Johnny Musselwhite, in her opinion. I'm not sure where that gets us?"

"She wouldn't be the first member of the judiciary who distrusts politicians."

CHAPTER TWENTY-ONE

In Buckinghamshire, it was an early Wednesday-morning start for the police team, including the specialist armed squad, some of whom had come from the nearby London borough of Hillingdon. Detective Sergeant Harry Wardrop had been a little sceptical when he had been passed twelve addresses in his county with the information that one of them, Holly Cottage, was likely to be where the cook and her daughter, kidnapped from Beswick Manor, were being held. He and his team had been laboriously watching CCTV footage from places near the manor house, trying to establish the route the kidnappers had taken in their two white vans. It was proving difficult because this area of Buckinghamshire, being so close to London, had some major roads with good public and commercial CCTV coverage, but it also had a network of rural lanes that most certainly did not.

When Nigel from Special Branch had phoned through Mike's list, he had also sent aerial photographs, including the one Mike had accessed showing one white van. Harry Wardrop was wondering where these current satellite photographs came from, but he was very grateful that they could well save him and his colleagues days of work.

An unmarked police car had driven slowly past Holly Cottage, but there was no view of the rear area behind the brick walls and the garage.

While this was happening, Harry and his team were checking any available CCTV coverage from the roads, service stations and shops nearest the cottage at the time of the kidnap. The two vans, it appeared, had split up and approached the cottage a few minutes apart. Neither had left since, or so it appeared from other footage. With the appropriate search warrant prepared, the decision was made to send in an armed team, but this wouldn't be until they had received the layout of the cottage from the rental agent and a drone had been flown some distance away but so as to give a clear view of the rear of the property, including the one white van parked outside.

A separate team was busy searching the records for the numbers of mobile phones recently used in Holly Cottage. They found only one, and it was registered in a false name.

By lunchtime, everyone was ready and fourteen officers with various skills moved off in five vehicles, eventually parking them some distance from the cottage. The eight officers with firearms edged into positions around the property. The drone operator was ready to provide images of the action, and another officer was poised to activate a device that would block any mobile coverage and, probably, mess up any heart pacemakers.

At 12.30pm, they crashed through the front door, firing their stun guns, which delivered flash-bangs, disorientating anyone inside.

This was a textbook operation, watched by the supervising officers via body cameras and via the drone.

An enormous sense of relief washed over everyone involved as Gabriela and her daughter were brought out of the front door. Two kidnappers would be brought out later in body bags.

***

Victor was chairing a meeting that was meant to be his last formal preparation before he flew from Heathrow to Marrakech. The attendees, of which there were twelve, included Commander Ben Cox and Dennis from the FCO. They had reached item four on the agenda: security.

"OK, we move on to security." The PM leant back slightly. "Ben? Dennis? Alexander?"

Ben Cox moved some hair across his forehead and began, "Well, let me bring everyone up to date with some good news. A very successful operation has just been completed – I mean minutes ago – in Buckinghamshire. The two kidnapped women have been freed in a joint operation between police, MI5, MI6 and special forces. The two kidnappers are dead. I have no more details. It will take a little time, but we hope that the people behind Mr Musselwhite's poisoning, the shooting of Mr Flushing and the threats to Mr Yelland of Petronello have now been removed. We are, therefore, content that none of this will now impact your trip to the G20."

"How is Mr Flushing doing?" Victor asked.

"Still in a coma… and under French police protection," Ben answered.

"Good news on the operation to free the hostages. Not so

good news on Mr Flushing," Victor concluded, "Dennis, what are the troops on the ground in Morocco saying?"

"Well, the latest report from our ambassador says that there are no rumours of trouble – not that the Moroccans would tolerate it – and not even the usual demonstrations by the eco-lobby. The Moroccans are very appreciative that the G20 chose Marrakech."

"Alexander? Are Conrad and his crew happy? What are the jungle drums saying?"

Alexander, a tall man with tanned skin and a slight overbite, reported on behalf of the secret-squirrel community: "The Americans seem to be happy, as do the French. The rest of the EU are relaxed. We hear via Five Eyes what Canada, Australia and, of course, the US are thinking, and it all seems as expected. There are no reports of serious terrorist interest or anything from rogue states. The Americans, in particular, have people on the ground monitoring the situation."

"How is Conrad?"

"He's flying in early Thursday morning and out on Sunday lunchtime. You have a private meeting for one and a half hours set for Saturday afternoon," a voice added.

***

Mike Kingdom realised she was going to start attracting unnecessary and possibly dangerous attention if she didn't leave the *riad* and take in some of the sights of Marrakech. She needed to act more like a tourist. Unfortunately, her mind was completely obsessed with finding Randy and all the more so since she had been in his room.

The room and the choice of the *riad* had told her that he

was trying to blend in for the long term. This was an attempt to look like a slightly impoverished geologist working for a gas exploration company who was trying to save a few dollars of his fixed accommodation allowance. Hassan would have been happy to take a low rent for the unused room, which had been full of old furniture and stuff. Perhaps Hassan had kept the payments separate from the main hotel and pocketed the money? Randy would have been happy to have his own entrance via a shop and the lovely Karolina to take any messages.

While physically a little different, Randy and Dylan shared some family characteristics. Their ability to put things in perspective and to plan ahead came from their mother. Mike had met her on visits to California, and one thing she had heard a hundred times was, "What if?" Dylan applied this while working for the CIA, and it had treated him well until the trip to Holland. Sadly, he hadn't asked himself what would happen if the Dutch importers were tipped off about his investigations. The consequences of which he, and she, had paid for as they drove along that polder on their day off.

As she sat in her room with her feet on the internal windowsill, what she was thinking about was this: What did Randy have in mind as an escape plan? What were his plans B, C and D, as Dylan liked to ask?

Half an hour earlier, she had been eating breakfast on the roof terrace. The view of the Koutoubia tower from under the pergolas was beautiful, but immediately in front of her, every side wall was covered in fifty patterned plates of various sizes, in either blue or red, and hanging on hooks, which made her regret that she didn't have a gun. When the lukewarm coffee from a chipped, brown mug, enough fresh bread to feed an army, and an egg swimming in too much tomato and onion were served, she knew this was more than she needed. She didn't stay long.

Sitting with her feet on the sill had made her more than aware of the eggs, onions and harissa that she had just consumed. She dropped her feet to the floor, let her stomach settle and brought herself back to the task in hand: what was Randy's plan B?

If she could go and sit in his room for an hour, she might find it easier to 'pick up the vibes', but this was not an option. Instead, she took off her Cleopatra wig and called up the photographs on her phone. This is what she had been taught a long time ago in Seattle while on a two-week course on checking out a room. (Actually, the course was only partly about doing a physical tour – it was also about doing a virtual tour. It demonstrated how not to waste time by going back and forth, and why you pulled out the bottom drawer of a cabinet first, then the one above it, so that you didn't need to close anything to make progress.)

She put her hands together and spun the wig like a propeller. A virtual tour would have to do.

Mike started logically with the outside of his room. That didn't take long as there was nothing apart from dirt, rubbish and piles of discarded hotel junk. She made a note to explore the access/egress route, possibly by visiting the clothes shop. This might be less risky than approaching from the hotel end. In her mind's eye, she approached his unlocked door. She accepted that not having a key was unusual in the rest of the world, but the norm here in the *riad*. It did mean, however, that he was unlikely to leave anything of any significance lying around, surely?

Scrolling on her phone, she started with the first picture

taken just inside the door and looking to the right. It showed the window, the curtains and the cast-iron radiator. Did it get that cold in winter? There was a recess with large shelves, one of which had a small TV screen and another had a dull brass pot. The next couple of photographs showed the wall with the desk and bookshelves. There had been nothing of note in the desk's drawers. *In fact,* she thought, *there really weren't many personal belongings in the room at all.*

She used her thumb and forefinger to zoom in on the bookshelves. The fat spine of *1421* by *Menzies* was screaming at her.

"Michaela!" she rebuked herself, and she had to stop herself from going straight back to his room.

She flicked through the other photographs, but somewhat distractedly. The last one was of the bathroom, and there, sitting incongruously next to the washbasin, was the heavy, black safe. It was like a magnet to her. She zoomed in further and read the plate displaying the Parisian manufacturer's name. She broke off to google the name, and after a few minutes, she learnt that this old model had a combination lock using four numbers.

She collected up her shoulder bag, put her wig back on and made for the door.

At least she now knew her way through the rabbit warren and where to be careful (which was most places, as any noise echoed up and down the three floors surrounding each courtyard). Without seeing anyone, she reached the padlocked temporary door. She picked the lock more quickly this time, opened the makeshift door and pulled the sheet of board back behind her as quietly as possible. She stopped and listened, but she could only hear an air-conditioning unit, probably at the rear of the clothes shop, blowing out at the dying lemon tree in its dusty courtyard.

Going past the stacks of boxes, she reached the door and stepped inside. Not pausing in the bedroom, she stepped up into the bathroom, lighting her way with the torch on her phone. Her research had told her the sequence and directions of rotations that were needed to open this model of safe. With an ear pressed close to the silver dial, she rotated it clockwise to the number one, then anticlockwise to the number four. After going back clockwise to the number two she prepared for the final turn to the number one. Her hands were sweating and shaking gently. *I'm not cut out for fieldwork,* she kept hearing a voice in her head telling her.

She was waiting for the click before turning the three-pronged handle in the middle. Nothing.

She turned the handle both ways. Nothing.

"I'm really, really not cut out for fieldwork," she whispered under her breath.

She sat back on her haunches. Calm down, breathe and do it again.

Kneeling forwards, she re-entered the numbers. Nothing.

She entered them in reverse order. Nothing.

It was time to go. She stepped gently back down into the bedroom and living area. At least the luggage label in the bin had confirmed this was Randy's room. *That's progress,* she told herself. Passing his desk, she reached up and pulled out the book that had so raised her hopes. Why was there also one in Málaga? Perhaps he had bought a copy for his room-mate? Perhaps it was as innocent as that? How many pages was it? She flicked to the end: 650.

She froze. There on the last page written in biro were the

details of a meeting with a name and address. She tore out the page and replaced the book on the shelf.

It took her four minutes to get back to the point at the top of the stairs above reception. *Perhaps, I actually am cut out for fieldwork,* she mused. She could hear Hassan talking to Karolina below her and, with a sigh of relief, made it back to her room.

CHAPTER TWENTY-TWO

"Essaouira? Where's Essaouira?" Mike was sitting on her bed, staring at the torn piece of paper in her hand.

She was thirsty, but there was no bottled water left in her room. The solitary teabag with its green tag seemed to beckon to her. She walked to the bathroom and filled up the kettle from the tap. *I'll boil it twice; that should sort it,* she reassured herself.

Sitting there with the teabag still in the hot water, she opened her laptop. The images showed a port on the coast, 114 miles due west of Marrakech. It was three hours by bus, she noted. It looked attractive for a city; there were seafront ramparts with brass cannons, matching blue wooden fishing vessels moored in rows and an impressive citadel by the harbour. It was no wonder that it was a draw for tourists, but why would Randy have an interest in it?

The torn piece of paper gave a name: Aksil Zadi. It gave an address that looked as if it were in the fishing port complex. It gave a time and a date: midday on Thursday, 8th September. Now fired up, it took her forty minutes to check out the person, the place and how to get there. If Randy was intending to meet someone tomorrow in Essaouira, Mike wanted to be there.

Aksil Zadi did not take long for her to investigate. He wasn't on any of the blacklists that she had access to, and he wasn't on social media, as far as she could tell using translation technology. The only thing she found was a management chart of the Port Authority where he was shown in a middle-ranking administrative role. The address for Zadi on the torn page looked like his office rather than his home. This is where the meeting was going to take place. Whatever the circumstances, she couldn't find anything else and needed to pack her things and get a taxi to the bus station in Marrakech. The bus she was going to catch left in an hour and a half.

"You are checking out?" Hassan had approached her while she was being dealt with by the efficient Karolina.

"Yes, I have decided to go to Ouarzazate for a few days. I've never seen a desert," she said, hoping to leave a false trail.

"It is very beautiful. They have made many Hollywood movies there."

"Yes, I'm looking forward to it."

"Please come back here after your trip."

Over my dead body, Mike thought to herself and then regretted it.

Karolina went on processing the credit card payment, but she quickly raised her eyes to Mike.

"Where are you from, Karolina?"

"Poland."

"I'm Czech," Mike replied.

"Your passport is American," Hassan said it as a flat statement.

"Yes… do you have many Americans staying here?" Mike asked.

"Occasionally, but none at the moment. They have all left." Karolina looked up into Mike's eyes as she tore off the printout from the card machine for Mike to sign.

Hassan called to the boy lurking in the dark of the entrance hall to escort Mike up to the main road and the waiting taxi, which he did, not expecting a tip.

As she slid into the backseat of the small, yellow cab a short while later, Mike was still trying to work out what Karolina meant by her final look as they had said goodbye. Thereafter, for the short journey to the bus station, Mike was oddly obsessed with the creases in the weather-beaten face of her driver and his frightening habit of turning around to smile at her, despite the taxi being the centre of an attack by every moped, donkey cart and pickup truck in Marrakech.

Major arguments were taking place as she got out of the taxi on its arrival and boarded the bus to Essaouira, such that she was left standing there waiting while some problem with luggage was sorted out. Fortunately, she only had a rucksack and the smallest of cases. She took her seat and found she was resting her head against the window, counting down until the departure time. But more than that, she wasn't just looking at her reflection, as her eyes were inches away from the glass. The cropped, brown wig made her look frumpy, and the North African sun had made the pitted skin on her face turn pink. As if staring deep inside herself, she excluded the world beyond the window and wondered what the hell she was doing. Almost exactly one week ago, she had been in her cabin, where her biggest problem was that water had been leaking from her gable window when the wind direction was from the south. A week later she was, well, what? Where was she? What was she doing?

She was honest enough to acknowledge that she was flying by the seat of her pants. The brutal crash – which had killed her beloved Dylan, wrecked her left leg and traumatised her such that her hair had fallen out in clumps until it had eventually disappeared entirely – had given her a purpose beyond her love of sitting at a computer undertaking a database search. She was a desk-jockey, as they had politely called her in Chiswick when she had arrived from Washington, DC. However, why she was sitting on a bus on her way to a port on the west coast of Africa probably needed a little more examination. Actually, it didn't. Whatever she thought, and she had strong opinions on many things, the one person who seemed always to be the hidden conductor in her life was Leonard de Vries.

She had already noticed from her first hour in Morocco that the country was predominately brown (actually, a hundred varieties of brown, ranging from pinkish to dark chocolate), and the first hour of the journey had not dissuaded her from this opinion. She was sitting next to an old man wrapped up in brown robes that smelt of wood smoke. He seemed in a trance and didn't speak once.

About halfway to the coast, Mike began to feel a strange sensation in her stomach. She thought back to her mint tea and deeply regretted making it. She grabbed her rucksack, retrieved and swallowed an Imodium tablet, and then, as a distraction, proceeded to count telegraph poles for the next fifteen minutes while it took its effect. The last hour of the journey seemed interminable to her, and she felt every pothole and grimaced each time the driver braked.

When she finally arrived and stepped down from the bus

in Essaouira, she was expecting the smell of the sea. Instead, she was immediately overwhelmed by the diesel exhausts of the buses. Her stomach had calmed down a little, but finding a taxi to the *riad* was top of her list of priorities. The Riad Brouette de Ma Tante was near the port and, she hoped, it would be central enough for whatever she ended up doing in Essaouira.

"Are you going into the centre? Do you want to share a cab?" a female voice came from behind.

Mike turned around to see a thin woman, perhaps in her thirties or forties, who rather surprisingly had straight, greying hair. She was wearing a long, sleeveless dress and had a rucksack on her back. The woman had clearly tried to fight the sun for most of her life and lost badly. Mike had not seen a brown, lined face like that since, well, her taxi driver earlier that day, if she were honest.

"Sure, why not?" Mike accepted.

"Great. I'm Josie, by the way."

"And I need to get to a restroom, but that's another story."

"Where are you staying?"

As Mike was telling Josie the name of the *riad*, she wondered whether having a fellow traveller might be a good idea. Dylan would have been proud of her. He was big on 'tradecraft', as he called it.

"I have a large twin room for two nights. It was all they had available. Actually, it was ridiculously cheap. Would you like the other bed? It's paid for," Mike said.

"Bonzer," came the reply.

"That's a yes, I think?"

"Sorry, yes. I'm Australian. 'Bonzer' means that it would be great."

"I've worked with Australians. Let's get a cab." Mike looked around the bus station. "I'm not going to use the restroom here."

The journey to the *riad* was uneventful and quick. It took six minutes. Mike did glimpse the port and fishing harbour out of her window, but she had already planned to play the role of 'American tourist' later in the afternoon as she investigated the harbour before the anticipated meeting tomorrow. She might take Josie with her on her investigative tour as part of the deception.

On their arrival, the *riad* turned out to be a more modern interpretation of the traditional ones, built around a courtyard with a single Phoenix date palm. The bedroom walls were white, adorned with fishing scenes in wooden frames. Shutters rather than curtains over the windows closed off any views into the atrium. Mike noticed the smallest kettle she had ever seen and a box of mint teabags. She supressed a retch and continued looking for a place to hide her small but important bits of computer hardware.

After freshening up, Mike changed her wig, put on a loose dress like Josie's and picked out a sun hat. She immediately looked very different.

Josie had described herself as a 'seasoned traveller', using the word 'seasoned' in the 'like an old bit of wood' sense of the word. She was easy company, having been all over the world since something traumatic happened in her teens. She readily accepted Mike's suggestion to walk down to the harbour and fish market, where they might grab a coffee.

They were standing by the ticket office that was promoting sightseeing trips aboard some of the blue wooden boats, when a tourist coach pulled up in front of them.

The tour guide, who it transpired was called Tanya, stepped

down from the coach and invited everyone to leave the air conditioning and to experience Morocco in the raw.

Tanya began pointing out the boxes of silvery fish and the sharp knives in a monotonous voice.

Who could ever forget that splash?

"Oh my God!" Josie exclaimed.

A woman had tripped over her kaftan and had fallen head first into the large concrete channel used to collect the fish guts and various foul-smelling liquids. Several people off the coach had stepped forwards, but they had stopped short of offering a helping hand. She had clambered out with as much dignity as is possible when you have a fish head sticking out between your bum bag and ample stomach.

"There's a footbridge over the sluice down there," Tanya had helpfully pointed out.

An old man turned around to ask everyone if they would like a group photograph, only to be met with a range of stares. The woman from the sluice was standing with her arms outstretched, being given plenty of personal space.

Mike Kingdom's wig was itching on her sweaty, bald head. *Give me an office any day, rather than this,* she thought to herself as she cursed Leonard under her breath.

"Ealing Broadway, Slough, Reading, Swindon next stop…" the unfortunate woman had announced in her best station-announcer's voice, trying to relieve the embarrassment as she had climbed back on to the coach.

Swindon? Mike thought, *That's one of the places where I nearly died,* as she tried to push Leonard de Vries from her mind.

"Let's walk over here, and mind the sluices," Mike had said to Josie as they walked towards the port office, passing the men and women who were gutting the fish while others distributed their catches in handcarts or loaded plastic trays into small refrigerated trucks.

They found some shade under a white covered walkway with grubby hand marks on the walls and peeling plaster. The recessed doors were bright blue. Not betraying her interest, Mike spotted the sign on the wall that matched the address on the note she had torn out in Marrakech. She worked out where she might stand tomorrow to get a good view of Randy as he turned up for his meeting with Aksil Zadi.

They walked on back to the sea wall, just two female backpackers taking selfies against the backdrop of the raft of blue wooden fishing boats.

***

In Buckinghamshire, the police operation now changed from the freeing of hostages to the collecting of evidence. Detective Sergeant Harry Wardrop had just been congratulated by his superiors when four additional scene-of-crime officers turned up in a grey van, together with Commander Ben Cox, who was being driven in a dark-green Range Rover.

After they all got out of their respective vehicles, some introductions were made, and the commander walked over to the two body bags in the back of an unmarked police van. He was checking the faces of the two dead kidnappers with a man not in uniform who took some photographs.

"Are these the only two?" Ben asked Harry.

"Yes, there was no one else. We had drone coverage of the whole action. No one escaped."

"And there's no one hidden in the loft, the basement, or any other nook or cranny?"

"We haven't been in the loft yet, and I shouldn't think there's a basement." Harry had only had access to the cottage for thirty minutes.

"OK, we won't interfere with your crime scene, but my team need to check the place over."

With that, the commander went over and liaised with his colleagues.

Twenty minutes later, Ben Cox was sitting in his car, speaking on his phone. "Brendan Dowell isn't one of the two dead kidnappers, and he isn't hiding anywhere on the premises. Therefore, he must have left much earlier if he was ever here. We haven't found anything yet to indicate that this is a safe house, but the team is working on it systematically. I'm coming back to London."

CHAPTER TWENTY-THREE

They clinked their bottles of ice-cold Casablanca beer together, each took a swig and put them back down on the red-and-white plastic tablecloth. Mike and Josie were sitting in the shade outside a café with views over to the harbour in Essaouira. The blue sky was filled with gulls that had followed the boats back from their fishing grounds. The barman brought out some olives and cleared away the empty glasses and plates from the next table. Josie was sitting there in a sleeveless, red dress that showed off her leathery skin.

"How do you keep so fit?" Mike was looking at Josie's sinewy arms, which were resting on her head.

"I run… that keeps me fit." Josie had a gentle Australian accent.

"Run where? Not out here?"

Josie took another swig of beer. "Yes, I've run everywhere… and I mean everywhere."

"Why?"

"Why not?"

It was Mike's turn to take mouthful of beer. "I meant that there are other ways to keep fit."

"Some shit happened when I was younger. I started running… and I haven't stopped. When I run, I feel good."

Mike was evaluating the earlier answer. "Where's everywhere?"

"I've run marathons on every continent including Antarctica."

"No way."

"Antarctica was easier than running out here."

Mike had a quizzical look. "You really mean that you run out here?"

"In March, I did the Marathon des Sables here in Morocco."

Mike was trying to keep up.

"It's in the desert; 250 kilometres in seven days… through the sand," Josie continued.

Mike was too hot to try to work out the maths, let alone contemplate serious exercise. "Is that a marathon every day?"

"No, and if you want it in miles, it's only 150 over the week."

Mike almost choked. "How old are you?"

"Forty-three. There were competitors in their seventies, before you ask."

There was a natural connection between the two women who had both clearly come out the other side of some unpleasant phases of their lives; neither took any prisoners.

"You must be wrecking your body." Mike was gently shaking her head.

"How did you wreck yours?" Josie asked, but before she received an answer, the person that Mike held responsible for her injuries was calling on her phone.

"Hello," Mike answered.

"How's your holiday?" Leonard asked.

"I'm sitting outside with a friend, having a beer."

"Then, hey, I'll keep it brief. Our boss is flying in tomorrow to where you are, so things are getting more urgent. Have you found the person you're looking for?"

"Yes, I married him. You remember him, I'm sure." She paused for effect. "As to the other guy, I hope to meet him tomorrow at 2.00pm."

"Have you spoken to him?"

"No, but I have a name, the date, the time and the address of the meeting. At the moment, I'm sitting within half a mile of the location, drinking my well-earned beer."

"If I said I've had to change my underpants twice already today, would that tell you how nervous I am? It could all happen quickly."

"The idea that you own more than one pair of underpants has thrown me completely and may allow me to enjoy the rest of my beer."

"Call me after the meeting." He ended the call.

Mike put down her phone and picked up her beer. Josie could barely look Mike in the eye as she tried to control her smile, the evening sunshine turning her face the colour of caramel.

"Is this guy with the underpants an uncle, a sugar daddy or someone you met on Tinder?"

"Josie, if only one of those three disgusting options were true."

The waiter was obvious only because he walked in front of the setting sun.

"Same again, sport." This was the first time that Josie had sounded truly Australian.

"He's an old boss in case you're getting creeped out," Mike explained.

"And you have a meeting tomorrow?"

"Yes, over there." Mike was now reasonably relaxed and nodded towards the harbour offices.

"I'm guessing you're not here on holiday?"

"Sadly, not." Mike hesitated, but then continued, "I'm looking for my brother-in-law. He's gone missing."

"Strewth, I'm sorry. Is he Moroccan?"

"No, American... he's working out here for some energy company."

"What's this got to do with your old boss with the underpants?"

Mike hated the way that her job had made her suspicious of everyone she met – even a random backpacker from Australia whom she had met on a bus in the middle of Morocco.

"They know each other. He's concerned as well."

"So, what do you do when you're not tracking down relatives?"

"I have a boring job in IT. I sit at a computer all day." In most cases, Mike had found that this bland statement bored people into not asking further questions.

"I didn't have you down as a geek."

"What do you do?" Mike asked trying to switch the conversation.

"I was in the ADF, the Australian army," Josie replied.

"Is that where the shit happened?"

"In 2014, I was part of the first female intake into the special forces. Unlike in the movies, not every job goes according to plan." Her voice rose at the end of most sentences. She took a large mouthful of beer. A coldness had come into her eyes. "What wrecked your body?" Josie asked.

"Car accident that killed my husband. It messed up this leg, and my hair decided to start falling out."

"Sorry. Shit happens."

There was a mutual respect growing.

"Why do you have such long hair if you spend your life running marathons?"

"Because I spent so many years with my head shaved. Why do you wear a wig?"

"After the accident, I wanted to be someone else, and different coloured wigs meant I could become lots of people depending on my mood, which was normally foul, I should add."

"Do you ever go out bald?"

"I do, but not if I want to blend in with the background… and not if there are any horses that might be frightened. I feel most content in my red wig. Don't ask me why."

"Would you like me to come with you tomorrow for a bit of moral support?"

"No, thanks. I think it will go one of two ways. Either he turns up and I talk to him to find out what's happening, or else he doesn't turn up and I go back to the drawing board."

"Fair enough, but the offer stands."

***

Walter Flushing thought he was back in Cornwall, surfing with his friends. He had been riding a wave into Sennen Cove beach, which seemed oddly a long way off. Then, suddenly, he was underwater with a roaring and bubbling in his ears. The need to get to the surface became more pressing, and he pulled back some bedsheets. He opened his eyes to see not the sky over Cornwall but an array of medical equipment in his peripheral vision; his surfboard was no longer attached to his ankle, evidently. Thankfully, there were various tubes helping him to breathe – the currents can be dangerous off Sennen Cove, he remembered.

It took him a long time to work out that he was in a ward, but not one in Derriford Hospital on the edge of Plymouth. Why were the nurses speaking to him in French? He drifted in and out of consciousness.

Unbeknown to Walter, there had been a security scare earlier that had the armed police shouting at each other down the corridor and calling for back-up. A man had run up the corridor, opening doors and peering in maniacally. He had been calling for a stop to the invasion across the Mediterranean Sea, although whether this was about migrants, North African footballers or malarial mosquitoes was not clear. It had been a false alarm, and the man was escorted back to his ward and sedated.

Walter had called out to someone in his confused state, and a nurse had checked him immediately. She put her hand on his arm and calmed him down gently, explaining that he was in hospital. After he had drifted back to a happier place, she walked out to her office and a doctor was informed of the developments. He immediately undertook his own checks on the patient, who was still surfing in Cornwall, according to his mutterings. Once back in the ward office, the doctor phoned the prosecutor's office.

After taking the call, Madame Bettancourt sat back and smiled; this was from relief that she might now be able to solve the case, given that the innocent Walter looked like he might pull through. She was also looking forward to him giving her first-hand testimony that would clear up what was, and still could be, a high-profile political nightmare. Privately, she was looking forward to calling Patrick Redwood and meeting up with him again.

***

Brendan drove past the entrance to the villa and spotted a man dressed in black standing on the roof. This in itself did not represent an impossible threat, but rather it shouted out that there were probably plenty more at ground level patrolling the grounds. The gatehouse appeared to be occupied, and there was no simple way of gaining access.

Long before the police assault on Holly Cottage, he had begun his circuitous route back to the Continent. He had flown from East Midlands Airport via Dublin on another passport, hoping that the face-recognition cameras hadn't picked him up. The two hired heavies, who were actually Turkish, had filled him in on most of the security arrangements and were waiting for instructions. These were the two men who had been successful in transferring the poison to Johnny Musselwhite. In their new hotel base, they had been joined not only by Brendan but also by a fourth member of the team who had driven down in a Range Rover that concealed an array of additional weapons now at their disposal. They wanted to complete the task and get paid as they had done many times for different, mostly Muslim employers.

The information he and his masters wanted hadn't been on the laptops or the wiped memory card retrieved in the two visits to the Auberge du Pont Neuf – this was a major setback. The murder of Johnny Musselwhite had removed a large part of the problem, but the project had yet to be cancelled permanently. The kidnap and threats had also failed so far. The British police had killed two of his colleagues and freed the two women, although they would never have given him the leverage that he would have acquired from having kidnapped Maria and Angelica Yelland.

Brendan needed to get inside the villa and remove the threat, such that the project would be well and truly dead.

He was sure the answer lay with the drone that one of the Turks had in pieces on the coffee table. He was doing something with a battery. The drone was state of the art. It was mostly made of see-through plastic so the ambient light passed through the main peripheral fabric, which meant it cast only a minimal shadow from the battery on the underside. With security at the villa so high, it could only be used judiciously. Multi-millionaires' villas were regularly buzzed by the paparazzi, hoping to get a photograph that would make them rich too. Everyone would be looking out for them. It was the location of the security personnel and any cameras that interested Brendan most – he already had the layout plans for the buildings.

He was weighing up whether it was better to attack the villa or wait for the gates to open and to attack the car. The first option would be on his terms and at a time of his choosing. It would be, however, the more difficult option; the second was unattractive because someone had to lie in wait with substantial weaponry and ordinance, continuously ready to make a split-second decision to attack. The timing would not be down to Brendan.

There were other options: one forming in his mind was to fire at the villa over the walls. The Turks now had with them some shoulder-mounted rocketry that would put the fear of

God into anyone in the villa, if it were fired against the large French windows overlooking the Mediterranean. Brendan could follow this up with new threats demanding that his requests be fulfilled. The other option involved the power and water supply. Undoubtedly, the villa complex had a back-up generator to provide electricity, but could he disrupt the water supply and say that it had been poisoned? After all, Johnny Musselwhite had been poisoned. This would, however, be an unfounded threat as the poisons he had at his disposal had to be applied to the skin, not watered down a million times.

His mobile rang.

A voice, speaking in Arabic, recited two coded phrases that gave him the go-ahead to attack the villa. It also specified that he was to use the rifle with telescopic sights and to take out the target on the rear terrace, firing from the adjoining villa.

Decision made.

CHAPTER TWENTY-FOUR

Thursday morning was fresh with an offshore breeze and a developing bank of cloud far out at sea. High up above her, there were white contrails left by planes flying north from Dakar in Senegal to Europe. Mike Kingdom wondered if one of these had been produced by the plane from the Falklands that refuelled every week at Dakar before passing over her cabin to reach RAF Brize Norton. *The world is so small,* she was thinking.

It was 10.30am, and she was sitting outside her hotel having a breakfast of eggs and hash browns. A brushed-steel pot had provided her with hot but bitter coffee. There weren't many guests, and this gave her time to think and prepare. She was currently in her black wig; *But this,* she was thinking, *may change.*

Her phone buzzed.

"Can you speak?" Leonard asked when she picked up the call.

"Yes, I'm alone. I'm eating my late breakfast in the sunshine," she replied, but she instantly regretted mentioning food.

"Boy, it's hours since I had breakfast. I might have to get something. Lunch is a couple of hours away."

"To what do I owe this pleasure, if that's what it is? I told you nothing happens until 2.00pm."

"That's about when POTUS lands at Marrakech; he's another person probably eating breakfast at the moment… over Greenland or somewhere." Food was always a major distraction to him – especially if it were on someone else's plate.

"What? Do you want me to meet him? Only, I'm busy and didn't bring my full wardrobe."

"I think Morocco has a king, or somebody like that, who's going to meet him, together with all the usual flunkeys."

"At least Randy hasn't done anything to upset the visit, yet? Has he?" she asked.

"So far, so good, but I'll feel a whole lot better once you've spoken to him."

She drank some coffee. "Why did you call? Unless you get turned on by listening to someone eat croissants – which you probably do, come to think about it."

"To do you a favour." He paused for effect. "The British police went to the address on the top of your list and freed the two women. They shot a couple of kidnappers."

"Was one of them Brendan Dowell?"

"That's why I'm letting you know. No, it wasn't, and the Brits can't find him. You might like to let your other client know."

"What nationality are the two kidnappers?"

"They're just hired help from Eastern Europe. The

connection between them and Brendan Dowell hasn't been established yet... but I wouldn't get excited about that."

"Will you let me know the second that they find Brendan?"

"Will you phone me straight after you crash the meeting... please?" He was speaking slowly and precisely.

The call ended, and she ordered another pot of coffee.

When it arrived, she reflected on Leonard's call. He was so easy to underestimate. He suckered you in with his, well, with his what? Faux incompetence? Personal idiosyncrasies? Political incorrectness? All of the above? He wasn't head of station for the CIA and chair of Five Eyes for nothing. He had *done the hard yards,* as he might say, although he now looked like he couldn't walk five yards. The more she thought about it, he rarely spoke about his past, so she had no idea if he had ever been fit. She doubted it. He did have a framed basketball shirt on his office wall; what did that mean?

Her thoughts returned to her task today. How was she going to play it?

He either turned up or he didn't.

If it was the former, she couldn't barge into his meeting, as that might put Randy in jeopardy. After all, she had no idea who Aksil Zadi was or whom he might be working for. He might genuinely work for the harbour or fishing authorities, but this could well be a front, and she hadn't found one picture of him or any meaningful specific reference. And why Essaouira? This was bugging her. Why come three hours west of Marrakech to a fishing port and tourist destination? Her best guess was that it had something to do with its import or export facilities. What was being imported? Was it from elsewhere in Africa or from the Canary Islands, which were only sixty miles out to sea?

Her mind went back to Aksil Zadi. She needed to intercept

Randy as he walked from his car, house or hotel towards the port office. It wouldn't take long. She needed to say that Leonard wanted him to stop what he was doing and ring Leonard, and on a personal level, she wanted to ask Randy to phone her later when this madness was over. If she achieved this, she could retreat into the background and get back to Spain and her other problem.

This reminded her that she needed to phone Charles to let him know that Brendan was on the loose. She needed to call Wazz as well.

The coffee was black and coated her teeth. She wiped her mouth with the back of her hand and picked up her phone. Five hundred miles to the northeast, a phone rang in the villa.

"Mike," Charles said, "how are you?"

"Well, thank you. How are you all doing?"

"Everyone is going stir crazy – by which I really mean Maria and Angelica."

"Have you heard from the police?"

"No, and I haven't had any further calls from the kidnappers."

"I hear that your cook and her daughter are safe. They were rescued by police this morning. Two of the kidnappers were shot during the operation, but I wanted to warn you that Brendan – or whatever name he uses – wasn't there."

"That's great news about Gabriela and Camila. So, we can all relax?"

"No, Charles, I think it's the opposite. You all need to be on higher alert. Brendan knows you're all in Spain, and you still have whatever it is he wants. Have you had any more ideas about what Johnny had on that memory card? Especially about anything other than PEGASUS."

"It could be anything. It might be stuff unconnected to me that the blackmailer thinks I know about. I'm in an impossible situation. My name is written all over the business card, but I don't know what Johnny loaded on to it."

"So, you need to stay vigilant."

"This can't go on indefinitely. I – we – all have things we should be doing."

"Well, if I were you, I would be spending my time trying to work out what could be on that card other than PEGASUS that has so preoccupied the Moroccans or Russians or whoever."

Charles made a sort of grunting noise, and they ended the call.

Mike picked up her coffee cup, realised it was cold and put it back down on the table. She dialled Wazz's number.

"Wazz up?" he answered.

It was good to hear his voice. She couldn't stop herself smiling. "Not much here, yet. Wazz up at your end? All quiet on the western front?"

"It appears to be. No more really suspicious stuff happening, and I have some good people helping me out."

Mike updated him on the UK police operation and explained that Brendan's whereabouts were unknown.

"Now that he doesn't have anything to bargain with, I hope this Brendan goes away." Wazz was sounding hopeful.

"Sadly, I think not. He's not a deranged individual or part of a criminal gang. He's just the front end of a very big organisation or country. If he's removed, the next one will step up to the plate."

"Charles did have one visitor who caused a bit of excitement in an otherwise dull day."

"Who was it?"

"I don't know. Charles isn't very forthcoming—"

"Tell me about it," Mike interrupted, "Who do you think it was?"

"I don't know, but his security was French."

"What security?"

"He turned up in a chauffeur-driven white Mercedes followed by three French apes, and I mean apes – it takes one to know one."

"He had three French bodyguards?"

"Yes, Charles didn't tell me until five minutes before this man arrived. I tried to ask about the security arrangements, but he didn't seem to know or care. At the gate, Diego wasn't in his friendliest mood, and he doesn't like the French, so I had to go down and sort it out."

"How long did Charles speak to this man, and did you hear anything?"

"An hour, and then he left, but I didn't hear anything. I did have a few minutes with one of the apes who was vaguely approachable. He wouldn't say whom he was protecting, but he was ex-COS and about six foot five."

"He was Greek?"

"No, Commandement des Opérations Spéciales – they're the French special forces."

"What did this visitor look like?"

"Short, cocky, forty-five years old, small feet and nice shoes."

"What? That's most of France."

"OK, he had wavy, black hair and distinctive eyebrows."

"You wouldn't make a spy, would you?" she mocked gently.

"Well, in that case, I'll just send over the photographs I took of him."

"Touché."

There was the sound of smirking across the airwaves. "Didn't Charles mention this to you?" Wazz asked. "Did he really think the risk was worth hiding it all from you?"

"I told you that Charles keeps it all close to his chest. He only tells you stuff if you pester him. Even then you get a redacted version. I'll do some research before I confront him."

***

The choreography began as twenty world leaders flew into Marrakech airport. The travel disruption was immense.

It was particularly bad when Conrad, the US President, was arriving in Air Force One, which today was a blue-and-white Boeing 747. An exclusion zone of ten nautical miles – under a temporary flight restriction that lasted from fifteen minutes before landing to fifteen afterwards – meant that there were no other planes in the air. The Office of the Military Advisor, the Presidential Advance Agency and the White House staff had done a good job of preparation over the previous week. As the plane came in to land, armed Secret Service agents were at the base and inside the control tower.

Already, a second plane – which would become Air Force One in case the first was incapacitated and POTUS had to make a speedy escape – was parked under armed guard.

Within minutes of arriving at the secure ramp, Conrad descended with the First Lady. He had spent the last minute checking his teeth. Who gives a President a spinach omelette just before he makes a major public appearance? After waving and descending the steps, they were met by the King of Morocco and a group of eight dignitaries. A military band was playing somewhere out of sight. The President got into one of the two identical armoured cars, and it was absorbed by a cavalcade of twenty vehicles as it swept out of the airport; these included doctors and ambulances, counter-assault teams, an intelligence vehicle and a hazardous-materials team among others. There were twenty motorcycle outriders up front in a delta formation, but these were unnecessary as all the roads had been closed for the short journey to the Glaoui Palace hotel, which had been completely booked by the American contingent. The President and First Lady had the entire third floor to themselves.

The arrival and transfer worked perfectly, much to the relief of all involved and to Leonard de Vries, who was watching it all nervously from his office in Chiswick.

**

Not fifteen miles to the north in Northwood, but several floors underground, Leonard's British equivalent, together with Dennis from the FCO, Lorna from MI6 and Commander Ben Cox were monitoring the arrival of the PM at the end of his three-and-a-half-hour flight in the Airbus A321 that was made available for such journeys.

The PM, his closest team and his security were heading for a palatial, ten-bedroomed villa in a gated community almost under the flight path of Marrakech airport. The remainder of the large team, along with the travelling press pack, were to occupy floors in several nearby hotels.

From the very beginning when Marrakech had been mooted as a location, there had been a general nervousness about the potential for terrorists, and four of the Five Eyes whose presidents and PMs were attending – the UK, USA, Australia and Canada – were all heavily focused on monitoring the internet, phone traffic and other sources for any indication of trouble.

Ben Cox stepped out of the London meeting to take a call from Patrick, who was standing outside the hospital in Colmar.

"What's new?" Ben asked.

"Walter has regained consciousness; well, sort of..." He paused as someone walked by. "He hasn't made much sense yet, but the doctors think that he'll be *compos mentis* soon. He is now off the critical list."

"Thanks, Patrick, let me know the second he tells you anything important."

"Will do."

"I'm just twitchy about Brendan. The Moroccan passport is probably coincidence or a wind-up by the Russians, but the PM is in Marrakech with the other leaders. I don't like it."

"I understand."

"When we find out whether Walter knows what's on the card and whether he saw something or has some information about Brendan, I'm sure it will all make sense. Nothing more from the lovely prosecutor?"

"No, I haven't seen her, more's the pity."

"I must rejoin the others. Bye."

CHAPTER TWENTY-FIVE

It was 1.30pm, and Mike had exhausted every diversionary activity to stop her blood pressure going sky-high. Her head was pounding, and she drank yet more bottled water. She had distributed her harmless-looking secret-squirrel gadgets around the room and put her laptop on the top of the wardrobe. She put her passport and spare money in the small safe. It was time to go. After all, Randy might be early.

In her brown wig, bandana and rucksack, she looked like any other tourist. She wanted to blend into the background, not fall into the fish gutter and draw everyone's attention.

She walked in the wrong direction for a few minutes, went past some shops and turned down a small alley. Next to a stack of mangled ironwork, she entered a clothes shop by a side door and knelt down, ostensibly looking at the soft leather shoes. Nobody followed or was watching out for her when she stepped back out of the front door onto the main sea-facing promenade. Dylan would have been proud of her, although he did always say to her that she put the 'anal' in 'analyst' and that she wouldn't last five minutes in the field. Well, so far so good. She had even bought a tourist map and guidebook on Essaouira so that, if she needed to, she could stop at any time without looking suspicious by pretending to consult them.

The thought that she might meet Randy had now assumed a disproportionate importance in her mind, and the fear that he might not show would represent a terrible blow; she tried to prepare herself mentally.

Retracing her steps from yesterday, she walked around the edge of the fish market and slowly approached the white colonnade outside the management offices. There were plenty of voices from behind the various doors and a few Moroccans in various modes of dress, from caps and aprons to full Berber scarves and *djellabas*, walking around or talking. She leant against an old pickup, which reeked from the empty plastic fish crates in the back, and waited.

She leapt up, only just managing to suppress a scream. A rough-looking black-and-white mongrel nuzzled against her leg before jumping into the back of the pickup. It smelt only slightly worse than the fish crates. It wasn't aggressive but more defensive and proprietorial. In a practised routine, it jumped in among the boxes and through the void where the back window of the cab should have been. It sat staring at her through the windscreen from the passenger seat.

Worried that her cover may be in the process of being blown, she stepped away from the pickup, only for the dog to start barking. She turned around and took two paces back. It stopped. Surely dogs start barking as you approach, not as you leave? The dog was looking at her with pleading eyes. She could hear Dylan laughing, and she looked skywards. Looking up at the sun-bleached sky in an exasperated way did not solve her problem, and she was too inexperienced to realise that the attention-seeking dog had given her a wonderful reason to be standing there. Instead, she spread the tourist map out on the bonnet while the dog turned its head on its side and looked back at her through the windscreen.

A grey Renault saloon pulled up fifty yards from her, closely followed by a rusting, white van. The car disgorged two tribesmen in Berber robes, and the van's door opened to allow a tall, black African in a shiny, grey suit to step out before he bent over to look at himself in the wing mirror. They were obviously all together, but they walked separately towards the shade of the colonnade. Standing under the first arch for a few moments, they began to light cigarettes and blow smoke ostentatiously upwards as they scanned the car park and bustling harbour.

As soon as they turned to walk, Mike used her phone to take pictures of them and their vehicles. She would never be able to hack into the Moroccan car registration system, which was, of course, in Arabic, but it might prove useful if she ever had to ask anyone who these men were. She began walking through the first arch of the covered corridor, partially in pursuit and partially to get a view of Randy coming to the meeting from any direction. The dog started barking again, but it stopped quite quickly with a strangled yawn.

It was 2.00pm.

She had watched the three men enter the door that she had identified yesterday, but there was no sign of Randy. She listened briefly at the closed door, but she could hear only what she presumed was Arabic; there was no American voice. She retreated to the end of the colonnade and got out her guidebook. It might be a long wait.

Her plan was simple. She would use one of the numerous taxis parked at the rank next to where the coaches dropped off the tourists for their photo opportunities and follow the three men. The traffic in Essaouira wasn't heavy. How difficult could it be?

By the time the men reappeared, she had begun to lose faith in her plan, despite having looked up 'right', 'left' and 'straight on' in her guidebook. They walked straight to their two vehicles, giving her no time to think. With a major change of plan, she opened the driver's door of the pickup, much to the excitement of the friendly dog, who was clearly missing human contact. She beckoned him out of the door, which he did eagerly and jumped in herself. Earlier, she had seen that the keys were in the ignition, and this proved a temptation too far. She drove off slowly, not because it was a stick shift, as she had driven one in London on and off for five years, but more because the steering wheel was on the other side. The irony that this was the same as in the USA was not lost on her, but she had only learnt to drive automatics in Oregon.

She was just leaving the car park when there was an almighty crash.

As she was weaving between two coaches full of tourists, the dog had jumped into the back, knocking over the plastic crates, and had then leapt through the rear window. It ended up sitting on the passenger seat like Scooby Doo, panting through the sides of its mouth. She drove off northwards, following the white van and grey Renault in the direction of the bus station.

The dog put its front feet on the dashboard as if up for the chase. The traffic was sufficiently light and slow moving that a mad dash was unlikely to take place. The pickup had no working air conditioning, and therefore the missing cab window was a blessing in disguise. It also removed some of the overpowering stench of fish that came from, well, everywhere in the vehicle, including the dog, which must have been playing in the fish gutter.

"What's your name?" she asked her new sidekick pointlessly.

It didn't answer and kept its eyes on the road ahead, unlike Mike, who had looked across at it while talking, which forced her to swerve to miss a moped. The rider in a long, black leather jacket shouted at her. *How can he wear a leather jacket in this heat?* she wondered.

"Now, what am I going to call you? What goes with fish? Chips!"

Keep your eyes on the road and concentrate, she heard Dylan's voice say in her head. "Fat lot of good it did you in the pickup in Holland," she said out loud, but she subconsciously took the advice.

The traffic was moving at a slow pace because of all of the handcarts, donkeys and overladen mopeds, which made it relatively easy for her to follow Aksil Zadi or whoever had been attending the meeting. She realised that she didn't actually know whom she was following, but this was now her sole link to Randy, however tenuous that might be. They turned off the main road, and she instinctively hung back, keeping two cars as a buffer between her and the van. The buildings began to thin out and some brown fields started to appear, punctuated by scrub and silvery-grey olive trees. They had been driving for less than half an hour.

Mike hadn't the slightest idea where they were going – a local village or, at worst, deep into the hinterland? She also had no idea what she was going to do when they stopped at their destination. If necessary, she would drive past a couple of times, take some photographs and head back to Essaouira. She could phone Leonard, and he would call in a CIA team in hours. Well, not many hours, to be precise, as there were probably fifty of them in Marrakech watching the President.

It dawned on her suddenly that she had an additional problem: Chips. If she stopped and got out of the pickup, he would bark and probably jump out of the back window and follow her. He wasn't wearing a collar, and there was no lead or rope anywhere. So much for undercover observation. *I'm not cut out for fieldwork,* she said to herself for the hundredth time, *Why do I end up in situations like this?*

She had no more time to reflect on this as the two vehicles slowed down and turned off down a short, dusty farm track to the left. The farm buildings were set about fifty yards back from the road under two palm trees. Mike had no choice but to carry on along the road until she could find a place to turn around. She parked and waited for a few minutes before driving back slowly. Apart from a lorry loaded with livestock and a local taxi, which drove on towards the east, there was no traffic.

She had her phone on her lap ready to take a couple of quick photographs.

At the farmhouse, there was no sign of human activity, which encouraged her to slow down to a virtual stop. She took a picture of the farm sign at the side of the road, although it meant nothing to her as it was in Arabic. In fact, she wasn't even sure it was a name and not a road sign saying "Slow down for camels". The main house was a whitewashed cube with shuttered windows and it was also attached to some buildings partly painted in peeling turquoise. The colour changed quite abruptly where the decorator had run out of the blue paint. There was a stone arch half-buried in the garden area to the front of the farm that had been partially blocked in by a loose stone wall. Mike had no idea what it was, but she thought it looked like the entrance to a Roman irrigation system.

Two terracotta pots containing spiky yuccas were positioned one each side of the old wooden door. Sadly, one was a healthy dark green, but the other was a crispy orange-brown. Mike was musing on why the pots, so lovingly positioned, had recently been neglected when Chips jumped out of the window and ran towards the farmhouse.

***

Walter had finally stopped surfing in Sennen Cove. There's never an obvious reason to stop surfing. You just go in and out of the water until the cold becomes unbearable or the light fades. Surfing is, after all, an obsession. He was becoming aware of his surroundings and the fact that it hurt to take a deep breath. A tube appeared to be draining his lungs, and there were patches stuck to his chest with wires coming from them that converged at the back of a device cantilevered over his hospital bed. Sitting alongside him were Madame Bettancourt, whom he recognised, and a man called Patrick Redwood, whom he wasn't sure he could place.

It had been an intense half an hour of diplomatic discussion when the French authorities' desire to interview a prime suspect in the murder of a British government minister conflicted with the British police's desire to interview a victim who was a national working in the British Embassy in Paris.

The compromise was achieved only through the working relationship that Patrick Redwood and Jacqueline Bettancourt had established over their lunch the previous day.

"Walter, I'm Patrick Redwood from the British police. Do you feel well enough to speak?"

"Yes," Walter answered in a surprisingly robust voice.

"You're in hospital in Colmar; do you remember what happened to you?"

"Yes, I was shot."

"Who shot you?"

"Brendan... from the embassy," he said slowly.

"Do you know why?" Patrick asked as the prosecutor sat quietly listening to the replies.

"Um... not really."

"Could it be connected to the poisoning of Johnny Musselwhite? You remember that, do you?"

"Yes." He moved his gaze over to Madame Bettancourt.

"It's OK to speak in front of the prosecutor, Walter; we're all working together to sort this out."

In the silence that followed, Walter's other senses took precedence, and he became aware of the whirring of a pump and that indefinable smell of hospitals.

"I phoned him." Walter put his head back against the pillow and breathed heavily.

"Johnny?" Patrick prompted.

"No, Brendan."

"When?"

"Um..." – Walter temporarily lost his train of thought – "after Johnny was killed, when I was in my room."

"Thursday?"

"I don't know." Waves started to crash on the beach, and he

needed time to pick up his thread again. "The afternoon after he was poisoned. Just before I was shot. I was in my room."

"Why did you phone Brendan?" Patrick was using the most gentle and encouraging voice.

"I found a memory card in Johnny's room and took it back to mine. I put it in my laptop to have a look."

The others sat quietly, letting him continue.

"It had some dodgy photographs – you know, porn; some emails; and a load of stuff about PEGASUS."

"The planned gas pipeline?"

"It's not just a gas pipeline. It's also an electricity cable and a pipeline for phosphates."

Patrick and Jacqueline looked at each other to see if this made any sense, but there was no recognition on either of their faces.

"There was a big specification describing the phosphate pumping process." Walter was now almost rambling.

"And you told Brendan all about this in a phone call on Thursday?"

"Yes, I was worried. I was worried about my position, you know? I rang him to tell him that I had picked up the card and what I had seen. He said not to worry and that he knew all about it. He kept saying not to worry about what was on the card, but I was to keep what I had seen to myself."

"What did you do with the card?"

"I wiped it straight away. I was worried that…" – he paused and tried to turn his head towards the prosecutor – "the French police would find it. It incriminated a British minister. Some of the stuff, some of the stuff… I couldn't leave it around."

"No, no, I understand. Had you downloaded it on to your laptop?"

"No, of course not." He sounded exhausted.

"Did Brendan say he would come down from Paris?"

"Was he in Paris? I don't know. He couldn't have been in Paris. It was only minutes until he turned up."

"What happened next?"

"What?" Walter was fading and lost his thread. "No, I didn't expect to see him at my bedroom door. It wasn't until he turned up that it came back to me that I had seen him in Algiers at the British Embassy. Small world, eh?"

CHAPTER TWENTY-SIX

"Conrad."

"Victor."

They sounded relaxed. The President and the British PM were now alone for twenty minutes – a rare luxury for people in their positions, which was perhaps something that's hard for the rest of the world to understand.

"I am so sorry. No, really, I'm so sorry. It's, well, so sad. Do you have to fly straight back home?" Conrad asked.

"Thank you and, no, not at the moment. I was going to be back on Sunday, anyway."

"Seventy years. It was seventy years, wasn't it? You and I are lucky if we get four."

"A hard act to follow and, may I say, the most internationally accepted world figure ever. She was queen to 2.5 billion people."

"So, you don't need to get back home?"

"It's possible, but I would like to stay until Sunday. She understood how the world of diplomacy works. She had met thirteen US presidents, I think. She would want the system to go on as before, and this G20 is pretty important."

"Let me know if things change and you need to disappear."

"Conrad, thank you and I know that, however much we all plan, nothing in life runs along rails."

"Victor, you're right, and may God bless her and the new king." He paused. "On to more mundane items, are your security guys as jumpy as mine? They almost pulled the goddamn trip an hour before departure. One of our agents in Morocco has gone missing, and everyone's waiting for the video to be posted."

"I'm getting the same; they had a meeting just before I left, but they couldn't give me any concrete reason not to come. I understand that they've cancelled one trip into the desert for all of us because it's too close to Algeria."

"Who picked Morocco? It was before my time."

"Before mine, as well."

"And it was before Poot'n invaded Ukraine, and things are a bit different now. From my perspective, apart from the neutrals in the G20, we have the US, the Brits and Spain behind Morocco, and the Russians, China and the French behind Algeria. Does that sum it up?"

"Yes, and the EU gets a big chunk of its gas by pipeline from Algeria... oh, and the UN has its longest-standing peacekeeping force in Western Sahara."

"Jeez, we might as well have met in Afghanistan."

They were in a large room with pink walls and arched recesses full of gravity-defying flower displays. The air smelt of rich spices.

"The Secretary of State visited Algeria back in the spring to see if we could start weaning them off of Russia, but, unfortunately, there was nothing doing," Conrad explained.

"You and I both want the Algerian gas to get to Europe, otherwise they're competing with us on the world market. Russia would rub its hands with glee if those pipelines were shut down. Actually, the Algerians have shut down the one via Morocco and a little explosion seems to have temporarily shut down another. It's very hard to defend long pipelines."

"Looks like, while I'm here, I have to say nice things about semi-autonomy for Western Sahara under ultimate Moroccan control while not slamming the door on the Algerians, who want it wholly independent. That should be a barrel of laughs."

"I'm told that the only fun on this trip is a visit to Yves Saint Laurent's villa nearby."

"Jeez, they showed me a picture. Did you see the garden? If I wanted to see a tall cactus, I could have gone to Arizona."

***

Patrick was back on the phone to Ben Cox, giving him an update on Walter.

"I finally managed to talk to Walter with the prosecutor. He was still rambling a bit."

"What did he say happened?" the commander asked.

"Walter said he took the memory card back to his room after Johnny Musselwhite's body was found. When he eventually looked at it, he found some emails, porn and detailed specifications of the PEGASUS pipeline – but not just the planned gas pipeline and power cable. PEGASUS also includes a phosphate pipeline. The card included a detailed specification, but Walter was beginning to waffle at this point."

"Does he remember being shot?"

"Yes and no, he remembered Brendan, whom he said he

had phoned on Thursday afternoon when he had looked at the contents on the card. This must have been not long before he was shot, and Brendan was already in the *auberge*. Walter wanted his superiors to know what Johnny was up to. He wiped the contents to protect Johnny. Brendan must have been searching the *auberge* that day and must have decided that Walter knew too much. If he had thought that taking Walter's laptop and this memory card would solve everything, then he would have been very disappointed."

"I don't think that this has anything to do with porn or blackmail, otherwise they would have kept Johnny alive. No, this is to do with PEGASUS and possibly the phosphate-pipeline element, which I haven't heard anything about, and I don't think is public knowledge. I'll get all this checked out at my end. Charles Yelland at Petronello must be involved and know all about this phosphate stuff. It's probably why Brendan is after him and his family," Ben concluded.

"But who's Brendan working for? Who cares about a phosphate pipeline enough to kill, or attempt to kill, twice and to kidnap and blackmail? It's quite a coincidence that Johnny Musselwhite and Yves Dubuisson, his French counterpart, were meeting in Colmar at a potash mine. Potash is phosphate, isn't it?"

"I have no idea, but I don't like coincidences. I'll get all this checked out. How was your friend, the prosecutor?"

"She was fine. The French are busy tracking Brendan's flights in and out of France over the last seven years. I didn't mention the potash/phosphate connection, but she'll probably have thought of it herself."

"Does Walter still have an armed guard at the hospital?"

"Yes."

"When he comes around a bit more, chat to him again. You could take the prosecutor for lunch again. What do you think?"

"Great idea."

***

Ben Cox walked along a corridor, knocked and entered a room in which there were five people, including Dennis from the FCO and Lorna from MI6, who were busy looking at screens. While the technology looked cutting edge, the furniture and room decoration were standard UK government issue circa 1965. There was even a wooden coat stand and wicker wastepaper basket. He updated everyone on Walter's ramblings. Someone called Vanessa took on the task of producing a briefing note on phosphates, potash and the relevant transportation methods. Someone else began the task of checking key words, such as 'phosphate', in the communication traffic of Johnny Musselwhite, Brendan Dowell and others.

It was Lorna's turn to update Ben on the events at Charles Yelland's villa in Spain. "Look who turned up at the villa with some serious protection."

Ben didn't bother to ask who had put in a surveillance camera watching the Yelland villa. Instead, he looked at a monitor and saw a white Mercedes approach the gates only to be met by a one-eyed man dressed like Lawrence of Arabia, who walked out to the car. Before he could speak to the driver, the gates opened and a thick-set man with a crewcut orchestrated the car's entrance.

"Who's that?" Ben asked.

"Yves Dubuisson, the French Minister of Energy," Dennis

answered, "He came from Paris and is now on his way to his home in Cannes."

"Strange route… via Málaga?" Ben was beginning to make a series of connections that he could never have made a few hours before.

"We thought initially that he was hopping across to Marrakech, but that wasn't what happened. The French President is already there, of course." Lorna picked up a phone, looked at some message and put it down on the table again.

***

It took a few minutes to put on the handcuffs before releasing the chain from the iron ring on the wall. The prisoner didn't bother struggling; the odds of escape weren't worth thinking about, and he was feeling weak from the lack of food and water. His back was aching despite standing or half-standing as often as he could to relieve the pain and stress.

"*Vamos*," one of his jailers said in a heavy North African accent, "Let's go."

The prisoner looked at the bucket that he had used as a toilet for a week and hoped that this wouldn't be one of the last images of his short life.

He had tried to think of all the reasons that they might chain him up, but most importantly, keep him alive; he was about to find out.

The few paces across the room to the three stone steps were only achieved with the support of the two men who were wrapped almost head to foot in brown cloth. They manhandled him up through the doorway, despite his inability and, perhaps, his lack of enthusiasm to move nearer to his death.

The adjoining room was also whitewashed and was probably a storeroom for fruit or winter feed for the animals. There were some boxes in the corner, but not much else. What he did see was a flag draped over two sawn-off branches that was acting as a backdrop and the video camera on a tripod.

It was time to film the video.

The bottom of his stomach had fallen out, and he craved his private access to his bucket – something he couldn't have contemplated thinking a few weeks before.

They propped him in a chair with the black, white, green and red flag of the Western Sahara as the backdrop and left him alone with his thoughts – the one place a hostage does not want to be.

He was just mentally tidying up a few things, as if this were his last opportunity for redemption. He processed a series of thoughts that weren't sugar-coated or, indeed, coated in anything. They were the honest feelings of someone who would never again have the luxury of speaking to his partner, a member of his family or his friends. Oddly feeling at peace with himself and not morbid, he was moving on to the two things in his past life that he really regretted when something leapt through the window opening.

A scruffy, black-and-white dog landed in front of him and started running around.

He almost burst into tears, not because he had said goodbye to this earth and the dog had brought him back to the present, but just to see a free spirit unconstrained by handcuffs and chains. It leapt up and started kissing him.

"God, you stink of fish."

The noise attracted three new people into the room: a large black man in a shiny, grey suit, plus two local Berber tribesmen. They hurriedly chased the dog out and closed the door behind it. A few seconds later, it jumped back through the opening, much enjoying the game. One of the Berbers led it by the scruff of its neck out of the door and, presumably, locked it away somewhere. The remaining Berber spoke in broken English.

"I am Aksil Zadi. Mr Ramirez, now we meet. Time for video."

"You will be a big, international star." The man in the shiny suit spoke in good English and what sounded like a Nigerian accent.

"I'm not looking my best," came the reply.

"You read this." Aksil Zadi produced a sheet of paper from inside his *djellaba*.

"Mr Ramirez, my English is good. Do not waste our time trying to put in anything extra. If you do, it will upset us. Please don't upset us. We will come back soon to begin the filming," the man in the shiny suit said.

The sheet of paper was handed over, and they left the room. It read:

The Sahrawi People's Army (SPA) supports the legitimate liberation struggle waged by the Sahrawi people against the illegal Moroccan occupation of parts of the Sahrawi Republic and the continued acts of aggression carried out by the occupying Moroccan state on the Sahrawi Liberated Territory.

Despite terrorist attacks in London, Paris, Barcelona, Brussels and Finland, which were almost exclusively carried out by terrorists of Moroccan origin, the US continues to support Morocco.

The Moroccans blew up an Algerian gas pipeline on Wednesday last week, but there has been no international condemnation, apart from by our friends in Russia, India and China.

The US and its allies insult the Sahrawi Republic by holding the G20 meeting in Marrakech and sending its spies to destabilise the region.

The US and its allies must agree to support the complete independence of the Sahrawi Republic immediately.

If it does not announce this publicly at the G20, American hostages will be killed.

***

Two hundred yards away, Mike Kingdom was sitting in the pickup, cursing Chips – a thought that, until an hour ago, she never believed would ever enter her mind. Now she had a dilemma. Common sense said that she should leave the dog, drive back to the port, call Leonard and leave the rest to the professionals. They would quickly trace the three individuals and any connection they might have with Randy. Another side of her wanted to check whether Randy was in any of the farm buildings. If challenged, she was just looking for her dog.

The approach to the right-hand corner of the first building was reasonably well hidden, and there were no windows – only whitewashed walls and a rotten, old wooden door. She muted her phone to avoid any noise occurring at some embarrassing moment and got out of the pickup, trying not to look suspicious. After fifty or so paces, she found herself next to the wall and could hear nothing apart from the blood thumping in her ears. She thought it was odd that she couldn't hear or see Chips, who seemed incapable of sitting still or not barking for more than ten seconds.

To her right, away from the house, she could now see the free-standing stone arch, of which one was half-filled in with a much later wall; it appeared to be a dark entrance to something underground. There was no door, and it was partially overgrown. It didn't look as if anyone had used it for years. Unfortunately, she would have to cross open ground to check it out, and she felt safer up against the whitewashed wall of the main buildings.

She leapt when Chips came running around the corner only to bark when he saw her. He skidded on the loose sand and charged back out of sight.

CHAPTER TWENTY-SEVEN

"How long is this going on for, Charles?" Maria Yelland was beginning to get tired of her gilded cage in Spain. "I might as well be back in Mexico. Nobody will find us at the *hacienda*."

This was probably true. Her family was descended from the conquistadores and were now landed gentry with an income effectively coming from a drug cartel. Security around the family was extensive, and strangers could get nowhere near.

"Anyway, I want to go home." Angelica did not want to be in Spain or Mexico. She wanted to be in Beswick Manor with handy access to London. "Or, like, Dubai. Like, half of my friends are there at the moment."

Charles was sitting eating some cold meats and bread that Paco had just placed on the table, together with a glass of white Rioja. "Mexico might be a possibility, Maria, but it's easier if we're together until these crazy people are caught and we can go back to normal. And by easier, I mean it's easier for Wazz and the rest of his security team to look after us."

"What is it that these 'crazy people', as you call them, want? Is it really worth it? Why don't you give it to them? We're not exactly down to our last peso."

"Gabriela and Camila have gone back to Mexico. I don't blame them." Angelica was talking while tapping the keyboard of her phone.

"These people were asking that I give them something I didn't have." Here, Charles, as usual, was playing games with the truth or, more accurately, with the tense of the verbs, because he now had it in his possession since Yves Dubuisson had visited.

***

Conrad was not a happy man.

"The three of you had better give me a good reason not to get on Air Force One and fly out of this godforsaken hole right now. I don't want any BS." He paused, but the other people on the video call were wise enough to keep quiet. "This smells like Stan Turner and Carter in 1977. The CIA was completely asleep back then, with its foot off the gas and putting all of its eggs in one basket – the Shah of Iran. Suddenly, it was revolution under an ayatollah and sixty-six Americans were held hostage for over a year. The CIA got Iran all wrong. Now tell me it's not the same here in Morocco?" He paused again. "The US has been supporting the Moroccans and their kings since the Founding Fathers. What if this is about to go belly up? Why did we let the Russkies cosy up to the Algerians? Why not let the Algerians control Western Sahara in return for a whole slice of their gas?"

It fell upon the Secretary of State, who was in a separate

hotel not far away, to try to calm the President down. "Mr President, trust me that we're backing the right horse. It's better that Morocco has tacit control of Western Sahara. If the Algerians get control via the Polisario, then the Russians have control as well. We'll have lost out big time."

"But what if there's an Islamic revolution in Morocco? Like Iran. Or an Arab Spring?"

"That would be unfortunate, but we're doing everything we can to stop that. Morocco has the best intelligence service in Africa other than the South Africans. They're on the case."

"Carrying out attacks in Europe and bribing EU Commissioners?" Conrad was not appeased.

"Nobody in this region of North Africa is as pure as the driven snow, even the Moroccans, and especially not the Algerians."

"Why are half the leaders at this G20 getting warnings from their intelligence agencies that there's going to be trouble?" Conrad was darting all over the place.

"Leonard?" the CIA director of operations (DO) in Langley prompted his man in London, who was also on the call, to respond.

"Mr President, the potential trouble might come from the Sahrawi People's Army, which wants independence for what we call Western Sahara. It has the support of the Algerians and the Russians. There are no specific threats yet. We have our best men in the field checking." Leonard was on his best behaviour.

It was, perhaps, a blessing that Mike Kingdom couldn't hear how Leonard was describing her.

"What's so damn special about a pile of sand where nobody lives? Why are we all getting so worked up? This sounds like the Brits over the Falklands." Conrad wasn't buying any of this.

"Well, the Falklands was, firstly, about principle and, secondly, about the potential for oil."

"Principles can be retrofitted, and Western Sahara doesn't have gas – unless you guys haven't told me something. So why should I get worked up?"

"Phosphates," was all Leonard said.

"Great, we need fertiliser real bad, but there are other places."

"It has seventy per cent of the world's known reserve," Leonard continued.

"Damn." The President was digesting this fact.

"That's why the Algerians, the Russians and, I might add, the Chinese (who are building a port in Algeria) are all behind the Sahrawis." The DO, who was oddly very politically aware for an operational director, had put his head above the parapet now Leonard had prepared the ground.

"No, Mr President, this is about phosphates. The Algerians sell us gas anyways." The Secretary of State knew the reality.

"Is this like the Contras in Nicaragua and the money from Iran?" Conrad paused. "Is this where the President shouldn't ask any more questions?" He could see the word 'impeachment' appearing out of a desert mist.

"Mr President, I can assure you that the US is not actively involved in any illegal activity." The DO knew the truth that it was the Moroccan secret service, the Direction Général de Surveillance du Térritoire (DGST), doing the dirty work for them.

The President had heard the word 'actively' and wisely let the whole of this pass.

"We just publicly support the UN-led peacekeeping force and objectives. We sit on the moral high ground and look down." The Secretary of State was happy with the way this meeting had gone, given its starting point.

It was only Leonard who had begun to piece together the implications for the UK and French nationals who were caught up in the crossfire. As one of the casualties was a minister, the proverbial had not yet hit the fan.

"I said I wouldn't ask any more questions, but I want reassurance that any terrorist threat to me or to the G20 is being dealt with by the CIA," the President demanded.

"As Leonard said, we have our very best men on it, with full support, Mr President." The CIA DO was very clear about this even if, in truth, he would have had kittens if he had been aware of the mess behind the scenes and that success depended on Mike Kingdom.

***

At that precise moment, the very best 'men' that the CIA could offer were completely unsupported and were either chained to a wall or standing outside a farmhouse, looking for a black-and-white dog. Was this the consequence of billions of dollars wisely spent? Who knows? But it was most certainly for the best that the President and 300 million Americans didn't know the thin thread on which so much hung.

The CIA spent most of its billions of dollars enabling its operatives to operate and its analysts to analyse. This was not a glib statement, as despite various name changes, confusing the two was the surest way for both of them to fail. Mike was an analyst masquerading as an operative; this broke every rule and every protocol in every handbook.

She was cursing Leonard under her breath as she tried to work out what to do.

Never having read a CIA operational handbook, she was

unlikely to benefit from their pearls of wisdom. Dylan had never been that complimentary about them. As to the analyst's handbooks, she had read most of them and was very proud of her input to the one on database searching. She applied her analyst's mind to an operational problem: what could go wrong?

She decided that the weird stone arch that looked like a mine entrance was the likeliest place to find Randy. Here, she was confusing the luxury of the analyst who can sift through twenty possibilities in any order without any direct consequence with the operative's position that if you choose the wrong one, you're compromised, tortured or dead. If Dylan was shouting from some distant place, Mike was not hearing him. It was a stupid decision.

She ran to the stone arch over the open ground in full sunlight. Halfway across, she thought about her exposure to anyone in the buildings and bent over in a strange, hunched gait that would have had no effect apart from slowing her down, simultaneously blowing any story that she was looking for her dog and concentrating her body mass so that a shooter was sure to hit her core organs. But she hadn't read the handbooks.

She made it to the entrance, which resembled a cave, with the left half blocked in by an old stone wall. She stepped inside and waited for her eyes to adjust to the dark. There was no sound inside or out apart from some crickets on the dry bushes and the occasional vehicle on the road. She pulled out her phone and turned on the torch. She was right: it was an old irrigation system, and it disappeared away to her left, but the sides began to close in quickly and there were dust-covered cobwebs stretched across that hadn't been disturbed for months. She turned around, choosing where to place her feet among the piles of stones.

The noise when Chips ran into the cave barking was deafening. It echoed down to the aquifer and back. He ran out and back to the farmhouse, only to be captured and finally tied up. Mike didn't know this, and she crept up to the entrance as if there were an alternative to walking out into blistering sunlight in full view of the house. She ran back across to where she had started from and massaged her damaged left leg, which was beginning to hurt (she normally never ran anywhere). Rubbing her leg reminded her of the precariousness of life, and she took off her brown wig and wiped away the sweat before repositioning it.

Chips must be with people or he would be barking, she thought to herself. She edged towards the rear corner of the building and peered around it. There were two connected small sheds that looked as though they contained goats or cows. Voices were coming from one of them through a window, which was really just an opening with a large wooden shutter tied back against the wall. They were speaking Arabic, but she picked up some English, although not enough to make any sense.

Oddly, she couldn't see any doors into these sheds. This should have set off alarm bells – it's essential to always know where all the windows and doors are. They were actually at the back of the sheds, out of her sight, which meant she never saw the men appear until it was too late. There was no time to run.

"Have you seen my dog?" she asked as they approached.

"That is not your dog. We know that dog; it is Kella. It belongs to Meddur, the fish gutter." The man in the shiny suit was now standing next to her.

"I know; he jumped into my car," was her last pathetic attempt to extricate herself.

One of the Berbers, now behind her, was saying something

in Arabic and pointing at the fisherman's pickup, partially hidden in the trees.

"Why don't you come inside and tell us why you have Meddur's pickup?" This was asked in a way that did not allow for refusal.

There was no point trying to fight all the men. She smiled and walked between them as they went around the back of the sheds and in through a solid, faded-blue door. She found herself in a room with a chain attached to a ring on the wall and a bucket that smelt disgusting. Chips began barking, having heard human voices.

"Are you American?" The man in the shiny suit appeared to be the only one who spoke any English.

Mike did not need any of the operational manuals to know that, in this sort of situation, the last thing you say is that you're American. She thought quickly; would being British be better? Probably not. "I'm Canadian; I'm touring Morocco with a friend."

The three men in the room communicated in Arabic or some Berber dialect.

"Please take a seat."

She turned around to look for somewhere to sit, and before she could think, she had been grabbed, pushed onto the floor and chained to the wall.

"Look, I just want to go back to Essaouira." Mike's voice was sounding desperate.

"Don't worry, we will make sure that Kella and Meddur's pickup get back to the harbour. Some of us will drive it back to Essaouira now."

"I don't want to stay here." She was now frantic.

"Are you scared of being alone? We will bring in someone to keep you company."

CHAPTER TWENTY-EIGHT

They had taken Mike's phone, so she never knew that Leonard was trying to contact her. He was annoyed that it was turned off. Didn't she realise he was up against the wall and facing serious heat from the President downwards, as well as from the secret services of Canada, Australia and the UK? Something was brewing, and no one was sure what. Her phone had been turned off for nearly an hour. He checked the time in Morocco and thought this was strange. Wasn't it a couple of hours after her meeting? If she had made contact in Essaouira, she would have let him know straight away and not turn her phone off.

He called in Tom, who was an extremely useful assistant, from a nearby office. Tom's stammer meant that he usually took longer to acknowledge an instruction than to carry it out. "*Tom!*"

Leonard had decided some time ago not to wait for him to speak as he entered the room. Instead, he just delivered his request.

"Tom." He wrote out Mike's number on a pad and handed it across. "Check this phone's locations over the last twelve hours and tell me where it was when it was turned off." He paused. "ASAP." He pronounced it 'A-SAP'. "And I'm not calling you a sap, just in case HR is listening."

***

Mike was also up against a wall, not that Leonard was aware. She had been left alone for half an hour, in which time she had tried to free her tied and chained wrists as well as manoeuvring herself as far away from the bucket as possible. It stank more than Chips, which was a barely conceivable thought. She heard him barking occasionally nearby and had visions of him leaping through the window opening, chewing through her ties and sitting in the passenger seat on the journey back to the harbour car park. Unfortunately, none of this happened, and a melancholy began to set in.

***

In the main farmhouse, one of the Berbers was discussing the situation in Hassānīya, a version of Arabic that was the common language between the three of them. The video with the American, Ramon Ramirez, had been filmed exactly as planned and would be broadcast tomorrow morning at Friday prayers. Was it worth filming the Canadian woman? Possibly, possibly not. They debated this over mint tea and some sweet biscuits. They came down on the side that it was. The more pressure on the G20, the better. It was agreed that the man in the shiny suit and the older of the two Berbers would film the interview that evening while the other men drove the pickup back to Essaouira with Kella. They had already called Meddur, and he was thrilled at the thought that he would get his dog back.

"Take the woman's phone with you. Turn it on when you get to the harbour and give it to the first driver taking fish to Marrakech. Tell him not to use it or answer it for twenty-four hours. He can do what he likes with it after that." The man in the shiny suit was called Toumi and he wanted there to be a false trail at least until Saturday. He was sitting at the kitchen table where he was writing a short speech for his female hostage to read out on the video. Naturally suspicious, Toumi couldn't work out who she really was. He would find out later when the filming was over, but until then, he did not want her to appear beaten up. In truth, it didn't matter who Ramon Ramirez or the woman worked for. He and his fellow Sahrawis weren't interested in any potential ransom money; there would be too many risks attached. What they wanted was the world's media and, specifically, social media to understand their cause and the Americans' role in backing Morocco. Then, on Friday the bombing would take out the world leaders at the G20, and the US, UK and the others would truly wake up – or possibly not.

Toumi wanted to get the message across that the Sahrawis didn't want Morocco or Algeria interfering in their country. He was grateful for the help Algeria had given the Polisario, which had fought to get an independent Sahrawi nation, but things had evolved and now Morocco was a front for the US while Algeria was a front for Russia. He didn't want his nation to become a political football. They should be independent and, through the phosphates, would be financially independent – or indeed, wealthy.

The proposed PEGASUS scheme was the last straw. It would take the phosphates out across Algeria and into Europe. It had to be stopped. He was completely unaware of the irony that his arch-enemy, the Moroccans, did not want PEGASUS either because they wanted to control the production of phosphates, which was the reason that the country's operatives were currently trying to stop it.

He picked up his piece of paper and walked across to the sheds. Together with his friend, he carried the unconscious man they knew as Ramon Ramirez into a different room and made sure he was secure; his reluctance to record the video had been regrettable. They walked back through to the room where the woman was chained to the wall.

"Are you CIA?" Toumi asked.

"Do I look like I'm CIA?" Mike was trying to push back against the inevitable. She moved her head against her raised hand, which was held by the chain, and pulled off her wig. "I'm a Canadian backpacking around your country."

"This is not my country," Toumi said firmly and slowly.

Damn, she thought.

"We are Sahrawi... not that it matters to you or your president."

"Canada has a prime minister not a president," she corrected him.

He shrugged and continued staring at her bald head. Her shock tactics had fallen on deaf ears.

"I came here for the Marathon des Sables; my name is Josie – check it out if you want."

"Why did you steal Meddur's pickup? Don't tell me you were entering the Paris-Dakar rally, because it stopped years ago."

His English was good – too good. It made her pause. "Where did you learn your English?" She thought she should try to build a relationship.

"At university… in Vancouver."

Double damn! she thought to herself.

Despite his normal facial expressions, there was a deadness behind his eyes, but she persevered: "What did you read?"

"Geology, like your friend Ramon," he added. The rhythm of his voice emphasised his sub-Saharan roots.

She didn't comment, but she tried to read something, anything, in his expression. Despite not having read the manuals, she knew instinctively not to reveal anything unless pressed. She had grown up 400 miles from the Canadian border and was therefore quite capable of pretending to be Canadian, having been there many times. Her accent was pretty much Canadian to anyone not from North America. What she took away from this – albeit bald-headed with her wig on the floor while chained to a wall and next to a slop bucket – was that she had been right (although 'right' may have benefitted from some definition). Randy was coming to Essaouira for a meeting with Toumi and Aksil. Clearly, he had been compromised, possibly by being suckered into some gas/oil/phosphates discussion, thinking he was talking to mainstream Moroccans or Algerians.

"We are going to video you while you read this statement." He waved a piece of paper. "If you mess about or try to add some words or other meanings, I will leave you in a room with Gwafa, after which you will talk, so do not fight; it is useless… *and it will hurt*." He emphasised the last four words, displaying emotion in his eyes for the first time.

She must have also displayed some venom in her eyes

because Toumi stopped moving and bent down closer to her. "Ramon finally recorded a nice video for us, but this was only after Gwafa spoke very, very nicely to him – I think that's the right expression. Well, after all that excitement, Ramon is now asleep – I think that's the right word. I'll let you know if Ramon ever wakes up."

I'm not cut out for field work, she heard over and over again in her head.

She began to read the piece of paper that was being held in front of her:

My name is Josie; I work for the CIA.

I would like to read a statement.

I was captured while supporting Morocco's illegal claim over the Sahrawi Arab Democratic Republic, known in the US as Western Sahara.

On 10th December 2020, Donald Trump supported the annexation of Western Sahara by Morocco.

The US wants to steal the natural resources of Western Sahara and secure 100 years' worth of phosphate supply for itself.

Russia and China also want to steal these natural resources and are supporting the illegal transportation of phosphates through Algeria to a Chinese-owned port and across the Mediterranean Sea to France by a pipeline called PEGASUS.

The Sahrawi Arab Democratic Republic is recognised by forty-five members of the UN. At the moment, we only control twenty per cent of our land – the Liberated Territories. The US, Russia and China must reverse their policies and avoid a major international conflict by supporting…

She read on until the end.

Bizarrely, her first thought was about the word choice and grammar. Her second thought was, *What's the US thinking?*

and her third thought was about that spineless shit, Charles Yelland.

Was it only nine days ago that she had first heard of any of this?

The mention of spineless shits brought Leonard de Vries into her thoughts. She quickly got back to reality. What was the point of resisting? They would torture her to the point where she would make the video anyway. Resistance seemed futile. If they were going to kill her, they might as well do it in three hours' time as in six after a lot of pain. She shuddered. If there were any chance she might be rescued, it might be worth trying to delay, but no one knew where she was.

"OK, let's go," declared Toumi.

With that, Gwafa came in, and he and Toumi dragged her into the next room. She was sat, bound hand and foot, at a simple table with a big flag that she didn't recognise draped behind her. A video camera on a tripod was directly in front of her. The statement was on the table.

"OK, put your wig on straight, act normal and start reading." Toumi was standing there with his arms folded.

Act normal? What was he talking about?

She started reading, but her mouth was dry, and she messed up her lines. "Sorry, I need some water. Let me start again."

Without saying a word, Gwafa walked into the next room and came back carrying an iron bar. Toumi picked up his half-drunk water bottle and held it to her mouth. A photograph of the Atlas Mountains on the label came into her view. She liked mountains. She thought about Mount Washington and her childhood, but she decided this might not help.

"Thank you." And with that, she completed reading the statement, unable to add anything that might help any rescue.

Leonard's office may have looked like any other in London, but it concealed the latest protection against eavesdropping. For one, it was quadruple glazed: one layer was coated in a metal powder and the inner glass was half an inch thick. Air was being pumped between the outer two layers so that conversations could not be monitored from outside using surface vibrations.

The room was pale grey and white and surprisingly clean, if you ignored the marks on the wall just above the wastepaper basket. Each evening, the cleaning staff moved it back next to his desk in the vain hope that he would put his copious food wrappers and other rubbish straight in the bin as opposed to throwing them at the wall so that they could drop in – or not. The framed and signed Alabama Crimson Tide basketball shirt above the bin should have given a clue to his aspirations, if he hadn't been five stone overweight, two feet too short, unfit and totally lacking in hand-eye coordination.

He was chewing what looked like a dried sausage in a green wrapper and sweating. The latter was from nervousness. He was head of the most important CIA station outside the USA and head of Five Eyes, to boot. The protection of the presidents and PMs at the G20 had been high on his list for a long time. With his man on the inside, he had felt he could fend off any problem – until he went silent. Leonard had believed there was ample time for Mike Kingdom to find him and report back on any threats in Marrakech. Time was running out, and now Mike had gone AWOL as well. He could sense something was wrong.

Leonard now had the President himself, together with the Secretary of State and various CIA directors, on his back. He sweated some more. With his sausage finished, he screwed the wrapper up into a ball, wrapped it in a cardboard carton and aimed it at the bin. It hit the wall, but when it fell, it missed its target.

There was a knock at the door, and Leonard asked his visitor to enter. He had told Tom to come straight across if he had any news. Time was of the essence. "Tom, give me the low-down."

Tom had been the interface with Mike on a previous job and so he was aware that this was her mobile number even if Leonard hadn't mentioned her name. "I have printed this out as a m-map with time p-points," he said in a singsong voice.

Leonard looked at the printout. "This must be her hotel or Airbnb; I don't know if they have them in Essao…" He gave up trying to pronounce Essaouira. "She was here last night and up to 1.40pm. Then she walks around and doubles back. Good girl," he interjected in a patronising way, "Are these shops? Then she walks across this car park to… what's this building?"

"Some h-harbour or p-port office, I think. Give me a s-second."

"Then she stands still just before 2.00pm, presumably waiting for the meeting?"

"Yes, it's the h-harbour office. Here." Tom showed Leonard a series of images of the colonnade and the wider view.

"Now what?" Leonard asked. "Is she in a taxi? Is she driving? Driving in Morocco? What's she up to?" These were rhetorical questions, and Tom wisely kept quiet. "What's this next place? After thirty-two minutes?"

"This is the s-satellite p-picture. I can get m-more detail back at my desk, b-but it will take a few m-minutes."

"Is it a farm? There are lots of outbuildings." Leonard was

just rambling, "Then what? After twenty minutes, she drives back to Essao… whatever, stays there twenty minutes and… what?"

"She's on the road to Marrakech. That's about two and a h-half hours away."

"But not answering her phone? So, is she driving, on a bus or what? Was it all a wild goose chase?"

Leonard stood there thinking for a few beats and, finally, said, "OK, thanks, Tom. You get me the best pictures of the harbour office and this farm and make them available to me. I'll have a team look into what is going on there, although it looks like she found nothing and is on her way back to Marrakech. Damn!"

CHAPTER TWENTY-NINE

"*Randy?*" Mike was standing, still chained to the wall, but twisted around to project her voice through the gaps created by the rotting rafters. She was speaking in a very loud whisper, which was a self-defeating exercise. Being vertical provided her only relief from the back-aching sitting position. She had lost track of time, but there had been neither sight nor sound of her two captors. Apart from a rat that had an unhealthy interest in the bucket, she had heard and seen nothing.

"Randy?" She thought she could hear some movement, but she also thought he might have tape across his mouth. Mike tapped the wall and listened.

There was a weak tapping in response.

"Randy, are you OK? It's me, Mike." She had made the decision that she didn't care if she blew her cover; she might not have long left alive.

There came a very mumbled and distorted male voice, but whether this was because of tape or damage to his mouth, she couldn't tell. She thought that she heard, "I can't speak," but she wasn't sure.

"OK, one tap for 'yes', and two taps for 'no'. I'll ask the questions."

There was one tap that sounded like a chain against the wall.

"Randy, are you all right?"

There were two taps followed by another frustrated attempt to speak. He tried several times repeating over and over again the same three words.

She felt terrible that she couldn't help. "Oh, Randy!"

There were two taps. She paused and it began to dawn on her. "Randy?"

Two taps.

"Are you Randy Kingdom?"

There were two taps, and her heart sank. Who was next door? He began to repeat two words over and over, the first with two syllables and the second word with three.

"Are you Ramon Ramirez?"

One tap.

She was confused and, temporarily, her life fell apart in front of her. *But Ramon Ramirez is part of all of this,* she kept saying to herself, *He's key to finding Randy. Don't give up.* "Do you know Randy Kingdom?"

Two taps.

Her heart sank. She felt even more devastated, but she tried to keep herself together. "You're CIA?"

One tap.

"And you work for Leonard in London?"

One tap.

"I'm ex-CIA, and I'm working for Leonard too." She was

trying to think what the important questions were. She might have only a few minutes. "I found your flat in Málaga and your room at the *riad* in Marrakech. I found the time and address of the meeting with Aksil Zadi in the back of your copy of *1421*. You understand?"

One tap.

"You were obviously compromised. Leonard sent me to get you to stop what you were doing and to ring him. Had you found out anything important?"

One tap.

Now what? How could she find out anything if she didn't know the questions to ask? He could only tap yes and no. At this point, he started tapping. She counted seven taps.

"Do you mean seven or the letter G?" She realised he couldn't reply to that question. "Do you mean the number seven?"

Two taps.

"Do you mean the letter G?"

One tap. And then, he began tapping and tapping.

"Was that twenty taps?"

One tap.

"For the letter T?"

Two taps.

"You mean the number twenty?... Oh, G20!" She calmed herself so that she didn't raise her voice unnecessarily.

One tap.

She paused. How to find out what he knew? "Is there a threat to the G20?"

One tap.

Now what? "Can you tap the first letter of the threat?"

Two taps.

"Was that a no or the letter B?"

Two taps.

"You mean the letter B?"

One tap.

"What's the next letter?"

There were fifteen taps.

"Shit! A bomb?"

One tap.

"When? Today? Thursday, 8th?"

Two taps.

"Tomorrow, Friday, 9th?"

One tap.

"Shit. At what time? Tap the hour."

He tapped twelve times.

"At midday?"

One tap.

"I presume in Marrakech, but where? Give me the first letters."

It took him a long time to tap out Y followed by S and L. He stopped.

"You just tapped out YSL, is that right?"

One tap.

They both heard a noise like a door opening and stopped communicating instantly. Mike slumped back onto the floor. Her wig caught on the chain and fell to the floor.

***

Walter had woken properly from his coma and had begun asking his own questions, with the first being, "When can I go home to the UK?" The FCO in London was already putting in place the arrangements to fly him back in order that he could be protected on British soil from any external threats. He could see the bright sky out of a window to his right and was imagining his flight back to London. It was a beautiful day in Colmar.

***

"It's a pizza."

A mile away, as they sat at a table in the Restaurant Magritte, the relationship between Patrick Redwood and Jacqueline Bettancourt was blossoming. They were having a very late lunch that showed no sign of ending any time soon, but this, perhaps, was no surprise – it was France, after all.

"Shhh!" she whispered, "You must never call it pizza in the Alsace. It's *tarte flambée*, and it's different. It's Alsatian flatbread topped with *fromage blanc,* bacon and thinly sliced raw onions."

"It's a pizza." He looked up at a Magritte painting of a pipe. "You see that? '*Ceci n'est pas une pipe.*' Magritte would agree with me: 'This is not a pipe.'"

"He was Belgian."

"A pipe is not always a pipe. Look at PEGASUS." He paused. "Is Alsatian cuisine based on stealing other people's ideas? *Tarte flambée* is just pizza and *raclette* is just a Swiss fondue."

She smiled at him benevolently. "How have you lived this long?"

He ate a slice of *tarte flambée* and almost burnt the roof of his mouth. He started breathing out rapidly trying to cool the red-hot cheese.

"You see, there is a God," Jaqueline declared.

"Wrong René; that's René Descartes not René Magritte."

"At least he was French."

There was contented silence as two like-minded souls communed over a simple meal. After some sips of wine, their conversation inevitably returned to the case in hand.

"And you don't think this is about pipes?" Patrick enquired.

"*Mais, certainement.*"

Their eyes met.

"Sadly, I shall be flying back once Walter is on British soil. There's not much more evidence to gain here. It's now about finding and prosecuting Brendan and his cronies. Mind you, we have to catch him first," he clarified.

"It depends on who catches him, I expect. We will want to prosecute him for murder and attempted murder on French soil, and you will want to prosecute him for the same and spying, I expect."

"Either way, it will be delicate given he has a Moroccan passport and appears to be working for Moroccan intelligence."

"Thank you for passing on to me the information about his history and movements from your FCO. We will keep it very confidential." She looked up at him.

"Thank you for giving me the information on his Moroccan passport and his movements in France. My commander is very happy."

"Do we presume that he is on his way to Morocco via Ireland and Spain?"

"We're still checking. The fear is that he has gone after the Yelland family in Málaga. Actually, the bigger fear is that he's about to do something at the G20, but surely not; I can't believe that Morocco wants anything other than good publicity from the meeting?"

"In confidence" – she leant a little closer and spoke quietly – "our investigations into Yves Dubuisson are taking precedence at the moment. He and Johnny Musselwhite stood to gain very substantially from this PEGASUS project, not just from the gas and electricity but also from the phosphates. There are others high up in the French government who quite like the idea of all of this coming to France."

"It would sort out your energy, heating and agriculture problems for decades and decades."

"True."

"It is a clever idea."

"It will make some people very, very rich."

"Not Johnny Musselwhite, unfortunately, but perhaps Charles Yelland and Yves Dubuisson, I think?"

However, they had moved on. The look they gave each other had absolutely nothing to do with the investigation or pizza but more to do with the painting on the wall above them: *The Lovers* by René Magritte.

***

Mike heard a creak. Was it a door opening?

She was at a low point and, oddly, it was worse to get so close and fail; it would almost be better to get nowhere, moan for five minutes, go for a walk through her pine forest and come back to a cold bottle of beer. She now knew there was a plot to blow up the G20 tomorrow at midday – but she couldn't tell anyone about it. If only she could tell Leonard.

Thinking of Leonard was a mistake. It hit her like a brick. *You fat, lying bastard!* It began to dawn on her. *You… you…!*
She had been set up by him – again. How could she be

so naïve? Everyone fell for the fat, stupid façade with the lack of social skills. Clearly, he was no idiot. He had retained his position under two presidents and three CIA directors – this was unheard of. He was accepted by the leadership of the other countries in Five Eyes.

When he had turned up at her cabin just over a week ago, he wanted her to find out the threat to the leaders of the G20 in Marrakech. This was his objective. He wanted her and no one else to find Ramon – and quickly. Leonard did not leave his office in London, even when chauffeur-driven, to have a cup of coffee. The newspaper had not been dropped accidently by her armchair. He knew she wouldn't accept the job if he asked directly; therefore, he had fooled her into searching for her brother-in-law, Randy – an offer she could never refuse. He knew all along that she was looking for Ramon Ramirez. All along, he knew the cell phone number, the address of the CIA flat in Málaga and probably the room in Marrakech. He gave her this information when she asked for it.

He needed her to find Ramon Ramirez and uncover the plot – which she had done successfully, but all to no avail.

Leonard had acted his role to perfection. He had poked fun at her for not spotting Dr Rose Delavine. It was all to provoke her into getting involved.

You... you...! But this all got her nowhere. There were still some sounds nearby, but she couldn't identify them – probably rats. Of everything, it was the Berber that she feared the most; he seemed psychopathic. The one who spoke English and had been to university in Vancouver seemed more reasonable, but this might be a major self-delusion.

She could definitely hear movement. She looked at her

watch – it was almost 5.00pm and she was hungry. It had been a very long day.

"Ow!" She heard a muffled shout from somewhere nearby. It made her try to stand back up, pulling on the chain.

At that moment, someone came through the door looking quickly left and right. It was Josie.

"Quiet!" she whispered as she assessed the situation. The situation she met was a bald, exhausted woman, bound at the wrists and feet and chained to a ring on the wall above her head. "Shit," was her follow-up assessment of Mike's circumstances.

"Josie, get out of here and ring everyone you know. Tell them there will be a bomb tomorrow at midday in Marrakech. Ramon next door said, 'YSL,' but I don't know what that means."

"The guy next door can't walk, and I can't free you. I'll be back – trust me." With that, she left the cowshed.

There was silence again, and Mike was left working out what had just happened.

"Mike?" came a mumbling voice from next door.

"Ramon?"

There was one tap and a mumbled, "Yes."

"Are you OK?"

"My legs aren't working, and my jaw seems a bit loose. Who's that woman?" Despite having had the tape torn from his mouth by Josie, he was having trouble speaking.

"She's Josie, a backpacker from Australia; I met her in Essaouira. She told me she was ex-special forces. I have no idea how and why she's here."

"Did you understand YSL?"

"No."

"It's the Yves Saint Laurent villa in Marrakech. All the

heads of state will be there on Friday, with a group photograph being taken at midday. They've planted a bomb."

"We need to tell Leonard… the shit," she added, "We will – if Josie comes back. I told her to ring everyone she knows, but I think she has her own plan."

They fell silent, but that didn't last long.

"Why the two copies of *1421*? It's been bugging me."

"I suffer from dyscalculia; I have trouble remembering numbers. It's my PIN."

"You are joking? I thought it was the number for your safe in Marrakech or that you were interested in early Chinese exploration of Africa."

"That's Hassan's safe, not mine." He sounded as if he was dribbling as he spoke.

"Are you American?"

"Florida. You?"

"Portland." She paused to catch her breath. "What a… mess."

"Tell me about this Josie."

"We caught the same bus from Marrakech." She stopped mid-flow. "Crap! It never went through my mind that she might have been following me."

"The DEGD, the Moroccan intelligence agency, is really switched-on – that much I discovered. She could be working for them." He seemed to be getting his speech under some sort of control.

"Is that good? I can't work out who are the good guys over here."

"I don't know if they're the good guys, but they sure as hell hate the Sahrawis and won't want world leaders blown up in Marrakech. It would wipe out the tourist industry." He was still speaking slowly and slurring.

"What about PEGASUS?"

"The Sahrawis hate it because they think the phosphate belongs to their nation. The Moroccans hate it because they think that Western Sahara is theirs, so it's their phosphate and should go out through their ports." He paused while he wiped the saliva from his chin. "And they hate the Algerians, backed by the Russians, for getting involved."

"This region is an utter mess."

"Nobody would care if they didn't have gas, phosphates and oil."

Across the yard, there was an almighty crash.

CHAPTER THIRTY

Josie had been watching the harbour car park when Mike had left her hotel and made her way through the bustle towards the shade of the port building. She had seen the black-and-white dog running around and the arrival of the three men in the white van and car. At this point in time, she had moved next to the taxi rank, from where she could get a better view of the colonnade. She had almost felt the disappointment in Mike when Randy had failed to show up for the meeting at 2.00pm. Josie had been only half-prepared for what happened next. She had seen Mike get in, start the pickup and begin to follow the two vehicles out of the car park. Out of the corner of her eye, Josie had caught the dog leaping into the back and going in through the rear window, but at this point, she herself had been jumping into the taxi at the front of the rank.

It had taken some time for the driver to understand that he was to follow her friend in the pickup ahead, which he knew very well belonged to Meddur, the fish gutter, as did the dog Kella, which everyone in Essaouira loved.

It had been a slow and uneventful journey until the van and car had turned off towards the farm. She had asked the taxi driver to turn around and park under some thorn bushes about five hundred yards away. Josie had watched Mike sneaking around the barren area at the front of the building and emerging finally from the stone arch. When she had seen Mike creeping along the sidewall of the farm, Josie had jumped out and paid the driver. She had taken his crudely produced card and said she may call him. With a *shokran*, she had pulled the small rucksack onto her back and disappeared over the sandy, red soil, going down through the scrub with an easy stride that had served her well in the Marathon des Sables.

Mike had been making such fundamental mistakes that Josie knew she was likely to run into trouble. Her desire to find her brother-in-law had clearly been stopping her thinking straight. Who takes a dog with them when they're trying to blend into the background and sneak around? From her vantage point, Josie had seen the debacle and the three men escorting Mike around the back of the sheds. Unfortunately, the dog charging around the place, jumping through windows and barking had made it difficult for her to get close. Josie had been faced with no choice but to sit it out under a very old olive tree, much to the annoyance of a hoopoe, which had flapped away after having been disturbed while feeding on bugs in a large hole created by a broken branch.

Eventually, some men had taken the dog and driven off in the pickup, which wasn't a good sign. It also wasn't helpful. The vehicle had also been part of Josie's hastily cobbled together escape plan for the two of them. While she could run back to Essaouira, if necessary, over several hours, Mike and most of the population could not. She had decided to face that problem when she had found out what was going on.

Mike had not reappeared.

Sitting against the ancient tree, she had swigged some water and then checked the small knife in her bum bag, the three-inch plastic stiletto hidden next to her calf at the bottom of her combat trousers, and the cheese wire around her waist, hidden in her trousers behind her belt. This was all she would need, although her hands were probably her best weapon.

She had retied her ponytail and waited. The peach-coloured hoopoe had flown into the next tree, checking whether it could continue its meal.

Josie had thought she would be glad when this mission was over in a couple of days' time, and she could fly back to Melbourne. It would be cooler there. Over the last few months, she and her three colleagues from ASIS, the Australian Secret Intelligence Service, had been preparing the ground for their PM's attendance at the G20. They had picked up rumours of some terrorist threat, but pinning down the details was proving elusive. They were sharing their intelligence through Five Eyes in London, but the dots just wouldn't be joined up. On Tuesday, she had been directed by her controllers in Canberra to watch Mike Kingdom from afar and make sure that she didn't fall into harm's way. This had proved relatively easy while she was in Marrakech, but things had got progressively messy once she had booked the bus journey to Essaouira. Josie couldn't risk losing her, and the G20 leaders had already flown in. She needed to stay close to Mike. The woman was clearly an analyst not an operative; this was patently clear. Normally, in the intelligence world, these two fundamental divisions never mix; she had wondered if this was different in the US. *What are the Americans thinking about? They're chalk and cheese.*

She had been warned via the head of Five Eyes in London that Mike was brilliant at searching but stubborn, and also completely ignorant of why she was looking for Ramon Ramirez. Josie had guessed that Leonard de Vries was the 'concerned uncle' who had telephoned Mike while they were sitting outside the café, and she had hoped that Mike would accept her offer to accompany her when she went to the meeting with her brother-in-law. This hadn't worked. Josie and Mike were both under the illusion that Ramon Ramirez was Randy, Mike's brother-in-law.

Sitting under the olive tree, Josie had been unaware that Ramon Ramirez was, in fact, in the shed nearest to her, badly beaten up and shackled. Her one concern had been freeing Mike; everything else, including Ramon could follow.

After sitting and waiting next to the farm buildings, she had concluded that a long enough period of time had passed since the two captors had left, and she had returned across the yard to the main building. Josie had decided it was time to look inside the sheds. Using the available cover, she had made it to the first door. Inside was a man bound and chained to a ring on the wall with a piece of tape across his mouth. His white shirt was dirty and covered in blood. She had run over to him and pulled off the tape.

"*Ow!*" he had shouted as she had tugged at his broken jaw.

"Shh!" she had said before going outside and into the next shed.

It was here that she had seen Mike, chained to the wall, and where she had learnt about the bomb on Friday at midday in Marrakech. Josie had turned, left the outbuildings and moved back behind some trees that gave her some screening. She had sent a message to her controller and, separately, to one of her colleagues in Marrakech. It had warned of the bomb tomorrow, the coordinates of her current location, and that Mike and Ramon were chained up. It was almost late afternoon, and the heat was disappearing out of the sun, but it was still being radiated from the sandy ground.

***

Toumi had decided to change his plans. He would release the video with the man immediately. The one with the woman he would save until before Friday prayers tomorrow. The video showing Ramon Ramirez reading the statement went viral in a matter of minutes. Moroccan TV, which had also been sent the video, was reluctant to show it at first, but once it started appearing on newspaper websites and international news agencies, it had no choice. The G20 was thrown into turmoil.

"Make a note," Conrad said, "This is the last time we have a G20, G7 or G-anything in a godforsaken, two-bit country like Morocco. Next time, it's somewhere safe like in the US, UK or Germany."

The assembled group of about twelve people were letting the President vent his spleen – again.

He continued without taking a breath, "Who are these Sahrawis? I thought this was all being dealt with by the UN and its peacekeeping force. Isn't there meant to be a referendum soon?"

"The United Nations Mission for the Referendum in Western Sahara, MINURSO, has been there since 1991. Its mission has been extended forty-seven times. It's basically a failure," someone tried to explain.

"The Moroccans have been building and resettling its population in Western Sahara for decades – a bit like the Israelis have been doing in the Palestinian areas. They're now in the majority over the native Sahrawis and would, therefore, win any referendum," someone else continued the explanation.

"That's good for the US, right?" The President wasn't interested in lengthy explanations.

"Yes, if Western Sahara were part of Morocco, it would be great as they are heavily pro-USA."

"But we're watching the creation of a new terrorist group. This Sahrawi People's Army, or SPA, are far worse than the other arm of the Sahrawis, the Polisario Front. This video shows us that Americans will be in danger at home and abroad. It's just ISIS all over again." The President's security adviser was nervous of the future.

"Who's this hostage?" the President asked.

"A CIA operative, Ramon Ramirez, who's undercover here in Morocco."

"Damn." Conrad put his head in his hands. "How's this playing out with the rest of the G20?"

"Two are thinking of going home. The rest are waiting for you, I think."

"Well, we're not running away. We are only here a few days. Are we safe at the remaining meetings?"

"We've all done our best. We believed you to be safe before this happened and this doesn't change anything in that regard."

"OK, we stay. What statement should I put out?"

"We are drafting some options, but they basically repeat our support for the UN, for a referendum and for respecting the result. They state that taking and killing hostages will not change policy and will harden the world's view against the Sahrawis, with whom the US has no beef. The G20 will continue with reinforced solidarity."

"The Moroccans are going crazy behind the scenes. Every person they have is looking for this poor hostage," someone said.

"OK, that's it. Get me the text ASAP." The President had had enough.

***

Across Marrakech, a very similar series of discussions was taking place between the British PM and his team.

"Right, what do I need to know? What do I need to say? Are we all safe?" Victor asked the three questions on his mind.

"With regard to your first question, in one respect, we can sit back because it's the Americans who need to sort this out. What's worrying is the evolution of a new terrorist organisation that's going to be anti-West and anti-anyone who supports Morocco. What makes them different from the Polisario – basically, their predecessors – is that they aren't quite so enthusiastic about Algeria, despite all of the Sahrawis that live in camps there. This new group, SPA, is definitely vehemently against the USA, but it doesn't like the Russian and Chinese backing of Algeria either. They truly want independence." His adviser continued by answering the second question: "As to what you say, I think you should condemn hostage-taking; support the UN, which is seeking a referendum; and express solidarity with the other G20 members." The adviser looked around. "As to your final question, I'll hand over to Lorna."

Lorna began to give MI6's view on the situation: "The hostage is a CIA operative. The Americans have been very active in Morocco, especially in the build-up to this G20. The Moroccans want this G20 to be a success, so they're doing everything behind the scenes to find this hostage and to nip this new terrorist organisation in the bud. You'll be aware that any US President is severely restricted by executive orders. These are circumvented by tacit agreement with the President. Basically, he isn't told about certain things so that he cannot be impeached or prosecuted. In reality, this means that the CIA doesn't actively undertake certain actions abroad; instead, these are done by third-party organisations supported indirectly by the CIA. One of the most actively used is the DEGD (the Moroccan intelligence agency). The fact that Morocco is so strongly anti-Algeria, anti-Russia and anti-Chinese makes them easy bedfellows." She paused for her words to take effect. "It hasn't been necessary for us to be overly active here because we get everything from the Moroccans via the Americans through Fives Eyes in London. The general thinking is that this G20 meeting is safe and this hostage-taking is a small group using the opportunity to grab some headlines. If anything changes, we'll hear it from either our monitoring of various sources or via Five Eyes. Of course, the Canadians and Australians are worried about the safety of their leaders too."

With that, Victor moved on to the agenda for a series of one-to-one meetings with other G20 leaders.

**

In a grey office in Chiswick, someone else was watching the video of Ramon Ramirez filmed against a backdrop of the Sahrawi national flag. Leonard de Vries was so frustrated. He hadn't heard from Ramon for so many weeks that he had begun to believe he was dead. Ramon had struck up a relationship with the SPA terrorist group, and Leonard was desperate to hear what he had discovered. The video came as a shock. He had so hoped that Mike would find him.

One of his phones rang. It was the brief update from Josie, patched through from the Australians.

So, Mike had found Ramon; he smiled to himself quietly. He didn't have the luxury of wallowing in self-congratulation, however, as his priority had to change quickly to letting key players know about the bomb threat. The event at the Yves Saint Laurent villa would, no doubt, be cancelled and security increased. Next, he made a call that would lead to two helicopters, containing special forces personnel from Morocco and the USA, taking off from near Marrakech for the forty-minute flight to the coordinates provided by the Australians.

If only they could rescue Ramon and Mike Kingdom, he would have had a good day and he might treat himself to a meal at his favourite Greek restaurant – only the Greeks and Americans understood portion size.

CHAPTER THIRTY-ONE

Josie had passed on the message.

The bomb threat would be dealt with, and special forces would soon be on their way to the farm by helicopter and by road. She now needed to take out the two remaining men and get the keys to release Ramon and Mike. It was no use waiting too long. The failing light or darkness would favour them: they knew the farm; she did not. Although a gun would have been useful, she hadn't seen anything to suggest they were carrying anything either. Inside the main house, there probably were guns, but not immediately to hand.

It was also likely that they would get ever twitchier. Ramon was CIA, Mike was effectively CIA and she had found their hideaway. They would know that their cover had been blown. They would be worried about who else was on the way and would be getting ready to disappear soon, she guessed, and this might involve silencing any witnesses. The other Berbers had already gone off in the pickup with the dog.

She approached the kitchen door. In her left hand, she had a handful of dusty sand, and in her right, her knife. If someone was to come out unexpectedly, the sand would give her the one-second advantage she needed to disable them, with or without the knife. As it happened, she looked through the window and saw the back of the bigger man hunched over a laptop. This was good news, but she didn't know where the other man was, and he might hear her and turn up with a gun.

Always expect the unexpected, she had been taught at her base at Holsworthy Barracks in New South Wales and when being hunted in the jungles of Brunei during her training. She suddenly heard the sound of someone walking fast around the side of the building, coming towards her. He turned the corner. The sand was thrown up into his eyes and the side of a hand struck him in the throat. She caught hold of him to control any noise as she lowered him to the ground. She listened – nothing.

The bigger man in the shiny suit was sitting four paces inside the door. She opened it with her left hand, and he began to say something, assuming that she was his colleague. He didn't turn around and died instantly from a single thrust of her knife. She pulled out his opened laptop from underneath him, so it wouldn't get covered in blood, and also picked up his phone. The keys for the padlock and car that she needed were in his jacket pocket, and as soon as she'd extracted them, she raced back to free Mike and Ramon.

***

It took one person under each arm to get Ramon across the yard to the grey Renault, and this wasn't easy as Mike was very stiff with a weak left leg. With Ramon in the back and Mike in the passenger seat holding the big man's laptop, Josie drove the car back towards Essaouira.

"Thank you so much." Ramon was still slurring his words from having a broken jaw.

"You've been amazing. Are you going to tell us exactly who you are?" Mike was inquisitive.

"I told you I was ex-special forces, and that's true. I was hoping that you would let me come along with you for moral support when you thought you were meeting your brother-in-law," Josie said.

"Are you a freelancer?"

"No, I'm in the ASIS. I'm in intelligence... like you two."

"I'm not complaining, but did you purposely follow me from Marrakech?"

"Yes, I've been watching you since you arrived. You almost threw me when you booked the bus journey. I had to think on my feet."

"Why are ASIS interested in me?" Mike was puzzled.

"I'm part of a team of four that's checking the ground before our PM attends the G20. I've been here a few months."

"But how did you know about me?"

"Your fat uncle put in a request via my boss for me to watch that you didn't get into trouble."

"*The...*" Mike was about to rant against Leonard, but she realised that, yet again, he had been right. She hated him.

"He said you're the best analyst ever to go into the field." Josie turned and winked at Mike.

"I'll kill him."

Josie changed the subject: "I've called in a helicopter that will pick us up in just over an hour to take us to Marrakech. Mike, I assume you have stuff at your hotel in Essaouira?

Ramon, USAF is flying you straight to the Landstuhl Hospital in Germany. I need to hand over this laptop and phone to your colleagues… they're very interested in them."

"Have they broadcast anything yet?" Mike asked. She felt helpless without a phone.

"Yes, they've released Ramon's video, as I understand it."

"And mine?"

"No idea there was one. I guess it's on that laptop."

Before long, they were approaching the outskirts of Essaouira.

***

Friday 9th September was a momentous day for more reasons than one.

For Brendan, a decision had been made.

He had previously been weighing up his options and had passed these over to his controller. They had decided that poison wasn't a realistic possibility – it would be difficult to get past the villa gate, let alone administer it and get out safely. The rocket grenade had a certain appeal, but it was felt that Brendan would then have to negotiate, threatening further attacks. They would have to vacate the area quickly – and, presumably, even more security would be brought in. Instead, his controller had looked at the drone footage again and reassured himself that the villa next door was unoccupied. If Deniz – one of the Turks, who had recently served as a sniper for the Saudi Army in Yemen – could gain access to the roof, he should have a direct line of sight to anyone on the rear terrace or kitchen area. The controller had instructed Brendan to go to the villa with Deniz in case anything unexpected happened, and Selim and the man who had driven to Cannes could stay in the car. Selim would be the get-away driver.

Brendan went through the plan, choosing where to climb the boundary wall by identifying a spot that was only covered by one security camera. Deniz could take this camera out with one shot from a silenced gun, and this would give them a route up the external staircase to the solarium on the roof. He preferred this route to the alternative of cutting the electricity supply, as the alarm systems and cameras would have back-up batteries. One camera failing was unlikely to draw immediate attention if all the other parts of the security system were working normally.

He only intended to be on the roof for half an hour or less, Deniz having established the rough routine of the household. They decided to clear out from their hotel and put everything into the hired Range Rover ready for a fast departure to the nearest border.

With the plan rehearsed, the four men left their hotel and drove the short distance to the adjoining villa. The bottom part of the rear door of the Range Rover folded down and provided a step up onto the car roof and, from there, up onto the high boundary wall. Deniz pushed through the tops of some cypresses and shot out the one security camera. As he dropped down the other side into the garden to the side of the villa, Brendan followed him. All was quiet, and there were no unexpected gardeners or dogs and no locked gates or grilles. No alarms went off.

Brendan and Deniz climbed up the outside staircase to the enclosed roof area used as a suntrap and barbecue area. They were completely hidden by the parapet wall and not overlooked by any other villa. There was a warmth radiating from the red floor tiles, and there was a pleasant background smell from the junipers and cypresses. Deniz found a corner, created by a chimney stack, that helped to hide him and to give him somewhere to rest his rifle with its telescopic sights.

It was exactly fifteen minutes to midday, and now it was simply a question of waiting until his target stepped onto the terrace of the adjoining villa.

**

Early on that Friday morning, Mike had been sitting in a window seat aboard the first flight to Málaga. The sky had been graded from a dusty brown at ground level to a pure, pale blue higher up. She had held a plastic cup of water in both hands for most of the short journey. She had felt naked without a cell phone, but she would get one very soon in Spain. At least she had her laptop and special bits of computer kit.

Following her arrival at Málaga, she had come out of the terminal building into the heat and jumped into a taxi. Almost immediately, it drove past the San Miguel brewery, and she had experienced an odd craving for a cold beer at 11.00am. She had seen the reflection in the taxi window of her black wig. She always preferred to wear it when she travelled, as it matched her passport photograph and caused less hassle.

Wazz had been expecting her. She had sent a message from Marrakech that had conveniently left out almost all detail, including being chained to a wall – in fact, particularly the bit about being chained to a wall – and the video. He had messaged back, asking if she had found Randy to which she replied with a simple "No".

Mike had thought Diego had given her a smile as she

walked through the outer gate, having paid the taxi, but it was hard to tell. Wazz had helped to pull her small suitcase up to the villa.

"Hey, how was it?" He had sounded genuinely happy to see her back.

"If I said that having a cigarette by the bins with you could be the highlight of this trip, that might give you an idea."

"That bad?"

"Yes, and sadly, there was neither sight nor sound of Randy, but that's a long story. Probably a two-cigarette story. What's happened here in the last few days?"

"Drones; we've had a lot of drones until Diego used them for target practice."

"That means Brendan or his heavies are nearby. How are the Yellands?"

"Not used to people telling them what to do and not used to being unable to move. Maria has now sunk into some sort of deep depression and is on even more tablets—"

"That's nothing new," Mike had interrupted.

"As to Angelica? I really would give her a wide berth."

"Why?" Mike had asked, as if she couldn't hazard a guess.

"She arranged to have her nails done at some place in Fuengirola and booked a limo."

"Oh, for Fuck's sake."

"Luckily, Diego was keeping an eye on her."

Mike had burst out laughing. "I've missed you. How far did she get?"

"I don't think they had applied the topcoat of varnish." He had paused as she went on giggling. "What do you think? Diego stopped her, she complained that life wasn't worth living and he offered to apply the varnish himself. She screamed at him – a man who has survived more bullets, mortars and missiles than she's had hot dinners."

"Has Charles received any new threats or demands?"

"Not that I know of… but he's an odd character, don't you think?"

"I don't think he even trusts himself." Mike had tried often enough to work out if he was in control or just went whichever way the wind was blowing at that moment.

"I need a cigarette before lunch."

With that, they had walked around the villa to the kitchen bin area. It was almost midday.

***

The noise was deafening.

It reverberated off all the buildings, walls and hard surfaces. What looked like brains were splattered all over the walls and surrounding trees. Dogs were barking, and alarms were screaming from several of the surrounding properties. There was devastation. Hundreds of tall cacti had been destroyed in the bomb blast, and their pulpy flesh was sprayed everywhere. There was no Jardin Majorelle left. Instead, there was a bomb crater and open views to where the beautiful, deep-blue walls of the villa had stood since 1923. The front wall was completely gone, and the furniture and contents chosen by Yves Saint Laurent were in pieces, sitting on what now looked like the stage of a theatre.

The Moroccan bomb disposal unit had spent several hours searching for a device, but they had found nothing. This was because the explosive had purposely been buried very deep two months earlier, so no trace remained on the surface. The

Sahrawis had infiltrated the gardening staff, and long before the current terrorist campaign was launched, they had buried the explosives in anticipation of the G20 meeting.

The warning from Ramon and Mike via Josie had provided time to evacuate the area and move all of the world leaders to another venue. The hastily reorganised photo opportunity used a stretch of the pink city walls as a backdrop. They looked as if they were facing a firing squad. After a show of solidarity that lasted until the next day, there was an unseemly rush for the airport. Victor used the death of Queen Elizabeth II as the reason he needed to leave early; Conrad didn't bother to offer an excuse.

CHAPTER THIRTY-TWO

It was at the precise moment when the eighty-year-old cacti and bamboos were being reduced to pulp and splinters that, a thousand miles away, a gunman on a rooftop was preparing to squeeze the trigger of a state-of-the-art rifle; this was the gentle squeeze of the professional soldier. It was unlikely that anyone could hear anything, but he had whispered to Brendan, telling him that people had walked out onto the terrace of the villa opposite. Brendan had swivelled around and leant back against the chimney stack. Staring out across the trees to the Mediterranean Sea, he had warned Selim, using his phone, to bring up the Range Rover ready for the get-away, and then he had scrambled across the tiles like a crab so he was ready to retreat back down the brick stairs.

The crack from the rifle, when it came, wasn't as loud as the bang in Marrakech, which could be heard halfway up the Atlas Mountains, but it also echoed around the villas and boundary walls. Two dogs barked, but this wasn't an unusual occurrence in this neighbourhood. Deniz, given that his location was almost textbook, had a clear line of sight to his target and he didn't miss. From that distance, viewed through an eyepiece, it was as if watching a film. Over the years in Syria, Yemen and, once, in Germany, it had been more difficult; this was well within his capabilities. He worked as only a professional can, knowing where speed becomes haste and mistakes can happen. He turned, slung the rifle over his shoulder and followed Brendan down the stairs, two steps at a time.

It was only twelve paces across the gravel to the boundary. They knew that the camera had been disabled and there were no alarms. So, it was with a feeling of satisfaction that they prepared to climb back over the boundary wall. Using a bin to gain a three-foot advantage, they had reached for the parapet and pulled themselves up. Brendan was the first to begin pushing his way through the spiky cypress branches that projected up above the wall. His Turkish sniper was right on his heels.

Brendan and Deniz never made it to the pavement alive. Brendan was killed as he jumped and Deniz as he tried to throw his rifle down before lowering himself. Selim and his colleague had seen the bodies hit the ground. He had instantly assessed that there was nothing he could do for them and had driven off at maximum speed, well aware that the Range Rover didn't have bulletproof glass in the windows. This was proved when, in the mirror, he saw the rear windscreen's glass shatter.

***

Jacqueline Bettancourt was stretched out in bed when her phone rang. It was her department in Paris telling her that

Brendan and one of the Turkish hitmen had been killed after shooting Yves Dubuisson at his villa in Cannes.

She and her colleagues had always suspected the Minister of Energy, but nothing could ever be proven against him.

The French authorities had discovered that Yves Dubuisson and Johnny Musselwhite were part of a group standing to gain substantially from PEGASUS, which turned out to be a Russian-funded project masquerading as another Algerian gas connection to Europe. The Russians were trying to control yet more of the energy pipelines providing Europe with gas and oil.

If that weren't bad enough, the third element of PEGASUS would have brought France into direct conflict with the rest of the EU, the UK, the USA and the UN. As much as France would like to receive and process such a reserve of phosphate, it was effectively being stolen from Western Sahara.

PEGASUS was, to all intents and purposes, cancelled. The French government wouldn't permit the pipelines and cables to enter its territorial waters around Corsica or elsewhere, and permission wouldn't be given for any phosphate-processing plants or distribution facilities.

A statement would be released to the effect that any French-funded scheme to deliver gas or electricity from Algeria in the future would be considered, but nothing backed financially by a hostile state or involving the transportation of phosphates would be entertained.

It had been decided to let the British search for the man known as Brendan. He was very likely to be working for the Moroccans, and it would be the Brits who had to deal with the political fallout. However, unless he was caught and he confessed, this story would quickly be kicked into the long grass.

The problem never arose. MI6 had traced Brendan via Dublin to Nice and on to Cannes, where Yves Dubuisson lived. The UK and French working together had monitored his and his colleagues' phones at their hotel. Yves had been tracked all the way back from his clandestine visit to Charles Yelland in Spain.

A special unit of officers and an armed response team had been keeping Yves under surveillance. This meant that they had also begun monitoring Brendan, his two Turkish mercenaries and the other driver at their hotel. They watched them check out and load their car. They never saw Brendan and Deniz enter the villa, having anticipated an attack through the front gate. By the time the armed team arrived, it was too late to save Yves Dubuisson, but they were in time to shoot two of his killers. The driver of the Range Rover and one other man escaped, but they were tracked to the Italian border fourteen miles away, where they were stopped and arrested.

There would be political fallout for a few days, but France no longer needed to worry about Yves Dubuisson and whatever else he had been up to. The explosion at the Jardin Majorelle in Marrakech would be the main story in the media.

She put the phone back on the coffee table, turned and smiled at Patrick, who was lying in bed next to her.

***

It was after lunch when Mike took the phone call from Tom who was passing on a message from Leonard. He explained what had happened in Cannes and that Brendan had been shot and killed. Leonard had also wanted her to know that the PEGASUS project had been very publicly cancelled by the French government. Tom told her that the bomb had gone off in Marrakech, but no one was injured, thanks to her efforts in Essaouira. Relief swept through the Yelland villa.

When Charles announced that they were flying back to the UK in two hours' time, Angelica screamed and ran upstairs to pack – although what she was packing, as she had duplicates of almost everything in the villa that she had in Buckinghamshire, was not obvious. Maria was still half-sedated, but even she seemed to go up a gear.

"My work here is done," Wazz said as he passed Mike on the stairs.

"One last debrief?" she asked.

"What you actually mean is that you're looking for an excuse for a cigarette before getting on the plane, am I right?"

"True."

And with that, they made their way to the space that wasn't at the forefront of the Spanish architect's mind when she had designed the whole villa complex and surrounds.

"When you said your work was done, did you think that you had actually done anything?" She was at her most provocative, to the extent that she had reversed their positions and was leaning on the large waste bin on which Wazz had been resting his elbows when they first met.

He inhaled and breathed out an enormous white puff from his e-cigarette, which smelt of rotting strawberries.

"At least they don't need to worry about mosquitoes tonight," she said, but he just smiled. "Does anything phase you?" she continued.

"Small spaces; otherwise, not much."

"What's next for you?"

"A trip to Agadir – ironically, to make sure three women aren't molested on the beach. Then, I'm going to finish my degree. I can't do this" – he looked around at the villa and gardens – "stuff for much longer."

Mike removed a bit of paper from her lip and looked suspiciously at her cigarette. She was wondering about parallel lives and how, at that moment, she would like one in order to see where more time with Wazz might lead. Good men were hard to find, in her experience.

***

"How's my favourite agent?" Leonard was at his most smug and annoying.

"You set me up… again."

"No, that's not true. Strictly speaking, it was that Dr Rose Delavine, if you remember. You need to be careful who you invite to your cabin."

"I think you invited yourself."

"Nah, strictly by invitation only, you said. You were waiting for the good doctor."

"I'll be more careful next time. What am I saying? There won't be a next time."

"Who knows? Never say never, but I need to work on another anagram – dear Rose needs to hang up her surgical gloves. But, hey, I just wanted to say a big thanks for finding Ramon and giving us all the heads up on the bomb plot. You were the only person I thought could find him."

"I could have died… again."

"I'm pretty sure you can only die once and, anyway, I sent the Australian to watch out for you."

"She was great. She's what's called an 'operative'. I'm what's called an 'analyst'. You seem to get them confused."

"Nah, operatives walk about and analysts sit down, otherwise they're the same."

"God, you're annoying. How does the President put up with you?"

"Because he likes people that get results. Oh, he says thanks, by the way. He and his team want me to send some money to you from the President's special account."

"I might use it to move house with no forwarding address."

"Don't worry, I'll find you. I employ lots of operatives, or is it analysts? I can never remember."

Mike was gripping both of her hands into fists so hard that her nails were digging into her palms. "You are a—"

"Hey, I told Tom to phone you once I heard about that French minister, didn't I? That was classified information. You should thank me for that. I bet your client is real pleased?"

"He is, and so are his wife and daughter. We're all flying home in an hour's time."

There was a pause in the conversation. Mike walked around her bedroom at the villa to relieve the ache in her left leg. "What was Ramon doing that you wanted him to stop?"

"Are all of your gizmos plugged in?"

"Yes."

Leonard was establishing that all of the little pieces of hardware were plugged in and that the line was, therefore, secure.

"You know all about executive orders that restrict the President? The CIA has to bypass them on behalf of the President so he can then claim deniability. We've been using the Moroccans a lot."

"You mean that they carry out our dirty work?" she interrupted.

"Well, that's a cynical view."

"That's what we operatives – sorry, analysts – are paid to take, isn't it?"

"The Moroccans have been doing a great job. They are a little bit 'all guns blazing' for my taste, but they've killed off the Russian-backed pipeline, PEGASUS. OK, they made the Sahrawis pissed, but they do have most of the world's phosphates, and the US wants it big time."

"Was the G20 the problem?"

"That and the Russia-Ukraine thing. The US finally had to choose between Morocco and Algeria. It chose Morocco, so it wants all of the Western Sahara phosphate to be under Moroccan control and for Algeria and the Russkies to be shut out."

"And that's going to happen?"

"Yes, blowing up those gardens was the best thing those Sahrawis could have done for the US. Nobody will talk to them now. When Morocco has resettled enough of its people into Western Sahara, there will be a UN-led referendum, and Morocco will keep ultimate control. And everything in the garden is rosy. That's the Rose Garden at the White House, by the way."

"Has anyone told you how smug you are?"

"I'm a glass-half-full kind of guy."

"You've never seen a glass or plate half-full."

***

Two hours later, there was a party atmosphere on the Gulfstream, and Mike was sitting on the leather sofa with Charles, drinking Louis Roederer champagne. Not that anyone was aware of it, but they were, at that moment, flying over Reims (near Paris) where the champagne had been produced. They were less than half an hour from London.

"You don't seem very upset about your PEGASUS project being cancelled," Mike suggested.

"It's a shame, but these things happen. There are plenty more fish in the sea."

"Will you try to use the new technology for pumping phosphates somewhere else in the world?" She was looking sideways at him with a knowing smile. She sipped the pink champagne and tilted her head so that the bright-red wig hung down at one side.

"Probably," he said with that sheepish grin that he seemed incapable of hiding from her.

"Who thought it was funny to call the other project MEDUSA, by the way? Surely, the last thing you want when pumping phosphate down a pipeline is for it to turn to stone."

His expression changed from sheepish to one of disbelief. "That's not the reason that project is called MEDUSA." He had rather unnecessarily lowered his voice on his own private plane.

"Nothing to do with the Mediterranean Sea – the Med – and the USA, then?"

"Could be. I take it that you read my confidential file… as usual?"

"Could be. I take it that Johnny and Yves weren't involved in this one?"

"No, no. In business, you need to cover all the bases. I want that phosphate, whether it goes out via Algeria or Morocco. The Americans are very keen on the Moroccan route. That's MEDUSA."

***

Mike's phone rang. The caller's name was withheld. She hit the green button.

"Hi, Sis, how are you?"

"Randy?" There was joy in her voice.

"Yeah, I'm just back and got your message. So, what's the good news?"

She had to think for a second. "That you're alive. It's a long story. Where have you been?"

"I've been trekking in the jungle down south. Just got back to Los Angeles."

"Work or pleasure?"

"Work, unfortunately; it was a waste of time."

He had probably been undercover chasing the Colombian drug cartels on which she had worked for her first few years as a CIA analyst. She began to see a pattern here. "Who sent you?"

He couldn't speak freely over the phone, so he just said, "Your old boss. The one before you went to London."

"You mean Leonard's friend at head office?"

"Yes, I'll tell you another time. But, funnily enough, Leonard did phone to tell me that you would be away for a few weeks."

"When did he phone?"

She could already guess the answer.

***

Sitting in the Gulfstream, Mike was drinking copious amounts of champagne; this was both to celebrate her success and also to relieve the tension building up in her from having to deal with Leonard. She frowned as she looked up the aisle at Charles laughing and joking with Maria and Angelica. What was it that attracted men like Charles and Leonard to her? Or was she attracted to them? She was soon to get her answer.

Her phone lit up. It was an invitation to have a Zoom call next week with a new client. When she saw that it was from Sir Donald Reeve, she smiled and, against her better judgement, pressed to accept.

ABOUT THE AUTHOR

After going to art college in the 1970s, David Jarvis set up an international planning practice, which he ran successfully for forty years. His canvases just got bigger and bigger. He has now retired to Wiltshire.